MORE

"Smart and fast paced
Raffel who has writte
thriller."—M. J. Rose, in
incarnationist and *The Memorist*

PRAISE FOR DOT DEAD, THE FIRST BOOK OF THE SERIES

"Without question, the most impressive debut mystery of the year."—Bookreporter.com

"A fast-paced, truly witty mystery set in the maze and madness of Silicon Valley."—Stuart M. Kaminsky, Mystery Writers of America Grand Master

"Raffel knows his way around the high-tech industry. A well-plotted mystery … you can't go wrong."—Library Journal

"*Dot Dead* is a fast-paced, twisty ride."—Peter Abrahams, bestselling author of *Crying Wolf* and *Oblivion*

"Keith Raffel's debut novel is a great read. Although the book is fast paced, each of his characters is distinct and well developed … Set aside a day to read this book—once you start it, it's hard to put down."—Crimespree Magazine

smasher

smasher
a·silicon·valley·thriller

keith·raffel

MIDNIGHT INK
WOODBURY, MINNESOTA

First Edition
First Printing, 2009

Book design and format by Donna Burch
Cover design by Ellen Dahl
Cover images: woman © PhotoAlto, background © BrandXPictures
Editing by Connie Hill

Midnight Ink, an imprint of Llewellyn Publications

Library of Congress Cataloging-in-Publication Data

Raffel, Keith, 1951–
  Smasher : a Silicon Valley thriller / by Keith Raffel. — 1st ed.
      p.   cm.
  ISBN 978-0-7387-1874-3
  1. Computer industry—Fiction. 2. Santa Clara Valley (Santa Clara County, Calif.)—Fiction. I. Title.
  PS3618.A375S63   2009
  813'.6—dc22   2009021700

Midnight Ink
Llewellyn Publications
2143 Wooddale Drive, Dept. 978-0-7387-1874-3
Woodbury, MN 55125-2989 USA
www.midnightinkbooks.com

Printed in the United States of America

To my wife and children.

"Who is rich? He who is happy with what he has."

—Shimon ben Zoma

PROLOGUE: FEBRUARY 17

I WAS CHASING A ghost. My wife Rowena's white UCLA sweatshirt and matching baseball cap floated in the moonlight, but I could make out neither the exposed skin of her legs nor the bouncing ponytail that had to be there. On the ground in front of her, I did see a shimmering cone cast by the flashlight she'd velcroed to her arm. She was younger, faster, and in better shape than I was. Listening to her iPod, she glided along without worrying about me. Experience told her I'd keep up.

We were out running earlier than usual. Even though court was not back in session till ten, Rowena had an eight o'clock meeting with the big boss, the D.A., to discuss trial strategy. I myself had a call at nine with plenty to sort out before then. So here we were running in the dark through the Stanford campus at five-thirty—an hour-and-a-half earlier than usual—on a cold February morning. For her, it was training to defend her title in next month's Napa Valley Marathon. For me, it was time to think.

Rowena loped along toward the foothills, and I continued to follow. We crossed under I-280 and turned on Arastradero Road. At the first cross street a car squatted with its right turn signal flashing, ready to head west like us. Waiting for it to pull on to Arastradero, we danced up and down at the corner. I welcomed the rest.

The car didn't move, though, and I waved for it to turn. It remained motionless. The driver was probably on his cellphone. We ran across the intersection, lit up by the car's high beams like convicts in a prison break. After another hundred yards, I heard the sound of rubber on asphalt approaching. A moment later an engine growled, and I turned to see the car from the intersection a few dozen yards behind us, traveling at least twenty miles per hour over the speed limit. Then its front tires swerved right.

What the hell?

"Rowena!"

She couldn't hear. Two long strides and I was up to her. I pushed hard on Rowena's left shoulder and heard a surprised cry. I remember leaping to avoid the onrushing vehicle and I remember the corner of the bumper smashing into my right leg. Then I went flying.

———

I didn't know how long I'd been there, dazed on the path, but I was roused by a bright light shining in my eyes. As I blinked, it swung away.

"A car hit you?" the voice of a woman asked. She flashed a light toward me, and I could see she was straddling a bicycle.

"Oh, my God," she said.

I followed the beam and saw white bone sticking out below my knee. That cleared my head.

"Rowena, where's Rowena?" I shouted. All I felt from my leg was a distant throbbing.

"Take it easy. You were with someone?"

I hoisted myself up and teetered for a moment. Groping for the light around my left arm, I sliced open my index finger on shattered plastic. I extended a hand, now dripping with blood, and she slapped her small flashlight into it. I managed to walk to the edge of the path. There in the beam was Rowena, motionless, her head against a tree trunk at the bottom of a six-foot gully. Where my push had sent her. Out of peril and back into it.

As I went into a head-first slide down to her, I heard our rescuer call out that she was dialing 911.

Then I was cradling my wife's head in my lap.

"Please God, not Rowena. Not Rowena, too."

PART I

ONE

HEISENBERG ESTABLISHED THAT TWO electrons could not occupy the same space at the same time. Nor could I be at two different places at the same time. Dammit. I was supposed to be on my way to a Stanford reception to meet my mother and wife. Instead I was in a rocket ship of an elevator on the way up to the office of Ricky Frankson, America's seventh richest man and the CEO of Torii Networks.

My ears clogged as the elevator accelerated past the fifteenth floor, and I felt a pop of relief as I swallowed. Much better to be smiling and nodding at a passel of professors, but I had no choice. In this morning's *Times*, Matt Richtel had reported Frankson's threat to crush Accelenet, what he called a "piss-ant little company." If Frankson followed his usual script, the initial threat would be followed by more bullying pronouncements to frighten potential customers about our viability, then would come price-cutting, and finally hiring away key employees. When the company cried for mercy, Torii would offer to buy it for a fraction of what it would have cost the year before.

So why did I care? Because I was the CEO of that piss-ant little company, responsible for the four hundred people who worked for the company and the ninety million dollars invested by venture capitalists. We'd been well ahead of our two-year plan until six weeks ago, when Samsung indicated it was about to pull out of our technology licensing deal, and rumors spread that Cisco was not going to renew our distribution agreement. I flew over to Seoul to play little Dutch boy and stick my fingers in the dike, but failed to calm the storm. Now I understood why. Frankson's huffing and puffing had kept the winds blowing.

Without the cash flow from our distribution deals with Samsung and Cisco, we were screwed. We'd need more cash soon, very soon. I considered myself fortunate that our board members didn't wet their pants when they read the morning's *Times*. Or maybe they had. In any case, during a conference call a few hours ago, they'd made clear that when it came to additional investment in the company, their wallets were sealed by superglue.

Off the elevator, I was met by a guard whose blue blazer bulged on the right side. He asked to see my driver's license before sending me through a gray metal archway that would detect firearms, poisonous gas, radioactivity, or explosive materials. Awaiting me on the other side was Frankson's admin, who flaunted the hallmarks of a 1950s Technicolor heartthrob—a slash of blood red lipstick, a dusting of blue and gold sparkles on her eyelids, and a hairsprayed helmet of cornflower blonde hair. Frankson had made her predecessor his fourth wife.

"I thought Ricky was famous for his open door policy," I said to her after introductions. In conversation, everyone in the Valley referred to Frankson by first name alone. Just as in basketball everyone knew who Kobe was—no last name required—the high tech world knew who Steve was without the Jobs, Larry without the Ellison, and Ricky without the Frankson.

"As you can see," she said, a crimson-tipped finger pointing to the end of the hallway, "the door is open. It's just hard to get to. *You* got here, though."

She made it sound like I'd made it to the tenth level of a video game. I smiled out of courtesy.

"He'll be up soon. Can I get you something to drink?"

"Hot tea?"

"Green or black?"

"Green, please."

The door to Frankson's office was framed by a pair of weather-beaten pieces of wood and the top was capped by two matching crossbars. According to Valley lore, Frankson had found this old *torii*, gateway to a Shinto shrine, during the year he'd studied in Japan back during the '70s. A stylized vermilion version of this antique now served as his company's logo, almost as well-known in high-tech circles as the once-bitten fruit of Apple or multicolored letters of Google.

A few minutes later, I was sipping from a cup and looking through the smog at the hills across the Bay. Straw brown, they thirsted for the tardy winter rains. As I turned around, my elbow hit Frankson. I hadn't known he was there, and the surprise, together with the collision, caused me to let go of the tea. I'm not sure how he did it, but his right arm flew out and caught the cup by its handle halfway to the floor.

"Here you go, Ian." Not a drop had sloshed out.

"Thanks, Ricky."

"Let's sit down." His voice was Zen-calm.

He had his own take on the geek uniform—black jeans, almost certainly custom-made, and a shimmering black T-shirt, probably made of silk spun by twenty-three virgins in a village at the foot of Mount Fuji.

All in all, Frankson looked about as good as a man of sixty-one could look. A field of wavy black hair showed nary a gray strand that might betray his age. A deep notch divided his eyebrows, but the forehead above them was unlined and his cheeks were smooth. The girth of his biceps, half-hidden by the sleeves of the T-shirt, substantiated the rumor that his early morning routine included weightlifting in a home gym. Scuttlebutt also had it that he invested tens of millions in biotech companies researching life extension. Maybe he was a beta tester. Or maybe he had a portrait up in his attic that aged in his stead.

On the other side of the table, Frankson took a swig from a clear glass of gooey, brownish liquid reeking of broccoli. Then he rolled back his chair and placed the soles of his shoes on the edge of the table.

Thirty-five years ago, some researchers playing around with network protocols at AT&T didn't know what they had come up with, but Frankson did. He left, founded Torii Networks, beat AT&T in its patent suit, and still owned about a sixth of a company valued at one hundred eight billion dollars at market close last night.

"So you want to sell Accelenet?" Frankson asked. No preliminary niceties for him.

"I was more interested in an investment. Ten percent of the company for fifty million." The figure left some room for negotiation.

"Two hundred fifty million for the whole kit and caboodle. And a three-year employment contract for you to work here for me. Best and final." He stood up.

So did I. "Nice talking to you, Ricky." A low-ball offer with the added bonus of serfdom. Nice.

"The price will go down twenty-five million a week," he said, bowing toward me with his hands clasped, a gesture used by the well-bred of Japan—and, apparently, by the samurai of Silicon Valley as well.

TWO

An hour late, I did a quick survey of the courtyard along Stanford's Serra Mall. I spotted my mother holding forth to a bespectacled man with the vague look of an academic. I took the coward's way out and found Rowena, squeezing her arm as I slid beside her.

"Oh." She jerked her head back and at the same time her right hand let go of a flute of champagne. I thrust out my own hand, but the glass hit the concrete with my outstretched fingers still a foot away. No shattering of crystal, just a crackle of plastic and a golden splash that missed Rowena's pumps by an inch or two.

From a crouching position, I looked up. "Hello, dear."

You know how when you're talking to some people at parties, they're always surveying the crowd to spot someone more interesting or influential. Not Rowena. She focused—focused to the extent of shutting out much of the rest of the world. My touching her arm, coming as it did for all intents and purposes from another galaxy, was bound to startle her. I should have known better.

"Where have you been?" Rowena asked. "Your mom figured you'd been in a ten-car crash on 101."

She didn't sound mad, but not exactly pleased either.

"I texted you I'd be late and asked you to tell her, too," I said, moving a napkin around the wet paving stones. There had been no way to forewarn my mother. Her technological aptitude had been frozen in the late 1960s. She'd stretched her capabilities to use a TV remote control—a cell phone was out of the question.

"Oh, you did?"

Rising, I leaned toward Rowena to offer the customary obeisance of a kiss on the cheek. She turned away. Okay, she *was* mad. She'd shown up at my mother's behest even with a murder case coming up. Why couldn't I be on time?

"Françoise," Rowena said to her conversational companion, "this is my husband, Ian."

"Her clumsy husband," I added, extending my hand.

"So enchanted to meet you," Françoise said in a lilting French accent.

"Professor Roux is doing exciting work on gravitons," Rowena explained.

"Please carry on," I said.

After a few minutes, I gathered that the professor was studying, not a just-add-water mix to produce gravy, but particles that conveyed gravitational forces. No experiment had ever detected them, but that did not stop her from building a theoretical proof of their existence. To make the math work, she'd posited an extra dimension of space beyond the normal three of length, width, and depth. Would there be life forms stretching across all four dimensions? What would they look like to us who lived in only three? Why

11

hadn't we seen these creatures if they existed? Good questions, but even trying to imagine answers to them made my head throb.

When the good professor took a sip of champagne, Rowena asked, "Was it an important meeting?"

"I'll tell you later. How about here? What did I miss?"

Rowena, a deputy district attorney, was as out of place as I was at this synod of scientists, but she was here for the same reason I was—a command performance that came in the guise of a request from my mother.

A few raps on a live microphone kept Rowena from answering. "Thank you all for coming," intoned Jim Ono, the president of the university.

Stanford was on a campaign to recruit female undergraduates, Ph.D. candidates, and faculty to the natural sciences. My mother's late aunt, Isobel Marter, had been the first woman in the physics department back in the 1960s. In an effort to honor her and to appeal to what was still the second sex in the realm of natural science, the university was naming its particle physics lab after her. I'd lived in Palo Alto all my life and couldn't recall a building, library, school, or academic chair at Stanford labeled with a name except in return for a donation of dollars, euros, yen, dinars, or other convertible currency. So maybe Stanford was really serious about recruiting women. Anyway, the university invited my mother to the ceremony as Aunt Isobel's closest living relative, and she in turn had dragooned Rowena and me.

Ono stood on brick steps at the closed end of a courtyard covered by canvas and warmed by mushroom-shaped propane heaters. "Of course, a champagne reception is always a good idea, but never more than today. We are here to honor the memory of one of the pioneers of modern physics." He called up our conversational companion who, I suspected, was chosen to speak because she was the only female full professor in the Stanford physics department.

What I knew about Aunt Isobel was that she'd been at the Stanford Linear Accelerator Center, or SLAC, four decades before and worked alongside several future Nobel Prize winners. She'd died in an accident before I was born.

"We all follow in the footsteps of our predecessors," Professor Roux began. "When I was a girl in France, I wanted to be Marie Curie. After two years as a graduate student at Stanford, after two years of hearing about her legacy, I wanted to be Isobel Marter."

Shit. My iPhone started ringing. Rowena took a step away. Heads swiveled in my direction as the crowd tried to identify the boor who'd failed to put his mobile on vibrate. I fumbled in my pocket and managed to stifle it after the first chime. No one could tell I was the perpetrator. Except Rowena.

When Ono came back to the microphone, he thanked a Professor Solenski for suggesting that the lab be named after Aunt Isobel. He peered out at the audience, but couldn't spot the good professor. Then he introduced Mom, who gave a Miss America-style wave from where she stood. That was it. The hubbub of chattering physicists recommenced.

Professor Roux returned to pick up her conversation with Rowena, and I was dispatched to refill my wife's champagne and fetch a Campari and soda for the professor.

I joined the queue at the bar at the same time as a bouncy man who appeared to be in his mid-sixties, clad in an extravagantly mismatched pair of checked reddish golf pants and a yellowish tweed jacket. I was turning my iPhone to vibrate and gestured for him to go ahead in line, but he stuck out a bony hand. "Bill," he said.

I introduced myself as Isobel Marter's great nephew. After shaking his hand, I looked down for only an instant before my gaze bounced back to his eyes. A long stare at his costume might cause retinal damage.

"A tragedy about your Aunt Isobel. She was such a competent assistant."

"You worked with her then?"

"Oh, yes. She made her contribution." Bill launched himself into a disquisition. I understood he was talking about atomic particles, but not much more. His enthusiasm expounding on leptons, bosons, strange, beauty, spin, and such precluded me from interrupting for any explanations. By the time we reached the barman, I'd gleaned that protons and neutrons were not the hard balls that Mr. Martin had taught us about in high school physics. Instead, they were made up of three infinitesimal particles called quarks.

I took the drinks back to Professor Roux and Rowena.

The professor thanked me and when a colleague came over to congratulate her, my mother materialized next to me. In a fierce whisper, she asked, "How *could* you shake that man's hand?"

THREE

"Hello, Mother." I moved to peck her cheek, but, like my wife, she leaned back to put it beyond the reach of my puckered lips.

Professor Roux thanked me for the drink and proved herself a woman of discretion by waving to someone else across the patio and gliding away.

"Who is he?" I asked.

My mother turned her back to me and gave Rowena a shake of the head. After an extravagant sigh, she swiveled around and said, "That was William Z. Tompkins." Each of the five syllables of his name rat-a-tat-tatted out of her mouth as if from the muzzle of a machine gun.

"Oh. No kidding. He just introduced himself as Bill." I'd just met one of the world's most famous scientists. Tompkins had done as much to popularize physics as James Watson had genetics.

"Oh, he won the Nobel Prize..." I began. Rowena flashed me a warning with a head movement closer to a shiver than a shake. I hung an oral u-turn and asked, "Um, what's wrong with him, Mom?

"Was that your cell phone that caused the disturbance?"

Talking with my mother was always a conversational odyssey.

"Yes, Mom. I'm sorry." My mother looked over at Rowena, who held up her hands in a what-do-you-do-with-him gesture. Or she might have been signing to my mother, "Look what I have to put up with."

My mother was three inches under six feet, my wife three inches over five feet. Mom's hair was wavy and light brown, Rowena's straight and black. Mom, conscious of the gravity of the afternoon, had abandoned jeans and Birkenstocks for a tweedy skirt and sensible brown tie shoes. Rowena was clad in her office raiments, a sleek navy suit and slingback pumps. External differences aside, the two had years ago formed an alliance in the struggle against my alleged obtuseness. I carried no resentment, though. In a world of over six billion souls, these two loved me.

"Rowena could get here on time," my mother pointed out in a voice of sweet reason.

"Living up to her example is beyond me, Mom."

She nodded.

I kept my mouth shut and waited the twenty or thirty seconds it took for my mother to start talking again. No sense throwing another match on the kindling of Mom's temper.

"You forgot about the reception?" she asked, as if she expected my tardiness to be one more example of my inability to run my life without direction from her, or, in a recent concession, from Rowena.

"No, something came up. Um, a meeting. A meeting with Ricky Frankson."

"Important?"

"Not as it turned out. Sorry it made me late."

"Have you read *Small Matter*?" she asked, the toe of a sensible shoe tapping against the flagstones.

"No," I answered.

Mom turned to Rowena. "Yes, I read it back in high school," my wife said.

Mom's look back at me said, "I knew you wouldn't have read it, and I knew Rowena would have." Aloud, she asked my wife, "And what did you think?"

Rowena deliberated on her answer. "That it made physics fun— no easy task? You read it, too?"

"No. Well, not way back when it came out. I knew Aunt Isobel despised the man. It would have been disloyal. But I knew I was coming today so I checked it out."

"No royalties to him if you got it from the library."

"Exactly," my mother said.

"What do you remember from the book?" Mom asked Rowena.

"Well, it was pretty self-serving. Tompkins was the center of everything. He made his partner, what was his name?"

"Solenski."

"Oh, right. The person who suggested that the lab be named after your aunt. Well, if Tompkins made himself the Sherlock Holmes of the physics world, Solenski was the Dr. Watson, you know, the sidekick. Now I read the book more than ten years ago, but I do remember that. Tompkins didn't hide his ego, didn't even try. He was so brash, it was winning."

"He's sixty-four now and still acts like a teenager," my mother said. "My God. He even dresses to draw attention to himself."

Rowena ended the next gap of silence. "How old was Tompkins when he discovered that particle?" she asked.

"The quark," Mom said and waited for Rowena to nod before continuing. "Twenty-four, but the way you asked the question, that's the problem. A team of people discovered the quark, not Tompkins alone."

"And Aunt Isobel was one of them?" Rowena asked.

Mom smiled. Rowena could do no wrong. "Do you remember her in *Small Matter*?" Rowena shook her head. "No, why would you? Tompkins described her as a stick-in-the-mud old maid with glasses and a bun, carrying a torch for her boss, Solenski, who was married. Tompkins called her Izzy. All lies. Aunt Isobel wore contacts, shopped for clothes in Paris, did a fair amount of rock-climbing, bit the head off anyone who dared call her Izzy, and was not in love with Solenski, nor was she his assistant. She had a Ph.D. from Columbia."

"And, as we just heard, she was the first woman ever on the Stanford physics faculty," Rowena said. "You knew her pretty well?"

"Not so well. She came to Stanford before we moved here. And she died before then, too. Hit by a car crossing the street while at a conference in Geneva."

"She died before Tompkins won the Nobel Prize then?"

Mom nodded. "Last night, though, I went up to the attic and found some of her old letters in a box from my mother."

"Just last night?" I asked.

"I'd forgotten about them. You need to read them," she said to me. "I'll drop them off for you."

"Okay."

"The way that man wrote about my aunt, it's a crime."

"Tompkins?"

Mom folded her arms and leaned close. "Yes, and I want you to do justice for her."

"Do justice?"

"Get her the credit she deserves for the work she did."

"Professor Roux just called her an inspiration."

My mother gave me a tight smile. "How many people are here today?"

"A hundred fifty?"

"And how many have read *Small Matter*?"

"Okay, okay. Probably millions. But what do I know about physics? How can *I* get her credit?"

Mom's eyes narrowed. "You know what I found out when I went through my mother's boxes? That Aunt Isobel sent my parents money to help pay for me to go to Northwestern."

"You didn't know that?"

"No."

"I'll get on it right after I've dealt with this crisis at work."

"This has waited long enough. Justice delayed is justice denied. She was family—flesh and blood—and family comes first, right?"

What could I do but nod?

FOUR

"I wish I could get you the money, but it's just not going to happen," said Margot Fulbright, the venture capitalist and long-time Accelenet board member. "The firm has only thirty million left in that fund for follow-on investments. Seven of our other companies will want a cut of that, and you need at least twenty-five by yourself." She folded arms toned by daily visits to the gym and tanned by monthly trips to her place on the Big Island.

VCs, bah. When you had no need for their money, investment offers would cascade over you like a tropical waterfall. When you could use a capital infusion—like now—the money flowed like water in a wadi, a riverbed in the Sahara. In other words, it didn't.

I just stared at her across the conference table in her downtown Palo Alto office, saying nothing. She picked the conversational thread back up. "Yes, yes, you did everything you said you would. You are on plan, your product works well." Last year, when all looked rosy, Fulbright referred to Accelenet as "us," not "you."

"Only what?" I asked.

"Okay, it works great. It could revolutionize telecommunications and networking. But my partners are tired of this. We backed Paul and then you. We've used up their patience. Nothing left in the tank."

Paul Berk, my best friend, my predecessor as CEO of Accelenet, had vanished just after the murder of Rowena's sister Gwendolyn. Reports of sightings showed up in the papers every month or two. I knew they meant nothing. Paul was gone—along with his wife. And he'd left me behind to run his company. If he didn't want to be found, he would not be. Damn him.

It was no fun following a legend. Did Steve Young have the same feeling when he replaced Joe Montana as the 49ers' quarterback? No matter what he did, even winning the Super Bowl, he'd never be Joe Cool. But my perverse nature had made me a Young partisan.

"We could look for a new investor," I said.

"You could, but once they find out that Samsung is pulling out of your deal, you're screwed. Maybe you'd still do okay if Cisco's going to renew."

Any sign of a smile was gone as I shook my head. "Torii buys a couple hundred million dollars a year in equipment from them. A hint that might go away, and Cisco will walk from our deal."

"You could sue for predatory practices."

"Sure. And in ten years we'd win. The company would be gone. Look what happened to Andersen."

She nodded. The feds had moved to pin blame for the Enron fiasco on its accounting firm. By the time an appellate court ruled in favor of Andersen, its employees and clients were long gone. "So?"

"You think we should do a deal with Ricky?" I asked.

"What choice do you have?"

"Tell me how you think a deal with him would play out." She would know. She'd been a vice president of marketing at Torii in the early '90s, and owed her first seven million to Torii's IPO. As a venture capitalist, she'd sold a dozen companies to Torii. She'd leveraged her experience sitting at the table next to Frankson *and* across from him to create this niche.

"Well, two hundred fifty million for Accelenet lets your investors, including us, make some money and get on with life. The employees wouldn't be Google-rich, but they'd walk away with something—a house in Palo Alto for the people who've been there for awhile, a down payment for a condo in Sunnyvale for the newbies. You yourself could take it easy, spend time with Rowena, travel. You deserve it, Ian. We've had a good run."

"What's it like doing a deal with him? What's the process?"

She leaned forward. Her hair was pulled up and back so tightly that her eyes had an Asian cast. In fact, her entire face had the taut look of someone who'd visited a plastic surgeon recently. "Ricky doesn't lose. Torii has twelve billion in the bank and tosses off another billion every quarter in free cashflow. You can't win a poker game against him, no matter how good your hand is. And yours is no pairs, seven high."

"I'm not on a mission from God here. I can be pragmatic, but I hate giving in to blackmail."

She reached across the table and tapped my shoulder twice with a pink-nailed finger. "Get the best deal you can from Ricky. He's got you by the balls."

———

Before I'd even reached my car, the bumblebee buzz of my vibrating iPhone began tickling my right thigh.

I pulled the instrument out of my pocket. The number of the caller was blocked. "Hello."

"Ricky Frankson here."

Had Margot called him before the elevator doors had even closed behind me?

"Hello, Ricky."

"I'm not sure I was at my most charming yesterday. Could we try again?"

"I have a pretty full schedule the rest of the day."

"How about a drink right now?"

"I'm just out of a meeting and on my way back to the office." I was walking past a California Pizza Kitchen on my way to the garage.

"Look to your right."

I turned and gazed across Cowper Street toward Il Fornaio, a favorite spot for Silicon Valley dealmaking. There at an outdoor table sat Frankson, with an oversized Bluetooth microphone wrapped around his left ear.

He'd known I'd be meeting with Margot. "Murder while lying in wait is a capital crime in California," I told him.

I heard the start of a chuckle and then nothing. He'd hung up. Pretty sure of himself.

Standing on the sidewalk in full view of Frankson, I dilly-dallied a few seconds and turned my phone back to ring. Then I jaywalked and sat down across from him at a small wrought iron table. I'd bet he'd changed clothes since yesterday, but he was dressed the same—in a black T-shirt and black pants. He probably had the biggest and most boring closet in Christendom.

At the next table sat a burly, crewcut man with the ramrod posture of an ex-Marine. When you're worth almost twenty billion dollars, you travel with a bodyguard.

Frankson took a sip from an oversized pottery mug. "Japanese sencha. Passable. What about you?"

"I'll have the same." Frankson raised a hand and a waitress materialized. He just kept sipping until my mug, a twin of his, showed up. I raised it to my lips, and he held up a hand.

"You should let it steep for another ninety seconds," He told me.

I took a sip.

"It's fine," I said. Of course, it wasn't. Too weak. "I just have a minute. Could we get down to brass tacks, please?"

"I spoke yesterday about two hundred fifty million for Accelenet. I offered you a job, too. I want to be more specific about that. You'd be put in charge, not just of Accelenet's product line, but all our board products. That would be a four billion dollar business. You'd also get a stock option grant of one point eight million shares of Torii."

"That almost sounds like a bribe. I'm just a representative of the company's shareholders and employees."

He smiled. "Excuse me. I should have mentioned the employees first thing. Anyone you wanted on your team at Torii could come across."

"And if I want all Accelenet employees to have jobs?'

"It's your business. It's your call. I'm not selling Ginsu knives here, but wait there's more. I'd also put aside two pools of fifty million, one for stockholders and one for the employees who come across. If the Accelenet product line does as well as we'd expect, both would be paid out at the end of three years."

Had Margot been negotiating behind my back? I sipped my tea and then my phone started playing—what else?—"Rowena's Song" by Unshine. "I don't mean to be rude," I said to Frankson, "but my wife's calling."

"Your first wife?"

"Yeah, one and only."

"If you want her to be your last, you'd better answer. Believe me. Divorces are expensive."

"Hello," I said.

"Ian. My mother's just called. Daddy, he's in the emergency room. They don't know if he's going to make it."

"I'll pick you up in five minutes and we'll fly down."

FIVE

"GOD, IAN." MY MOTHER-IN-LAW looped her arms around me. Whenever Rowena hugged me, her head nestled under my chin. Her mother, a few inches taller, could rest her head on my shoulder.

Nurses and doctors walked by us—some strolling, some trotting—as we just stood, holding on to each other in the corridor of Scripps Memorial Hospital in La Jolla. None of them stared. An embrace of hopelessness, a last grasp onto the slippery tendrils of life, must have been as unremarkable here in the cardiac unit as a newborn's cry in the obstetrics wing. I had a hand on Caroline Goldberg's back and could feel her breathing change from a series of gasps to a regular rhythm.

"How is he doing?" I asked.

"Not good. He asked for a few minutes with Rowena. We've been out here long enough. We can go back. He wanted to see you, too."

In the room Rowena sat on the right edge of the bed, holding her father's hand in both of hers. Two clear tubes snaked out of

Jack Goldberg's nostrils to a jade-colored canister of oxygen. The bluish purple bruises under his eyes contrasted with the cadaverous gray of his cheeks. Jack was closer to anorexia than obesity, but, still, the skin of his neck hung down from his jaw in slack folds like an elephant's.

I squeezed his forearm. "Hey, Jack."

"Hello, Ian. Thank you for coming." He did not speak in the whisper I expected. His matter-of-fact tone and everyday modulation seemed inappropriate in a room where death loomed.

He closed his eyes for a minute and then opened them. He focused on Rowena.

"Gwennie."

Jack was close enough to the grave that he mistook my ebony-haired wife for her blonde sister Gwendolyn, who'd been dead for four years.

Caroline gasped and opened her mouth. Rowena shook her head. She moved to the bed and put her hand on Jack's arm. "Yes, Daddy," she said.

He smiled and closed his eyes. Thirty minutes later, at twenty minutes to five, Jack Goldberg's heart stopped beating.

I stared at the now soulless body on the bed and then at the two weeping women he left behind.

———

Less than forty-eight hours after my father-in-law died, Rabbi Kahn, who'd buried Gwendolyn and married us, was conducting a memorial service. A graveside ceremony followed, ending with clumps of dirt clattering on the casket as parent was interred next to child.

At the family house, mirrors were covered as tradition required—a mourning period was no time for vanity. During *shivah*, the prescribed seven days after the burial, the front door stayed open and a stream of somberly dressed neighbors, friends, and synagogue members rolled in bearing comfort and casseroles. Sitting on kitchen stools, Rowena and Caroline greeted the visitors with tears and embraces, just as they had four years ago, after Gwendolyn's funeral. It was then, while a visitor myself, I had met both Rowena and her mother. This time, a member of the family, I sat with them and Jack's three sisters.

My own mother, God bless her, came down from Palo Alto to oversee the logistics and provide Caroline with the sympathy of a woman who'd also lost her husband. The rabbi helped, too. Each night of the *shivah* period, the gravel-voiced cleric conducted a short service that included reminiscences by Jack's friends and siblings. On the first night my sister Allison moved all of us to tears with her memories of Jack's pride when Rowena and I were married.

During *shivah*, one was supposed to leave behind the quotidian and focus on the transcendent. I was not a good mourner. The day after Jack was buried I snuck out of bed at five and sent an email to my staff explaining that I would be out of touch for a week. Each of the next six days, I took care of essential email via my iPhone. Two days after the funeral, I made a call to Bharat Gupta, the Accelenet CFO.

"Sorry to awaken you," I said

"You didn't," he said. "I was lying awake going down a list of possible sources of capital. I was at robbing 7-Elevens when you called."

I laughed. "We have enough for six more pay periods?"

"Yup. Without the cash flow from Samsung and Cisco, just three months."

A quick discussion on the quarter's forecast ensued, and then we hung up.

A man named Hobson had owned a livery stable in Cambridge, England four hundred years ago. He offered his customers a choice between the horse closest the barn door or no horse at all. Was doing a deal with Frankson a Hobson's choice? Was there an alternative to selling to Torii? I sent him an email apologizing for being called away during our meeting and promising to get back in touch next week.

At the end of the seven days, I was going to fly back to the Bay Area. Rowena and my mother were staying.

I gave Caroline a hug. "Sixty-two is too young to die."

"What I realize now," she said, "is that Jack didn't die at sixty-two. He died at fifty-eight. The knife that killed Gwendolyn killed him, too. It just took longer."

SIX

"Paul!"

The comforter fell away as I jerked up. I realized the scream had been mine. What was Paul Berk doing looking through our bedroom window? Had I awakened Rowena? No. Her side of the bed was empty. Was she already downstairs? I checked the clock radio—3:23. Wait, she was still down south with her mother.

I'd seen his face so clearly through the window. I knew the bedroom was on the second floor and unless Paul had shimmied up a tree, he couldn't have peered in. Yet his face had been so real, so there, so unchanged except for the crevices cutting deeper into his forehead, that I had to go look. My heart jack-hammering, I got up and gazed right through the mullioned glass—Rowena didn't believe in drapes or curtains. I saw the two pines outlined in the glow from the street lamp at the end of the cul-de-sac. A car down the block turned onto Hamilton Avenue. No Paul.

I climbed back into bed and lay staring at the ceiling. In the wake of Gwendolyn's murder, Paul had fled Palo Alto. An indicted fugitive, Paul might be gone in one sense. But in another, he was not. From the inside of my skull, he watched me. Watched me do what? Try to save Accelenet. Which as his successor as CEO, it was my job to do. I knocked the side of my head with my right palm. I didn't want Paul in there, but after ten years of working for him, of being obsessed with pleasing him, he was a constant presence. I hadn't seen him in four years, but he still haunted me. I suspected Gwendolyn's death was still haunting him.

At four-fifteen I rolled out of bed and went into the den. When Rowena and I had combined libraries, we'd had to go two deep on the bookshelves. While we hadn't exactly organized them according to the Dewey Decimal System, the books were roughly split between fiction and non-fiction. Even eliminating half the possibilities still meant that I might have to pull volumes off two dozen long shelves to find the book I was looking for. That task took twenty minutes. I found it out of place, behind a long row of Anita Brookner novels we'd inherited from Gwendolyn.

I flicked the switch on the pharmacy lamp, settled in my favorite reading spot, a brown paisley armchair, and began reading. On page 53 of *Small Matter*, Tompkins wrote:

> *At our meeting that Monday, Solenski introduced me to his assistant, Izzy Marter. From the outset, she had some sort of chip on her shoulder and repeatedly interrupted him. She might have been a good-looking girl if she had done something with her hair and worn more stylish clothes.*

Times had changed. Tompkins characterized Aunt Isobel more as an uppity secretary than a brilliant physicist. My mom would say we'd been right after all to shelve the book with the fiction. The irony of Tompkins' fashion criticism was that in a couple of photos in his own book, he wore the same kind of mismatched ensembles he had at the Stanford reception. Plaid bellbottoms and tie-dyed shirts were a far cry from sartorial sophistication even in the let-it-all-hang-out 1960s. I was grateful the photos were in black and white.

Slamming the book shut at seven-thirty, I headed back to the bedroom where I pulled on tee shirt, shorts, and Nikes. Good ideas came to me when I ran. It was almost Zen. When I focused on breathing and pace, my subconscious would go into overdrive. Seven good miles and maybe the answer to the puzzle of how Accelenet could survive as an independent company would come to me. Whether it did or not, I'd get some much needed exercise.

As I opened the front door, I heard my iPhone chiming in the bedroom. I reached my dresser in five rings and lunged for the phone. Dropped it. I scooped it up and pressed the button.

"Hello." Made it.

"I heard you were back in town."

"Hey, Ricky. You having me followed?"

"That was a dramatic exit last week. You playing hard to get?"

No apology for the early call forthcoming or expected. "Sure. The fast departure was playacting."

"Interesting stratagem. You're the ugliest girl in the school, and you say no to the football captain when he asks you to the prom."

Someone had been talking, probably Margot. In any case, Frankson knew we were short on cash and had no alternative on hand to Torii. "That's a little sexist, isn't it, Ricky?" I heard a snort. "Listen, we've got the hottest technology in networking since Vint Cerf came up with TCP/IP," I continued.

Bravado. I recognized that speeding up networks by four or five times wasn't on par with the breakthrough that led to the Internet.

He laughed. "Yeah, right. You're a real catch, aren't you? Listen, while you've been gallivanting, I haven't been sitting on my ass. I can buy a majority of the shares of Accelenet right now."

So he *had* been talking to Margot and other board members, too.

"Why talk to me then?"

"Protocol."

Bullshit. If Torii took over Accelenet and everyone left, it would be worth less, a lot less. The value of a Silicon Valley company wasn't in inventory or patents. It was in the brains of its employees.

"I see," I said.

"We can do this deal with you or without you. The offer I made at Il Fornaio stands. If you say no, I'll get the company anyway. You've got a week. You're smart. You'll see you have no alternative."

He hung up. "Thanks, Hobson," I said as I pushed the end button on my iPhone.

Twenty minutes later I found myself running uphill to the Stanford dish, an obsolescent radio telescope that crowned one of the foothills in back of the campus. Forty minutes after that, I stood hands on knees trying to catch my breath. As my respiration slowed down, the gears in my mind began whirling faster. An hour later fed, showered, and dressed, I climbed into my car, the same reliable Acura I'd had for half a dozen years. It was time to go to work. But instead, a sense of filial duty led me toward the Stanford Quad.

SEVEN

Through the windows of the Varian Building, I could see the courtyard where the reception had been the previous week.

Just outside the double glass doors of the physics department office were the mail slots for the professors. I sneaked an envelope out of Tompkins' and saw it was addressed to Room 313. I trotted up the metal steps of an inside stairwell lined with cinderblocks. His office door was open. I knocked and stuck my head around the corner.

Clark Kerr once said his job as president of the University of California was to provide football for the alumni, sex for the students, and offices for the faculty. Bill Tompkins' sanctum was twice the size of Professor Woodward's, an English professor I'd visited four years ago, but only a third the size of Leon Henderson's, a business school professor who also served on Accelenet's board. The way universities apportioned space reflected their academic values.

In the corporate world, you couldn't just amble into an office, but here I could. Through the wall of windows opposite me, I could see the science building next door. The wall on my left was covered by the same green chalkboards that I used in first grade in the late 1970s. I was no fan of whiteboards, and it was reassuring to think of scientific breakthroughs being sketched out with sticks of soft, earthy limestone rather than mephitic, headache-inducing markers.

The wall in back of Tompkins' desk was a shrine to his favorite idol—himself. The array of photos stretched from ceiling to floor. I'd seen a similar display of hobnobbing with the rich and famous in the office of a Washington lobbyist. It made sense there. A shot of the lobbyist with a senator or cabinet secretary was a credential just like the diploma from Stanford Medical School in old Dr. Dubitzky's office. But I'd bet almost any K Street influence-peddler would have swapped photo collections with Tompkins straight up. The White House photographer had snapped him with every president from LBJ to Bush the Second. In one 16x20 picture he was even dressed appropriately—resplendent in white tie and tails, his Nobel medal dangled from his left hand, while his right was grasped by the King of Sweden. If Tompkins were sitting behind his desk, this one would be the cynosure, the one that would draw the eyes of any visitor.

I walked around the desk and peered at the photos in the high left-hand corner of the wall. In one Tompkins stood outside the Stanford Linear Accelerator Center with construction equipment in the background. In another he was caught in earnest conversation with his co-Nobelists-to-be, Solenski, whose skull was encircled by a dark fringe of hair was then dark, and the SLAC director, Vansittart, who wore a Churchillian dotted bowtie. I spent a few minutes studying the shot of him writing on a chalkboard filled with sketches of nuclei-emitting particles.

Then there it was. Finally. Like the photo of the Loch Ness monster that was supposed to prove that it lived and breathed. Through the glass of the black frame I could see two tiers of physicists posing. In the middle of the front row stood Vansittart, who was easy to spot, thanks to his bowtie. To his right, grinning, stood Tompkins, dressed like a gawky teenager, long forelock swept upward and with—of all things—a pocket protector covering his heart. All he needed was a slide rule to fit the geek archetype. In the back row on the far right, with two feet between her and the next person stood a woman who was no nerd. It was the 1960s, and she wore a skirt that stopped eight inches above her knees and a pair of leather boots that stopped three inches below. Fashions from the era of Mary Quant and the Beatles didn't look so fetching four decades later. This woman carried it off though. With her shoulder-length dark hair, thin face, thick eyebrows, long legs, and fierce expression, she looked more like a sister to my wife than aunt to my mother. Aunt Isobel. Had to be.

"Hallo?"

I whirled around. "Oh, Professor Tompkins. Sorry. I wanted a word with you. I met you …"

"Yes, at the reception last week."

"I hope it's okay that I came in. I couldn't resist the photographs. What a career you've had."

"I've been lucky," he replied in a tone that said luck had nothing to do with it. Clad in a green-and-blue-checked short sleeve shirt, he sat behind his oak desk, leaned back on the chair, and asked, "What can I do for you?"

"I mentioned to you last week that Isobel Marter was my aunt."

"Great aunt, wasn't she?"

"Yes, that's right. Well, what with President's Ono's remarks, we realized we didn't really know her at all."

"She was a very bright woman."

"I recently re-read *Small Matter*."

"Well, I might have been less charitable in the book to her than I should have been. You know you write a memoir the way you remember things, and your memory can play tricks."

"How so?"

Tompkins took a letter opener off his desk and began tapping it against his desk blotter. "I always felt that she'd wasted her potential."

"And what was a waste?"

"There we were with this spanking new incredible machine that had cost the American taxpayer two hundred million and could shoot electrons at atoms darn near the speed of light."

"And what did Isobel think of it?"

"She seemed more focused on the math of the atom then on its reality. Instead of working with us on the machine, she would sit in her office writing equations on the blackboard. In today's terms, it was like trying to build a computer model of the Stanford-Cal game to determine who would win while the teams are playing at the stadium down the street. Watch and see what happens. No need to guess."

"She was misguided, then?"

"Well, there are two kinds of physicists, you see. There are theoreticians who spend time doing arcane equations trying to guess how the universe works, and then there are experimentalists, like me, who try to find out through observation."

"Solenski and Vansittart liked your way?"

"Of course. They didn't sit in their offices either."

"So you and Solenski and Vansittart shared the Nobel Prize in 1973," I said.

"Yes, we shared it for my experiment." He sighed. "Ah, yes. If you make one discovery like we did, people can consider you lucky."

"So since then, you have tried to win a second one?"

"Of course, but even Einstein won only one Nobel."

"Madame Curie won two."

"I only hope I live long enough."

"A posthumous Nobel wouldn't be worth much, would it?"

"No such thing. Nobel Prizes are only awarded to the living." Tompkins stood up.

"You don't have any letters or papers or lab work from Isobel Marter, do you?"

"And why do you ask?"

"I'd like to know her better."

"I'm no pack rat. I wrote what I remembered in *Small Matter*."

Taking his extended hand, I said, "Thank you for your time," I said and extended my hand. "I appreciated the opportunity to see your photos as well."

"My pleasure," he said grasping my hand. "It is tragic that Izzy died so young. I don't want to speak ill of the dead."

EIGHT

PLUMP DROPS OF RAIN were plopping against the sidewalk when I came out of the Varian Building.

Before he absconded with his wife, when I worked for Paul Berk, he used to make fun of me on days like this. I'd come into the office cold and wet, while he would be equipped with overcoat, hat, and umbrella. "What would you wear on a gloomy, wet February day in the forties on a business trip to New York?" he'd ask.

"A lined raincoat," I'd say.

"But here we are on a gloomy, wet February day in the forties and you're in shirtsleeves. What's the difference between Manhattan and Silicon Valley?"

I had no good answer. Growing up here in Silicon Valley, I'd been brainwashed. Just a few miles north of Palo Alto, an archway in downtown Redwood City proclaimed, "Climate best by government test" and I was not going to dress in a way that would undercut that assertion. My nieces, who lived a few miles farther up the Peninsula, went to elementary school wearing T-shirts and shorts all winter long. Paul was not a native—he grew up in Manhattan—and didn't get it.

All this explains why my protection from the elements consisted of cotton khakis and an Oxford cloth button-down in the French blue shade Rowena liked. I could have retreated back into the physics building and waited for the rain to let up, but that course of action didn't even occur to me. I strode out from beneath the overhang, turned my head up to the heavens, shut my eyes, and let the drops pelt my face. The rain itself had turned my mind to Paul, and maybe I was hoping it could in turn wash thoughts of him away.

No. Paul had shaped me, influenced my adult life as my parents had my childhood. He recruited me to Accelenet and gave me access to one of the two or three best minds in the Valley. He disappeared knowing I'd pick up the reins he'd dropped. For that matter, his disappearance and Gwendolyn's death had led me to Rowena and marriage. My fate remained wrapped in his invisible shackles.

After a few minutes, I settled on a bench and nodded out of courtesy to the white statues of a lesbian couple who embraced at the other end. The water soaked right through the seat of my trousers, but it didn't matter. I was as wet now as I'd been under the showerhead this morning. A gardener in a yellow rainsuit ambled by on the pathway, but he threw no more than a cursory glance at me and my companions, the alabaster women. Workers at Stanford must be inured to eccentric behavior.

I turned my mind to the present. What to do? Was selling the company to Frankson my only choice? How unjustly was my great aunt treated? Twin rackets swatted the questions back and forth across the tennis court of my mind as the rain continued to run down my face.

If the rain had persisted, I might have sat there until I melted, but after twenty minutes I realized I was sitting in no more than a cold fog. A small fissure opened between two charcoal clouds that arced over the foothills and a rainbow began to dance in the mist to the west. I decided to chase it.

———

I had the car heater and fan on maximum to dry me out as I drove west on Sand Hill Road. This was familiar territory, the Vatican of venture capitalism. In the bubble days of the late 1990s, office space on Sand Hill was the most expensive in the world. Here's where the founders of Google, eBay, Amazon, and Cisco had come, hat in hand, seeking the dollars required to turn the base metal of their dreams into stock market gold.

I took the entrance ramp south on I-280 and looked out the window. Just as tens of thousands of cars did every day, I was crossing over what looked like a two-mile long train of freight cars, stretching from the foothills back to the campus—the Stanford Linear Accelerator Center. I exited the freeway and came back north and went down Sand Hill the way I'd come. There was a sign I'd seen dozens of times and paid little attention to. I swung right and pulled up to a guard's shack and out came a gray-haired man who held John Irving's *The World According to Garp* in his left hand, thumb marking his place. He'd missed a swathe of whiskers on his cheek.

"Whom are you here to see?" Stanford evidently chose to teach its security staff the Queen's English rather than grooming.

"Is Professor Solenski in?" I asked.

"Do you have an appointment?" I shook my head. "An appointment is required."

"Could you check and see if he's in?"

"He's not. He doesn't come in every day."

I scribbled a note and asked the guard to make sure he received it.

Time to get back to work. Enough chasing rainbows—for now.

NINE

On the way into the office, I called Juliana, once our company's receptionist, now the executive staff's admin, and let her know I was on my way. When I arrived, a scrum of company executives was huddled outside my office door. I invited all five of them in and accepted their condolences for my father-in-law.

The others would have sat quietly for a minute to draw a distinct line between grief and business, but not Vince Lacquer, the VP of sales. He didn't wait two seconds before launching into what was on everyone's mind. "Torii's salespeople are telling our prospects we're going broke. Our guys tell me that they couldn't sell Accelenet insect repellent in the Everglades in July."

No surprise. That was just the way Frankson did business. In his way of thinking, Machiavelli was a wimp. He knew Sun Tzu's *Art of War* by heart, and applied its lessons to business. It wasn't enough for Torii to win. All its competitors needed to lose.

"I can get on the phone and talk to the prospects. We have money coming."

If sales dropped off a cliff, the price Frankson would pay for Accelenet would start plunging, too.

Four years ago, I'd resigned from Accelenet, ready to strike out on my own, start my own company, finally leave the nest. But after Paul disappeared, the board had convinced me to come back. The people in the room gave me credit for our success when I knew it was due much more to their hard work, together with dollops of luck and chutzpah. Now the dice had stopped coming up with sevens. Cisco and Samsung were backing away, and our winning streak was in danger. The team looked to me to find the solution to the crisis. They had more faith in me than I had in myself.

Shaking his shaved, chocolate brown head, Lacquer said, "Not good enough, Captain."

Lacquer had been an all-conference defensive tackle at USC. Four knee operations had ended any chance for an NFL career, but his competitiveness remained.

Ron Qi, the inventor of the Bonds technology incorporated in our TurboCom product line and now our head of engineering, looked down as if examining the polish on his shoes. The other three around the table, Samantha Maxwell, our Korean-born, MIT-educated marketing genius; Ori Mohr, the ex-Israeli para-trooper and kick-ass head of operations; and Bharat Gupta, the CFO, all moved their eyes from Vince back to me. Without turning around, I knew Juliana—loyal and patient, but concerned—was at the open door waiting for answers, too. Lacquer and Maxwell would be the ones doing the talking.

"We've been through this before," I told them as I swiveled my head to look each of them in the eyes. "We have money coming. I've met with Margot. The money is there."

"You going to sell the company?" Samantha asked.

"That's not our first choice."

Lacquer said, "We're going to have to be more specific than that to close some business."

I saw Ron, who'd been brought up in the more deferential milieu of Taiwan, wince at Lacquer's directness.

"Okay. Bharat and I will put something together. And then we'll have Samantha come up with a statement we can show prospects under non-disclosure that will reassure them about our viability."

"We still won't beat Torii," Lacquer said.

"If sales were easy, Vincent, we wouldn't need you." I reached up to clap him on the shoulder.

I would have loved to have told the staff about Frankson's offer. But I'd learned in the Valley that no more than two people could keep a business secret and that only worked if one of them was dead.

———

Bharat came back to my office just after two.

"You have something cooking, don't you?" he asked.

"I wouldn't be surprised if we get an offer in the next couple of weeks. We have a duty to get the best price."

"Why don't I check with our bankers and have them put out feelers to IBM, Verizon, Deutsche Telekom, and a few other customers? See if we can get competing offers."

Just what I'd had in mind. "Good idea. Let's do it."

I spent the rest of the afternoon reassuring our employees and sales prospects about our future. Back in the 1990s, IT departments of Fortune 1000 companies bought equipment from Silicon

Valley start-ups in a frenzy, wanting to surf the Internet wave. At the same time they wanted to foster competition among traditional IT suppliers like IBM, Cisco, Oracle, and Torii. With the bursting of the high-tech bubble in 2000, most of the smaller suppliers had gone belly-up and left the IT departments with orphaned equipment and software. So their concern was understandable. Once—or more than once—bitten, twice shy.

Each prospect I spoke to responded to my optimism with skepticism about the company's future unless we did a deal with Torii. But the terms were unacceptable. I looked out my window into the parking lot—quite a contrast from the vista of the Bay I'd seen from Frankson's office. Well, that's what Paul used to say: the key to success in business was being able to choose the better of two shitty choices.

TEN

MAYBE MY TASTE FOR pizza could be chalked up to genetics. I'd been born at Stanford Hospital, but both my parents were from Chicago with its long tradition of excellence in stuffing both ballot boxes and pizza. Patxi's in downtown Palo Alto did a pretty good facsimile of the real thing, so on the way home I hit the speed dial on my iPhone and ordered a deep dish mushroom and spinach for delivery. In a small concession to my absent wife's exhortations to eat healthfully, I specified low-fat mozzarella and a whole wheat crust.

I parked halfway up the driveway, just by the front door. We'd been living here in the old Crescent Park neighborhood of Palo Alto since we were married three years ago. Rowena found the house. She studied the real estate listings in *The Palo Alto Weekly* like my friends and I had scrutinized *Playboy*'s monthly offerings when we were fourteen. The difference, of course, was that the naked, chesty intellectuals with staples through their navels were beyond the reach of teenagers, while Rowena and I—with the help of Absolute Mortgage Company—could swing this ninety-year-old two-decker.

The house was bigger than what we needed, but who could blame Rowena for wanting to move out of the house where her sister was murdered? Each year we'd done some renovation—kitchen, den, library, laundry room. I was no good at saying no to Rowena. When we'd met after her sister's murder, I was work-obsessed, with no sense of what was really important. A couple of weeks later, in the wee hours of the morning, she'd just showed up on my doorstep. Or really in my bedroom. We'd made love. Since then, since that moment, she'd renovated my life.

As soon as my key touched the lock, the front door swung open. What the hell? Who could have left it open? Not Rowena—she was down south with her mother.

I reached into my pocket. There on my key ring was a small Swiss Army knife I'd received as a memento from an investment banker. I opened it and began tiptoeing up the staircase.

Three steps from the top, I heard a creak and then there on the landing, the person who'd left the door open appeared. She shrieked and dropped a laundry basket filled with a multi-colored collection of bras and panties. I was face-to-face with my wife.

With her right hand over her lips, Rowena said, "I didn't hear you come in." She looked down the stairs. "No wonder. You didn't close the front door." Then she looked down at my hand. "You thought there was an intruder in the house, and you were coming upstairs with a two-inch blade in your hand?"

I, too, looked down at the red pocket knife.

"A lot of good that would have done against an intruder with a handgun. Listen to me. I'd rather be married to a chicken who's alive than a hero who's not. Promise me you'll call 911 if ever you think there's an intruder in here."

"If I'd done that this time, I'd look like a fool, wouldn't I?"

She dropped her hands to her hips. "Promise."

"I promise." I put my arms around her. "What are you doing home anyway?"

"I sent an email. You didn't get it on that iPhone of yours?"

Looking down at the device hanging from my belt, I saw a flashing red message light.

A man's voice called from downstairs, "Hello? Anyone home?"

I felt Rowena's back jerk. "Pizza man," I explained. "Good news, too."

"What's that?"

"I ordered a large."

A few minutes later we were sitting at the kitchen table. Between bites of layered crust, cheese, and veggies, I asked Rowena, "Are you sure it was a good idea to leave your mother?"

She finished chewing. "I had no choice. She sent me away. She said she'd be fine with your mom. Your mom's going to stay there till next week, until she goes to Israel."

Mom was heading to the Holy Land with my sister and her family. Trying to finagle Rowena and me into going, too, she'd set off little 4.5 temblors on the Richter Scale of Guilt with queries like "When will we all have another chance to be together like this?" But with Rowena's trial and the squeeze at Accelenet, no way. Mom had sighed, "It will have to be enough to be with Allison, Harold, and my only two grandchildren." My mental seismograph registered 6.2. The words "my only two grandchildren" were sprinkled through Mom's conversations with me like salt on pretzels.

"Well, your mom wanted to cancel her trip, but mine wouldn't hear of it," Rowena said. "So after bickering for a couple of days, they settled on your mom leaving directly from San Diego next week and meeting up with your sister in New York for the flight to Tel Aviv. But as for me, Mom practically kicked me out. She said you needed me more than she did. So I jumped on a flight and took a taxi from the airport."

Rowena sipped from a glass filled with the under-eight-dollar Australian merlot she favored.

"Hmm." I took a swig from a bottle of Anchor Christmas Ale left over from our December Hanukkah party. "You think your mom will be okay?"

"You know how tough she is." Caroline's husband had been a successful player in the hurly-burly of the business world and she'd been a stay-at-home mother. But she had managed to carry on after Gwendolyn's murder, while he had fallen apart. She'd survive this, too.

"And you?"

She sighed. "I'm not as tough. Daddy is gone. It's just awful. You understand." My father had been dead for seven years.

"Yeah, I do." I touched her hand. We sat that way for a few minutes. Then she took another sip of the merlot.

"Mom said I should get back for the beginning of my case, too. So tomorrow we'll get started with the opening argument and probably get to a witness or two as well."

"Can I come watch?" It would be her first opening argument in a murder case.

"You must be too busy."

"What time?"

"Nine-thirty."

I had to make up for my tardiness in joining her at the Stanford reception. "I'll make it."

She smiled.

After the pizza was gone—I'd eaten six pieces, Rowena two—she asked what was going on at Accelenet. Even a quick review took twenty minutes.

"Can you hold the team together?" she asked at the end of my recital.

"We'll see."

As I put the plates and her glass in the dishwasher, Rowena said, "Your mom had me stop by her house to get Aunt Isobel's letters."

"Good. Thank you. I did stop by to see Tompkins."

"And?"

"He was Moses on the mountain, bringing word of his revelation about the quark to the awaiting masses below."

"An asshole, huh?"

"If conceit makes an asshole, yes. You know the person who makes a breakthrough isn't always the person who gets credit. That's life."

"Yeah, I know. Columbus didn't discover America, some Norseman did."

"Here in the Valley, forgetting the pioneer happens all the time, too."

"So you've told me. There's the guy up in the City who says he came up with the idea of providing software as a service. Your friend's company was selling it six months before, but since his company got bought, no one remembers. So it does happen all the time—that doesn't mean we should let it happen to your Aunt Isobel."

That night when we were in bed, Rowena had her back to me, and I reached over and cupped her breast through her T-shirt. She turned to me, kissed my cheek, and said, "I'm sorry, Ian. I'm glad to be back home with you, but not tonight, okay?"

There had been no lovemaking while we were down south. During the seven days of *shivah*, mourners are supposed to refrain from all pleasurable activities. We'd not gone this long without lovemaking since we were married.

I told Rowena, "Sure. I understand."

She turned back over, brushed her hair aside with her hand, and was asleep in less than a minute.

Understanding my mind might have been—her father had died, she had her first opening argument in a murder case tomorrow. My body, though, was less sympathetic. It took about half an hour for it to simmer down. I had a few seconds of serenity before my mind began to roil with thoughts of what needed to be done to keep sales going, to find an alternative source of capital to Torii. Then my mind went in another direction, and when I realized, after another thirty minutes, that I wasn't going to be able to fall back to sleep, I rolled out of bed, went to my office down the hall, untied the string around the two sheaves of Aunt Isobel's letters Rowena had left for me, and started reading.

ELEVEN

AUNT ISOBEL HAD GONE to elementary school in the 1930s and 1940s before kids communicated via words tapped out on a computer keyboard or cellphone keypad. Teaching handwriting was taken seriously in those days, and Isobel must have been a star. A pleasure to read, her cursive had a feminine flow with the backslant of a left-hander. The first few letters were from Wellesley, where she'd gone on scholarship in 1947.

I detected none of the homesickness you'd expect to find from a sixteen-year-old away for the first time. Although internal references indicated she wrote to her parents every Sunday, I could find only a dozen letters from those undergraduate years. While most of the letters focused on news of roommates and friends and extracurricular activities, one from her sophomore year expounded on a physics teacher. "The mechanics, electricity, and magnetism I learned about in high school physics could have been taught by Isaac Newton. Now I'm learning about the fundamental building blocks of the universe, invisible to the naked eye and even to the most powerful microscopes." With the advantage of hindsight, it was easy to see where her infatuation would lead.

I wasn't surprised to find a ten-year hiatus in the letters after college. From Mom's family stories I knew Aunt Isobel had lived with her parents while studying at Columbia with Nobel Prize Winner I. I. Rabi. It had been a shock to move from the all-woman world of Wellesley to being Columbia's only female Ph.D. candidate in physics. "Like a jump from sauna to ice bath," Mom said. Isobel stayed on at Columbia for a post-doc fellowship, doing experimental research using the university's state-of-the-art cyclotron.

Finally, the documentary trail picked up in 1965 after Isobel moved across the country to Stanford.

I wish I could be at SLAC full-time. Research is what I love. I don't understand how I won an award for undergraduate teaching. Most of my students have no interest in introductory physics and are taking the course only because medical schools require it. Lectures, grading papers, and office hours take most of the day. I do my research nights and weekends at SLAC.

As the old saying goes, shit slides downhill, and as the junior member of Stanford's physics department, Isobel was the one who taught introductory physics. Isobel's next letter made it easy to infer what Isobel's mother's number one concern was.

Mother, I am surrounded by men. The faculty as a whole is over ninety percent male. In meetings, when having coffee, or even when going out in the evening with friends, I am the only woman. More male attention, I do not need or wish for. If anything, I would like a female colleague in the physics department.

In 1966, the linear accelerator went live.

People call SLAC an atom smasher, but I think of it as an artificial eye. We need an incredibly big eye to see things incredibly small. Instead of using visible light to see the subatomic particles, SLAC uses electrons. A bundle of cables are the optic nerves connected to computers, the electronic brains, that interpret what we see.

The next year, Isobel wrote,

Bill Tompkins has just joined us from Berkeley where he earned his Ph.D. at twenty-three. He insists that students call him Dr. Tompkins, which is so funny because he looks to be the same age as the freshmen in my physics class. Any conversation with him, no matter the topic, turns into a debate where he seems determined to prove that he is the brightest person you know (or ever will know). If Einstein rose from the grave, he'd challenge him, too.

In a letter from 1969, she reported on a meeting with Vansittart, the SLAC director.

He came over to work on the Manhattan Project in World War II and never went home. He seeks glory like a free electron seeks a positive ion and figured that after the war the Europeans wouldn't be able to afford the particle accelerators needed for his research. Of course, he figured correctly and now has a leg up on Wilkinson, Ward, and the other British physicists in garnering a seat in the House of Lords. He both sounds and looks like he belongs there already with his plummy accent and bowtie and tweeds. Anyway, we're coming up on the due date for the annual report to our bosses in Washington, the Atomic Energy Agency. Vansittart had heard from Solenski that I might have some good news for the report. For the first time in months, he made some real time for me and I went over my mathematical model with him. *The very word "atom" comes from the Greek for "can't be cut." But then Rutherford—whose discovery did open the door to the House of Lords for him—found that atoms are made up of electrons, neutrons, and protons. I have some models that show neutrons and protons, too, might be divided further into particles I'm calling "quirks." I'll write this up. The quarter is over and I have enough to keep me busy at SLAC for June and July. Before fall quarter, I'm going to Yosemite to do some hiking and climbing.*

The next letter was dated two months later.

When dealing with the pieces of an atom, I try to put myself in the position of the Designer who has put together a model that reminds me of the wood puzzle boxes I had as a child. Taking it apart you find all sort of hidden keys, interlocking parts, and crevices. But whoever designed Yosemite works on a much larger scale. We climbed Half Dome and when we got to the top, I felt closer to the Designer than I ever had. Can there be a God who can work on such a small scale and such a large one? That's for the theology professors to worry about. My faith is expressed by doing my best.

A few paragraphs later, Isobel responded to a question her mother must have asked.

There were four of us on the trip to Yosemite. Besides me were Jake Cohen, a graduate student whose work I am overseeing, Candy Rabin, an old friend from Columbia, and Margaret Pierre, whom you know. We never had to worry since Jim is an expert mountaineer.

And a month later,

While we were in Yosemite, Bill convinced Vansittart to fire electrons at protons to test their ability to soak up virtual photons. Instead, just as my model predicted and thanks to the ingenious spectrometer Solenski built, they found that the protons are built of even smaller particles. Bill, Solenski, Vansittart, and I are racing to put together a paper for Physical Review Letters. *This might be the discovery that will get Vansittart his seat in the House of Lords. What a beautiful thing nature is! And how wonderful it is that I saw the architecture of the nucleus in my mind's eye even before we had any experimental proof.*

I rubbed my hand over the bristles on my chin. There were only about twenty letters left. Aunt Isobel had indeed been a full participant in discovering what she'd called "quirks" and what were now known as quarks. Close enough. Smaller and smaller particles got closer to the secrets of the whole universe. I shut my eyes.

The ringing of my iPhone upstairs shook me out of my reverie. Damn. Rowena was bound to awaken, and I wanted her to have a good night's sleep. Was it Frankson again? I galloped up the stairs and managed to get to the phone a half ring before it went to voicemail.

"Hello?"

"It's me, Bharat."

"What time is it?"

"Five fifty-two. I hope it's okay to have called."

"Go ahead, Bharat. I assume you didn't call to chat."

"Have you seen this morning's *Journal*?" he asked.

"No." This was not a good news call.

"Take a look at page A-3 and call me back, please," he said.

"Will do."

Rowena's voice wafted out of the bedroom. "What's up, dear?"

"Just a sec."

The gravel on the driveway bit into my bare soles. It was too dark to tell which paper was which so I picked up all three and brought them in. I laid the *Times* and *Mercury* aside and peeled the blue plastic off the *Journal* and spread the front section across the kitchen table and opened it.

Clad in tank top and nylon running shorts, Rowena padded into the kitchen.

"What's up?" she asked again.

I pointed to the headline.

Following my finger, she read it aloud. "Torii to Buy Accelenet for Quarter Billion, by Don Clark."

TWELVE

"There goes my morning run," I said, slapping the paper down on the kitchen table. "You can go, but I've gotta stay here and figure out the next move."

Rowena reached down and rubbed the top of my head as if I were a puppy and then said, "I'll boil some water."

A college friend of mine had written two critically acclaimed novels while fueled by a three-pack-a-day habit. In a noble gesture he forswore cigarettes when his daughter was born five years ago. My classmate had been ignoring the letters and voicemails from his publisher demanding return of a six-figure advance since the girl's third birthday. By contrast, all I needed to keep the needle of my brain's tachometer in the red zone was a steady supply of scalding hot tea.

I'd finished two mugs, while Rowena alternated between blowing on and taking a sip of her coffee. She raised the black streaks of her eyebrows.

"Ricky leaked it?" she asked.

"I'd guess yes. The only other suspect is Margot, and she's working with him anyway."

"Okay, let's go with the Ricky theory." Rowena's voice had taken on a modulated, hyper-logical tone. I knew what that meant. Like Clark Kent running into the phone booth, she was shedding her civilian identity. When she asked, "How does leaking this story bring him closer to what he wants?" she was questioning as Super-Lawyer, not my wife.

"First, it tells the world that Accelenet is in play. It makes it hard to get competing offers. Listen to what Ricky says in the article." I picked the paper back up and read, "'Accelenet will enable Torii to provide Global 1000 companies with a one-supplier solution for all their networking needs.'"

"Wouldn't HP or IBM or Cisco bid for Accelenet to keep Torii from getting it then?"

"Do you know how a male mountain lion stakes out his territory by leaving little mounds of dung and urine around its perimeter?"

She nodded in understanding. "And that's what Ricky is doing."

"Yeah. By pissing and shitting on us, he's telling all the other carnivores out there that Accelenet is his. On top of that, he's making sure our sales dry up. No one's going to buy diddly from us till they see how this works out. That will keep the price from going up."

"Will the Accelenet board accept his offer?"

"We're almost out of money. Margot seems to be working with Ricky, and the other investors—well, they're tired and gutless." I slapped the still-open *Journal*.

"Too bad. If Accelenet were a public company, speculators would be busy buying your stock."

"Right." I nodded. "So what I need to do is find someone who will invest now, who either believes in our future or figures that if we hold Ricky off, he'll raise his price."

"Yes. You need a white knight. In the meantime, you need to talk to your board, don't you?"

"You're right. Just a sec." I called Juliana on her cellphone and asked her to round up the board for a late-afternoon meeting. An offer for a quarter billion dollars ought to be reason enough for board members to reschedule late-afternoon appointments and navigate their BMWs and Ferraris down 101 to the Accelenet offices in Sunnyvale.

After I hung up, I asked Rowena, "You going for a run?"

"No. I'm gonna get going. Don't worry about not being able to make it down to the courthouse. Looks like you've got a big day, too."

"Everything will be hurry up and wait. I'll be there."

Thirty minutes later I walked out to the driveway with her, wished her good luck, and waved as she steered her car toward the courthouse combat that awaited.

———

"There is nothing that gets a lawyer's attention faster than a call from the receptionist saying your client is waiting in the lobby," Bryce Smithwick told me.

I'd made a stop on my way to San Jose. "Thanks for seeing me."

Vents on the ocean floor spewed a stream of minerals that included a small percentage of gold. Silicon Valley was the same. From the Valley floor bubbled up golden start-ups like Facebook and Google, but they were far outnumbered by their leaden brethren. As widely varied in technology, products, and management teams as these start-ups were, they usually had one thing in common—legal representation by Kaplan, Smithwick, and Dailey. Back in 1969, Michael Kaplan had been looking for a slower pace as he approached retirement. He left a big firm in San Francisco and moved down the Peninsula to open a law firm in Palo Alto. His plan for tapering off might have worked if he hadn't hired Bryce Smithwick straight out of Stanford Law to help him out. Under Smithwick's leadership, the two-man office had grown to nine hundred attorneys.

Moving with the lean, streamlined grace of a leopard gliding along the jungle floor, Smithwick looked twenty years younger than the sixty-five he was. He was Accelenet's outside counsel and a board member. Seeing him always reminded me of what he and I had in common—the vanished Paul Berk, best friend to us both. I silently cursed Paul for the thousandth time.

Smithwick was more a business advisor than a lawyer. He had been Paul's *consigliere* and now was mine.

"It will be close," he said. "Paul's trust owns nineteen percent of the company shares, and you control them as trustee. You yourself own seven percent. Other employees own fourteen percent. We'll assume they'll follow your lead. Darwin, Leon, and I own six percent." Smithwick hadn't had time to refer to any backup. He just knew the numbers. I bet he could spout off the ownership of a couple dozen other companies, too.

"That's forty-six percent. Not fifty. But what it comes down to is that the company is worth more than Ricky is offering."

"Right. But it won't be if we don't do something. Remember what Oracle did with PeopleSoft?"

"They said they were going to buy it and stop selling its products. Potential customers took the hint and put any purchases on hold."

Smithwick got up and started pacing. After a hundred steps that took him nowhere, he asked, "What do you think Accelenet is worth?"

"Four hundred million. Five, if we find the right buyer."

Smithwick grinned, and his sharp teeth gleamed. "Let's go find a white knight."

THIRTEEN

BECAUSE I'D STOPPED TO see Smithwick, I was later than I wanted to be. I peeked down at my watch and saw it was just after ten as I sneaked into the courtroom. Squeezing by the knees and stepping over the feet of five other spectators in the back row, I wedged myself into a small wooden seat.

Rowena, bent forward at the waist, had her hands on the jury box. Her head was no more than three feet from the first row of jurors.

"Daisy Nolan, the defendant, and Emma Singleton, the deceased, were known around the company to be very good friends," she was saying. Sitting in the back row, I had to strain to hear. By not raising her voice to address the entire courtroom, Rowena let the jurors know she cared about what *they* thought, not the other spectators or the judge. She focused on a pair of jurors for about ten seconds before she slid down the box and moved her gaze to the next two. She spoke with no Perry Mason histrionics, just quiet, compelling logic.

"When the vice president of marketing left the company to go to AMD, Daisy figured the job was hers. Why? Because Daisy was having an affair with the company CEO. Things seemed to be going her way. One Sunday Daisy invited Emma to go sailing on the Bay. Only Daisy came back. A horrible accident? So it seemed when Emma's body was found floating against a pillar of the San Mateo Bridge eleven days later."

Rowena paused. The jurors leaned even farther forward.

"Just one problem," she continued. "Despite the affair, the CEO was within two days of naming Emma, not Daisy, to the vice president position. Of course, with her competition gone, Daisy got the position. There was no reason to suspect foul play at first. Now though, the People can show that just before the tragic sail on the Bay, Daisy discovered Emma would get the coveted promotion and not her. The People will prove, prove beyond a reasonable doubt, that based on this new information, Daisy murdered her friend to get what she wanted."

A rustle on the other side of the courtroom diverted me from Rowena. There, at the defendant's table, I saw the defense attorney put his hand on Daisy Nolan's shoulder and push her back into her seat. He whispered in her ear. She settled back into her chair.

Rowena resumed her argument and did not look my way as she strode back to the defense table ten minutes later. She had been great. I could see worry lines around her eyes and creases running from her nose to the corners of her mouth—artifacts of her mourning. They gave her an aura of maturity.

Nolan's attorney stood up to ask if he could deliver his opening statement after the prosecution had rested its case. The judge consented and told Rowena to call her first witness.

A couple minutes later, the fourteen pairs of eyes in the jury box were locked on Rowena once again as she stood with her body at a forty-five-degree angle to a blue-suited woman in the witness box. That allowed her to look at the witness and then back to the jury just by swiveling her head.

"What did she say to you two days before the boating accident?" Rowena asked.

The witness said, "Daisy told me there was no chance she wouldn't get the VP of marketing job."

"When was this?" Rowena asked.

"On the Friday before the accident."

The judge sat enthroned at front of the courtroom, scribbling on a notepad. Over sixty, Marjorie Marks still wore her white hair shoulder length. A female pioneer in the office and on the bench, Judge Marks had a reputation for holding distaff attorneys to a higher standard than their male counterparts.

"Did she explain why not?" Rowena asked the witness.

"She said the CEO owed her."

"That's all?"

"She also told me she would get rid of Emma if she had to."

With a rattle of her chair, the defendant uncoiled herself and hissed, "It's just a goddamned expression."

Rowena held up her hands palm up. "Your Honor?"

A quick look at the jury members told me they were as uncertain as I was in determining whether Nolan's outburst was spontaneous or calculated.

The judge looked over her half-rims. "Mr. Guerrero, would you invite your client to retake her seat?"

Another gentle push on the defendant's shoulder was all it took.

"Please continue, Ms. Goldberg."

Rowena nodded and looked back at the witness. "That's what the defendant said to you, 'get rid of'?"

This time the defendant sprang up even faster. "What are you accusing me of?"

Her lawyer was up, but this time pressure on her shoulder had no effect.

"Listen, you." Nolan's eyes were locked on Rowena.

Rowena stared back, while the judge hammered her gavel.

The wood-on-wood thumping didn't stop Nolan. "Cut out your damn insinuations or..." she shouted at my wife. Her right index finger pointed at Rowena and then she pulled it inward as if pulling the trigger of a gun.

That did it. I was on my feet. Until that moment, I'd thought the expression seeing red was figurative, but a blood lust clouded my eyes like cataracts. "Or what?" I called out from the back of the courtroom. I started pushing through the five pairs of legs that blocked my passage to the aisle.

First Rowena, then the judge, then the jury, then the defendant, turned and stared at me. I must have been loud, real loud. With all watching me, I kept my gaze on Nolan. "You had better not try anything. Not anything."

"No outbreaks from the audience in my courtroom," the judge said in a clear voice. "This is a criminal trial."

By the time I made it to the aisle, the two khaki-uniformed sheriff's deputies who served as bailiffs were there to meet me. Ignoring them, I took another step toward Nolan. Each grabbed an upper arm and hauled me backward, my heels skittering over the linoleum. The strength of their grips helped clear the red cloud of irrationality from my mind. I saw Nolan sit down, her eyes glossed with surprise. Just before being hustled through the heavy courtroom doors, I looked back at my wife. The very placidity of her face boded storms ahead.

———

Rowena's right index finger pressed straight against my sternum.

"Ian, c'mon. Here I am. It's my first murder case. It's hand-to-hand combat. And my husband is acting like I need a nursemaid?"

The trial had recessed for lunch, and we were standing in a vestibule outside an empty courtroom. Her fingernail dug deeper into my chest. It hurt. As it was meant to.

"I'm sorry," I murmured.

"What in hell were you thinking?"

"I wasn't thinking, just reacting. Someone threatened you."

"And it's your job to protect me?"

"It was instinct. No one is going to take you away from me."

"Man protects his mate?"

"I couldn't help it." Didn't it make sense that men's DNA would be wired with some sort of protective impulse? Relying on Darwin right now was not a winning strategy, though.

"You couldn't help it? Get hold of yourself, Ian. You know you looked ferocious in there, like a monster in a hokey horror movie," she said. "You even had your lips bared."

"Shit. I'm sorry. You're pretty mad?" I wondered if the explanation for the pulsating pressure of my heart against my ribs was the memory of Nolan's threat or the immediacy of my wife's wrath.

"Good guess."

From around the corner into our little hideaway swooshed a woman of no more than five feet. Rowena dropped the accusing finger.

"Ah, I figured I'd find you two in conference," said Sally Huang, who'd been elected Santa Clara County District Attorney fifteen months before.

"Hello, Sally," my wife said "You know my husband, Ian."

"Nice to see you again, Ian," the D.A. said and extended a hand whose thin red-tipped fingers resembled five unlit kitchen matches.

"I was just telling Rowena how sorry I was..."

"You know, no matter how much you rehearse, something spontaneous blows up at every homicide trial," Huang said. "Most of the time it's bad news. This time I think it helped."

"You were there?" Rowena asked. "I didn't see you."

"I was in the back row on the other side of the aisle from Ian. Since it's your first murder, I thought I'd duck in and see how you were doing." Given the timing of her intervention with Rowena and me, I wondered if she'd been listening to our argument from around the corner.

"You think the jury will figure that Ms. Nolan has a temper and won't be crossed?" Rowena said.

"I do," the D.A. said. "That will help." She turned to my wife. "Keep up the good work, Rowena. Your opening statement made an impression on the jury." She turned her gaze to me. "Ian, as helpful as you were, it might not be a bad idea to stay out of the courtroom for the rest of the trial."

"Right," I agreed. "One thing, though. Nolan has threatened Rowena. Shouldn't we take precautions?"

Turning to me, Rowena said, "I think maybe it's you, dear, who needs to be confined and guarded..."

"No, no. I understand Ian's concern," Huang said, the politician trying to re-establish domestic tranquility. "But Nolan's in jail. You're going to convict her. She's not going to harm anyone else."

"Maybe she knows someone," I said.

Huang said, "She's not a gang member. I don't think she was making a serious threat. She got carried away, just like you did. She didn't really mean what she said."

I didn't tell Rowena's boss what I was thinking: That I had so meant what I said.

FOURTEEN

TWENTY MINUTES LATER, MY Acura had just carried me past the North First Street exit on 101. My iPhone started to warble.

"Hello?"

"Mr. Michaels, this is Ivan Solenski. You left me a note asking me to call."

Twenty minutes after hanging up on the call, I was at the guard booth at SLAC. I knew we had a board meeting that afternoon at Accelenet. Screw it, I didn't need to prepare. But I did need to tell my mother I was doing something about Aunt Isobel. Or was I just using Aunt Isobel as an avoidance mechanism? Whatever.

I saw *A Prayer for Owen Meany* in the well-read guard's hand as he waved me through, and I was shaking hands with the professor in his office five minutes after turning off the car's ignition.

If straightened out, Solenski would have been taller than my six feet, but as it was, the curled spine, hunched shoulders, and drooping head made it seem he was trying to get me to say "question mark" in a game of charades. A crescent of frizz above his ears and the back of his head left his crown shiny and bald. If his hair had been colored red instead of white, his skull would have made a matched set with Bozo the Clown's.

"What is your special interest in our work here, Mr. Michaels?"

"I am interested in learning more about Isobel Marter. She was my mother's aunt."

"Sit, sit," he said as he lowered himself into a desk chair. I followed his command.

"Some tea?" Solenski had a pot on his desk.

"Yes, please."

He watched as I took my first sip. This concoction was to the green tea I usually drank what 160-proof rum was to sugar water.

"You can get real Russian tea in the United States now. Tasty, isn't it?" my host inquired.

"Delicious. It's always a pleasure to sit down with a fellow tea drinker."

He give me a look and then a nod that said I'd passed a test. "So, what can I do for you?"

Even though he had lived in the United States for over sixty years, Solenski spoke with a noticeable Slavic accent—his "what" sounded as though it started with a vee sound.

"As you know, Aunt Isobel died at forty, the year I was born. Given the honor from Stanford, my mother and I thought it might be time to find out more about her. I understand it was your idea that the lab be named after her. Very nice. Thank you."

He nodded and pressed his fingertips together under his chin. "I was sorry to miss the dedication. Your great aunt was a beautiful woman. Very smart, too. And helpful."

"In his book, Professor Tompkins wrote that she was your assistant."

"He acted as if she were, yes. But she was not. Like us all, she worked for Vansittart."

"He died, didn't he? When was that?"

"The twenty-fifth anniversary year of proving the existence of quarks. Nineteen ninety-four."

"What *did* you do to prove their existence?"

"We shot a beam of electrons at what we used to call the beer can." He smiled at the memory. "It was really just an aluminum container of liquid hydrogen. If the protons were Rutherford's dense balls, electrons would have hit them and bounced off. Instead, we found most electrons just went right through the protons, but occasionally, the electrons hit something hard and ricocheted off it."

"And what they hit was a quark."

"Correct. Do you know about *matryoshkas*, Russian nesting dolls?"

"Sure, where one doll is found inside another."

"Correct. Rutherford showed us that an atom was not the last doll. Inside it was another, smaller doll of hadrons. Those are protons and neutrons."

"And you showed there's still another doll inside that." He nodded. "And what did Aunt Isobel have to do with all this?"

"She worked on the equations. But she was off hiking when the experiment was done."

"The Nobel Prize wasn't awarded for the theory?"

"No, it was for the experiment."

"I've seen some letters. Why did she call the particles you found 'quirks' and not 'quarks'?"

"A bad phone connection, I think." He grinned and leaned back.

"I beg your pardon?"

73

"News of what we'd discovered started criss-crossing the country. Richard Feynman was up from Caltech poking around, and Tompkins showed him the pictures of what we had. Next thing we knew the phone was ringing off the hook with long distance calls from MIT and Brookhaven. A few days later the transatlantic calls from Cambridge and Hamburg started coming in. No surprise then that Delany at *Zee Times*—he'd staked out particle physics as his own private beat—heard rumors of what we'd found out."

"*Zee Times*?" I asked. As soon as the words escaped from my mouth, I realized what he'd meant. What an idiot I could be.

Unfazed, Solenski said, "Yes, Vansittart called Delany at *Zee New York Times* and begged him not to write a story."

"Why not?"

"Because *Physical Review Letters* had a policy of rejecting papers whose results had shown up in the daily press. Delany agreed to wait on the condition that he'd get an exclusive. When Delany found out the *Süddeutsche Zeitung* was sniffing around, he took it as permission to run his story. What we'd called 'quirks,' Delany heard as 'quarks.' Probably Vansittart's accent. Once it was in *Zee Times*, quarks it was."

"I thought I'd read you named them quarks after a nonsense word in *Finnegans Wake*?"

"Billy-boy came up with that story after the fact."

Solenski put his hand up to his mouth and started hee-hawing.

I waited for the braying to stop and asked, "What?"

"Bill wasn't even mentioned in that first *Times* story. I thought he would reach critical mass and explode. He made Vansittart write a letter to the editor."

I wondered if Dr. Watson resented Sherlock Holmes. I wondered if Solenski had suggested naming the lab after Aunt Isobel as a needle intended to prick Tompkins.

"Tompkins did?" I asked.

"Yes."

"So no scientific paper ran?"

"It ran. The story was too big for the journal to ignore. We *had* found another nesting doll."

Half an hour later, I waved at the guard as I pulled out of the SLAC parking lot. Maybe I shouldn't have given up on physics so quickly back in college. God, I'd rather be looking for infinitesimal bits of matter than towering mounds of cash. So what? Gotta do what you gotta do. Back to the office.

FIFTEEN

When I pulled into the office parking lot a minute before the board meeting was to begin, Juliana was there at the door, giving me the kind of where-have-you-been, what-mischief-have-you-been-up-to glare that a mother would give to her rapscallion six-year-old.

In the boardroom, I slipped into the seat where my vanished predecessor Paul Berk had sat four years ago. I wished I could turn the clock back so Paul was still sitting at the head of this conference table made of tiger-striped tropical wood, his wife, Kathy, still skipping from one non-profit board meeting to another, and Rowena's sister, Gwendolyn, still writing novels of love won and lost. Through the picture window at my right, branches of birch trees, bereft of leaves, quavered in the February wind.

When I came back to the present and glanced at Margot, she didn't look away with a guilty conscience. She just narrowed her eyes and gave me a tight smile. Leon Henderson, the Stanford business school professor whose students had founded companies with a stock market value of over forty billion dollars, liked to sit at the other end of the table—playing center field he called it. He had all of us fanned out before him and could keep an eye on his colleagues. Bryce Smithwick sat across from Tim Yee, whose venture capital fund out of Austin owned a fifth of the company. The voice of Darwin Yancey, the technical brains at Paul's first company, came in crystal clear through the Polycom speaker in the middle of the table. He was calling in from his chateau near Aix-en-Provence, where it was after midnight. Bharat, the corporate secretary as well as CFO, sat behind me and to my left.

"As you all read in this morning's *Journal*, Torii is ready to pay two-hundred fifty million for Accelenet," I opened the meeting.

Margot spoke up. "It's a good offer. We should sell."

"Maybe," I said. "Let me go through the facts, and then we can discuss it."

I passed around a set of our latest financials and ran through a quick description of the cash crunch the company faced.

The moment I was done, Margot looked up from the papers and took off a pair of tortoise-shell reading glasses. I'd never seen her using them before. Without doubt Margot resorted to cosmetics, plastic surgery, and exercise to fend off the corrosion of middle age, but the glasses were overt in a way the other barricades to senescence she'd erected were not.

"If, if, if," she started. "If our fairy godmother appears, we can make a lot of money. And if she doesn't, we'll be sitting in front of the palace with our butt on a rotten pumpkin. We owe a fiduciary duty to our investors. We should take Torii's offer."

"And if we don't take the offer, what happens?" Tim Yee asked in the clipped English of his native Singapore. I saw his eyeballs stray to the left to look at Margot. She moved her head ever so slightly up and back down. They'd talked before the meeting. "May I speak frankly?" he asked, eyes back on me.

"Of course." I could never put all my trust in anyone who put the words "frankly" or "honestly" in a sentence.

"We—my firm—are not ready to put more money into Accelenet without assurances. I do not wish to be sitting around this table next month or the month after on the verge of running out of money with nothing changed. It will mean a fire sale of the company at a much lower price than Torii is offering now."

What with holders of over 50 percent of the company stock ready to sell, no wonder Frankson was confident.

"Tim, what are you looking for?" Leon asked.

"A higher offer from another company or another investor willing to put in twenty-five million with a good valuation."

Darwin's voice blared from the speakerphone. "How about a long-term contract to supply the TurboCom accelerators?"

Margot put up a hand and answered for Yee. "If it's iron-clad? Hmm. As long as it's at least a hundred million in the first two years." Then she laughed. She clicked her glasses against the table. "But who are we kidding? Not gonna happen, guys. If we delay in accepting Ricky's offer, we'll get closer and closer to running out of money and his offer will go down and down. I move ..."

"Before any motions are tabled," Smithwick interrupted, "could we agree to give Ian a month to try to find a higher offer, another investor, or a supply contract? Thirty days wouldn't matter much, would it?"

"A week from Thursday, I'm leaving for a month in China and India," Margot said. "My flight isn't till dinnertime. Why don't we have a meeting next Thursday afternoon and see where we stand?"

"That makes sense to me," Yee replied and folded his arms.

"Not a lot of time," Smithwick said.

"All we're saying is let's see what progress we've made by the end of next week," Margot said, with Yee nodding along.

"Makes sense," said Darwin's disembodied voice.

The way Margot had phrased the request made it impossible to say no. Of course, it was reasonable for the board to get a status report next week. But I knew that Margot had set it up so I faced a nine-day deadline. For all I knew, she'd start making arrangements for that Asian trip when she got back to her office.

"And of course, this meeting should be kept confidential," Smithwick said as the meeting began to break up.

I shook hands with Margot on her way out. She figured she'd won. Even without any crinkles around her eyes, I could tell she was smiling through the mask her plastic surgeon had left her—the ends of her mouth were turned up a millimeter or so.

SIXTEEN

As I headed down 101 the next morning at seven, my iPhone twittered. Awfully early. Probably Juliana calling to remind me of my seven-thirty call.

"Hello."

"Are you going to stand in the way of the only good exit route Accelenet has?"

"Ricky, how nice to hear from you."

"Why delay? You are not going to find a better deal."

If Margot was going to brief Frankson on every conversation I had with her, we might as well start inviting him to board meetings.

"Why talk to me? I read in yesterday's *Journal* that you were already buying Accelenet."

"Torii is a public company. The SEC says we need to disclose material facts to the market."

"But haven't you misled the market? It's not a fact that you are buying Accelenet." Yesterday Torii had closed up half a point—

that was over a billion dollars in market cap. The mere announcement of a potential deal had already more than paid for Accelenet.

"I think our chances of closing a deal are very high—you have no alternative—and therefore I had a duty to disclose the deal. We're just haggling about price now. The way you're acting, though, the price is going to start dropping."

"Ricky, I'm really starting to look forward to our little chats. Let's stay in touch. Hello, Ricky?" He'd hung up.

I got into the office just in time for the call with John Sutherland at Goldman Sachs. As I walked toward Juliana's desk, her phone started to beep. "Just a second, John. I'll put him on," she said into the handset.

I picked up the phone in my office. "Hello, John."

"Hello, sir."

"John?" John had been a year behind me in college and had a Darth Vaderish basso profundo.

"Yes, this is John."

Maybe so, but his tinny tenor did not belong to John *Sutherland*.

"What can I do for you?"

"Every so often my firm, Lawler, Fisher, and North comes across a stock with the potential to go up three times in less than two months and we reach out to executives like yourself..."

In boiler rooms across south Florida, thousands of Johns like this one were on the phone trying to defraud the greedy.

"Is Lawler, Fisher, and North interested in investing twenty-five million in a Silicon Valley networking company?"

"Um, no, but what better way to get the money you need than with good investments?"

Not a bad comeback.

Juliana stuck her head through the doorway and whispered, "I have Mr. Sutherland on the phone. The last guy said he was John, and I assumed ... Sorry."

Speaking into the receiver, I said, "John, when you can come up with the twenty-five mil, ring me again. Until then." I pushed a button terminating that call and pushed the flashing one to connect to the next.

"Hello, John."

"Ian." Ah yes, this was the right John, the one who spoke with the voice of God.

While Sutherland did not suggest I start buying lottery tickets, neither did he have any great ideas on where to come up with the scratch to free ourselves from Frankson's clutches. After we hung up, I started calling other investment bankers who had expressed interest in bringing Accelenet public. In fact, I spent the day doing the same thing the first John had been doing when he called me—dialing for dollars—and with little more success.

———

No self-respecting i-banker would still be in the office after five on a Friday. I left some messages and headed home by six. Since it was the start of the Jewish Sabbath, Rowena wanted to say *kaddish*, the prayer of remembrance, for her father. I would have been satisfied doing so during a quiet evening at home, but Rowena insisted on following the tradition of having a *minyan*, ten adults, for *kaddish*. On the way to the synagogue, I asked her a question or two about her afternoon in court. After a couple of curt monosyllabic replies, we rode in silence. She hadn't forgiven me for my morning outburst yet. From experience though, I knew I could count on patience paying off.

We arrived ten minutes before the service started and slipped into a pew near the front. This was the synagogue I'd grown up in, but I really hadn't had much to do with it between my Bar Mitzvah and marrying Rowena. She'd joined a Jewish book club there and went to Torah study Saturday mornings, and became friends with a swarm of women a couple of decades older than she was. Despite not having children, she'd been appointed chairman of the synagogue's youth education committee last year on the theory that she would remember what Hebrew school had been like better than fifty- and sixty-year-olds.

A queue of people conveying their condolences formed before us. We used to say most Jewish holidays could be summed up as "they tried to kill us, we won, let's eat." As the aphorism implied, Jews took refuge in food. Standing there in the sanctuary, we turned down over a dozen offers of home-cooked meals.

Rabbi Harold Frankel, who'd been the head rabbi at Beth El for forty years, who'd marched in the sixties with Martin Luther King, had retired and been replaced by, of all people, his brother's daughter, Shulamit. Rabbinical dynasties were still featured among the Orthodox, but there was no nepotism in this synagogue. The younger Rabbi Frankel, about my age, had finished first in her class at Hebrew Union College and had written *Commandment, Community and Commitment,* which *The New York Times* made an editor's choice book back in 2006.

Usually, I paid rapt attention to her sermons, but not today. The harder I tried to focus, the more I wondered where I'd find twenty-five million dollars. When I should have been thinking about the wonders of the world, I was running through a mental list of prospective corporate partners. I started listening only when the rabbi's tone indicated she was wrapping up. She reminded us that millennia ago her predecessors had taught that the world stands on three legs—study, worship, and acts of loving kindness. I wondered what leg running a company rested on.

After reciting *kaddish* at the end of the service, the rabbi came straight to us. "I will come see you," she told Rowena.

On the drive home, I drove with my left hand, while my right held Rowena's. She had a gift. Not even four years in the Bay Area, and she had more friends than I did after thirty-eight. I hadn't been adding many lately either.

"You glad we went?" I asked.

"Oh, yes. I'm glad to have found a community. Those sages knew what they were doing by requiring ten people to say kaddish."

"You shouldn't mourn alone?"

She squeezed my hand. "I know you didn't want to come to services. Thank you for coming with me anyway."

Nobody talks about it much, but Judaism is definitely pro-sex. Making love is a *mitzvah*, a blend of a good deed and a commandment. Most Friday nights Rowena reminded me that making love on Shabbat made it a double mitzvah. But the chance to multiply the virtue of the act was not enough to overcome her post-mortem celibacy.

"You understand, don't you?" she asked me again in bed that night.

"Of course," I said. She fell asleep with her head nestled in the crook of my arm. Was it just her father's death, was it the stress of the trial, or was she still mad at me? So I didn't really understand, but I did know I didn't like it much.

SEVENTEEN

THE JEWISH SABBATH RUNS from Friday at sundown till you could see three stars out on Saturday night. This never made much sense to me, but on the other hand, why should the day start at midnight?

Rowena's family treated the Sabbath the way Jewish tradition said you should—praying, relaxing, spending time with family. For the past three years, she'd been trying to teach me to do the same. When I got calls from a work colleague on a Saturday, she told me to tell them that I was available "twenty-four/six" rather than the Silicon Valley standard "twenty-four/seven."

On this Saturday afternoon, she and I were strolling hand in hand through our neighborhood. I knew part of Rowena resented the clear skies, the sixty-degree temperature—why should it be so beautiful less than two weeks after her father died? Was God mocking her?

"He was a good man and led a good life," I said.

"How do you do that? How do you know what I'm thinking?"

It wasn't that hard. We walked in silence for the next twenty minutes until we passed the main branch of the city library. I asked if we could go in for a minute.

"You've got plenty to read."

"I want to pick up a few physics books."

"So you can have an educated conversation with some of the professors about Aunt Isobel?"

"Educated? No way. That sets the bar too high. I'm going for un-imbecilic. I want to check the *Times*, too, for the first article on the discovery of quirks or quarks or whatever they are."

The reference librarian convinced me that a book by a Harvard professor named Lisa Randall was the best introduction to what was going on in particle physics. I thought microfilm had become obsolete around the time I traded in my typewriter for a personal computer, but not in the library of Palo Alto, capital of Silicon Valley. Ensconced in the corner just past a bank of online catalogs were three forlorn industrial microfilm readers. I scrolled through a couple of thick rolls before finding the *Times* article Solenski had mentioned.

I wondered if a new discovery in subatomic physics would make it to the front page in the philistine twenty-first century as it had in the twentieth. There in March 1970 on the far right column of page one ran the headline, "Scientists Find Proof of New Building Block of All Matter," with the byline Willard Delany.

Shoulder to shoulder, Rowena and I read the article:

Scientists have found evidence of a new particle that might prove to be a fundamental building block of the universe.

In experiments at California's Stanford Linear Accelerator Center (SLAC), the proton and neutron, once thought to be in-

divisible components at the center of every atom, are shown to be made up of smaller particles called quarks.

Professor Claude Vansittart, director of SLAC, said in an exclusive interview, "We appear to have discovered a new and smaller level of matter."

Stanford's two-mile long accelerator is the world's most powerful atom smasher. In the experiment, electrons moving at over 99% of the speed of light and carrying the energy of 20 billion electron volts are sent crashing into atoms of lead.

"Neutrons and protons are not minute solid cricket balls as we once thought," said the jaunty Vansittart who is English. "Instead they are like a Christmas pudding with three one-shilling coins hidden inside."

"Are you done?" Rowena asked.

"Yeah."

She turned the page. Inside the story ran another three long columns of text, along with a close-up photo of Vansittart, pipe in hand, and an aerial view of the linear accelerator itself.

"Look." Her long, tapered index finger stabbed a paragraph in the third column.

The experiments, overseen by Dr. Vansittart, were suggested by the theoretical work of Dr. I. L. Marter, an assistant professor of physics at Stanford.

"Wow," I said. "No wonder Tompkins had a fit."

"What do you mean?" Rowena asked.

"He isn't mentioned. Don't feel sorry for him though. He makes sure he gets plenty of credit in his own book."

"Didn't Aunt Isobel have anything to do with the experiments themselves?"

"Apparently not. Solenski said she was hiking in Yosemite."

"This was an incredibly big deal, wasn't it?"

"Oh, yeah. It threw the world of particle physics on its ear."

"Do you think she would have won a share of that Nobel Prize if she'd lived?"

"I don't know. Solenski said the prize was awarded for the experiments and not the theory."

Rowena retreated back into her shell of silence as we walked home. I held Professor Randall's book in my left hand and pushed the walk button under the traffic light with my right. Five seconds later, I took a step into the street, only to have Rowena haul me back on to the sidewalk as a car zipped through the intersection with no regard for the traffic light's glowing green stick figure. She yelled a few imprecations at the driver as the black sedan blithely sped on. Because of the car's smoky windows, there was no way to see the driver.

Until we arrived home, she held my hand as though I were a kindergartner too immature to be trusted crossing the street. Maybe the protect-the-mate gene was carried by both sexes.

After twisting her key in the front door, she turned around just as I stepped into the foyer. We collided, and I slipped my arms around her back in time to feel a shudder.

"That car scared me," she said. "Promise me you'll be careful."

"That's what's on your mind?" I asked.

"Before you almost stepped into oblivion, I was still thinking about Dad's death," she said into my ear. "I know I shouldn't, but I wish he had died a little sooner, before Gwennie did. Your Aunt Isobel died before she got credit for one of the great discoveries of modern science. Wouldn't it have been good if *she* had lived just a little longer, until after the Nobel was awarded. No justice, no sense."

I hugged her harder.

EIGHTEEN

MONDAY MORNING, AFTER OUR run, Rowena headed down to the county courthouse to try to do justice in her murder case.

I found Professor Leon Henderson on my iPhone's contact list and pressed the call button.

"Hey, Leon, Ian. Let's throw a Hail Mary."

"A what?"

In talking to non-Americans I was careful to avoid sports analogies, but I'd forgotten that I needed to do the same with Leon. My closest ally on the Accelenet board, he barely knew the difference between football and basketball.

"Never mind . . ."

"No, explain it to me, Ian."

"Okay. When I was little, my dad and I watched Roger Staubach—the quarterback for the Dallas Cowboys—throw a football as far as he could just before time ran out. His teammate Drew Pearson caught it, and the Cowboys won. After the game, Staubach told the interviewer that after releasing the ball, he closed his eyes and said a Hail Mary."

"So a Hail Mary is a desperation move?"

"Yeah, even for a Jew like me."

"Okay, let's hear what you've got in mind."

"I want to go see Barclay Corwin at Intel."

Leon was on the board of the chip giant, and Corwin was executive VP of business development there.

Two minutes later Leon called me back. "He's in an offsite meeting at the Four Seasons, but he'll step out to meet us."

"Us? You don't need to come."

"Can't hurt. I'm free till my one o'clock seminar. I'll meet you there."

"Good." He was right. It could only help to have him with me.

I walked the ten minutes from our house to the Four Seasons Hotel, located on the stretch of University Avenue once known as Whiskey Gulch. When he conveyed the land that became Palo Alto back in the nineteenth century, Leland Stanford had exacted a provision banning alcoholic beverages within a mile-and-a-half of the university campus. Five years ago, the block of bars and liquor stores that had grown up just outside the one-time teetotaling zone was demolished and replaced by a fancy office complex. The tilt-up concrete buildings populated by white-shoe lawyers and hotel guests from Europe and Asia could have been plopped down anywhere from Shanghai to Dubai without looking out of place. The old ramshackle Whiskey Gulch had fallen prey to global homogenization. I wondered where underage kids bought their beer now.

Leon arrived and stuck his head in the hotel's Runnymede Room. Two minutes later, Leon, Corwin, and I were sitting in the hotel café at a small table across from the fluttering blue flames of a gas-fed fireplace. A friendly and efficient waitress wearing a gold vest and necktie, and a nametag reading "Marissa" had placed a stainless steel pot of green tea in front of me and two French coffee presses in front of the other two.

Corwin smacked his lips and then looked skeptically at my tea. "I need all the caffeine I can get. It's deadly in there." Leon had warned me to look past the Intel executive's bluff, beefy, blonde exterior. He'd done a good enough job running operations for Intel that he was one of three contenders for the CEO scepter.

"I'll do my best to provide some non-caffeinated stimulation," I said.

He laughed. "This will have to be good. Yesterday morning at this time, I was at our plant in Israel and I am beat." He leaned back against the curved backrest of his Danish modern chair.

"You know we at Accelenet have a technology that will speed up digital transmissions up to eight times."

"It's laid out on a circuit board?"

I nodded.

"Why shouldn't it be a single integrated circuit?" Corwin asked.

"Why shouldn't it?" I responded. "Here, let me show you how the board is laid out."

There was a natural evolutionary process in electronics. Any innovation started size XXL and shrunk faster than a cheap cotton sweatshirt. The first computers occupied a room. More than a million times more power was now contained on a chip smaller than the nail of my little finger. I grabbed the menu and used the back to sketch the various components on a TurboCom board.

"So with a TurboCom chip you would have a product for every wireless-enabled PC," I concluded.

"And every cell phone and set-top box," he said. "Okay. Leon here did the prep work and told me to listen. I have. What are you looking for?"

"What do you think this would be worth to Intel?" I asked.

"Oh, no. I took Leon's negotiation course, too. I'm not going first. You tell me what you're looking for."

"Well, if you don't end up with the TurboCom technology, one of the big networking companies will."

"Like Cisco or Torii?"

"No names," I said. "But the technology should be worth more to Intel than to a networking company. If you have it, the networking companies will have to come to you. You become an arms supplier to everyone. If a networking company has it, it would be for its own use."

"Okay. So what are you looking for?"

"A fifty-million-dollar investment for ten percent of the company." That would value the company for twice what Frankson did. It would give us plenty of capital, too. And I'd left room for negotiation.

"Of course, for the sake of our discussion, I'm going to assume it works like you say it does. Would we get exclusive use of the technology?"

"That doesn't make sense for us."

"Unless we buy the whole company. How about that?"

"You don't have to put a severed horse's head in my bed to make me an offer that can't be refused, but an offer that can't be refused…"

Corwin completed my sentence, "Would be expensive." Ten years ago when I started working in the Valley, a reference like this to *The Godfather* was as common as a citation of the *AP Stylebook* in a newsroom. Now it marked me as an old codger in a society whose mores were set by twenty-somethings.

We sat quietly for a moment. Then Corwin raised his bulk and stuck his hand out to Leon. "Thanks for arranging this meeting, Leon. Very interesting. I've got to get back in there." He jerked his head toward the conference room. Then he turned his eyes to me. "I want to send some of my tech guys over to look at the Turbo-Com stuff."

"Under an NDA?" I asked. Non-disclosure agreements didn't usually do much good in the Valley, which was built on loosey-goosey dissemination of intellectual capital, but having one couldn't hurt. We had a raft of patent applications pending on the TurboCom technology, but if Intel stole what we had, Accelenet would be defunct by the time we won any lawsuit.

"Okay. I'll round up the right people and have them over there by next Monday," Corwin said.

"That's too late. We have another offer on the table."

"When do I need to get back to you then?"

"By close of business Wednesday," I said.

"Wednesday like the day after tomorrow? Shit," Corwin swore and rubbed his temples with index finger and thumb. "Hmm. Let me think. For deals less than two-hundred fifty million, we don't have to check with our board."

"There's some flexibility," I said.

Corwin smiled at Leon, the Intel board member. "Maybe they trust us. Anyway, I'll email you one of our NDAs. It's mutual and vetted already by our lawyers. That will keep us from wasting time. I'll have our technical people at your office at three this afternoon."

Nice to know that a quarter billion was chump change for Intel. I left a good-sized tip to make up for the ruined menu.

Leon had no passions beyond high tech except for fast cars. He drove me back home in his red Lamborghini Spyder, which went from zero to sixty in four seconds and managed a meager ten miles per gallon of premium gas. Leon expected some Silicon Valley breakthrough to solve the global warming crisis soon enough, and wasn't going to deny himself in the meantime. He'd said nothing during the negotiation dance because of his conflict of interest. As a member of Accelenet's board, he had a duty to make sure we received as much as possible from Intel. His duty to Intel was to help get them the best possible deal.

As I levered myself out of the low-slung seat, he said, "Good work. You know, you reminded me of Paul in there."

"It's still a Hail Mary," I said. "When I get in the house, I'm going to close my eyes and pray."

NINETEEN

The three Intel engineers didn't leave till eleven on Monday night, and they were back Tuesday morning at seven. Ron Qi, our chief technology officer, told me they had the impassive demeanor and expressionless voices he'd expect out of "Intel clones," but the questions they asked and tests they ran indicated strong interest. Other than a quick introduction, I stayed away from the lab. No matter that I wore khakis and a button-down; in the eyes of working engineers like the Intel folks, I'd be a "suit." Experience taught me that things would go better gearhead to gearhead.

Two irons in the fire—Torii and Intel—were not enough. I was in the office Tuesday morning even before the Intel engineers. Till nine I was calling potential investors in London, Boston, and New York. When I started calling VCs in the Valley at nine, most weren't in yet. They were probably out running or swimming or biking or breakfasting, enjoying what the Valley had to offer.

At eleven, Bryce Smithwick came by as we'd planned. It was unusual for him, the country's best-known high-tech lawyer, to have a start-up like Accelenet as a personal client, but he'd done it because of his long history with Paul Berk. Paul may have been gone, but Smithwick—always available to talk, always ready to offer advice—dealt with me as Paul's heir. It was almost as if he expected Paul to materialize one day and check on how I'd been treated.

Munching on the turkey sandwiches that Juliana had ordered, I told Smithwick, "I reached partners in eight firms. I found some interest."

"But not enough?" he asked.

"No. None of the three that nibbled is going to take the hook in his mouth by next week."

"Listen, why don't I draft a term sheet?"

"One we could use either for Intel or Torii?"

He stood up to leave. "Yeah. I'll have two draft term sheets to you by Wednesday morning."

I stood up as well.

"You have plenty to do," Smithwick said. "I can find my own way out."

A quick handshake and I watched him retreat through my office door. Nary a pucker nor a fold marred the hang of his navy suit.

What now? I had set up my email to scan and sort incoming messages automatically, so I checked the "ASAP" box on my laptop. By the third email, my mind had wandered, and I typed "Claude Vansittart" into the Google search bar at the top of my Mac's screen. More avoidance? Maybe. But I couldn't help myself. I needed to find out how Aunt Isobel had been cheated of her legacy.

Off I went to an entry in Wikipedia. Vansittart had been born in 1924 and, by the time he died in 1998, the Queen had knighted him and made him a member of the Order of Merit. Somehow, though, she'd neglected to bestow upon him that seat in the House of Lords. Hmm. It said he'd married Lady Penelope Healy, daughter of an earl, in 1957. No death date listed for her. I went to the AT&T online directory. She was listed. I dialed. When I hung up, I gathered my things and logged off my computer.

"Where're you going?" Juliana asked as I walked by her desk two minutes later.

"To the Stanford campus."

"Promise me that you'll keep your phone on and then you can go." All seventy-one inches of her were blocking my way.

I used my right index finger to make an X in the air. "Cross my heart."

Twenty minutes later, I pulled up in front of an adobe cottage with a red tile roof separated from the busy Santa Teresa Street by a serried file of eucalyptus trees. Stanford real estate existed in a self-contained universe. The right to live in hundreds of campus houses, many built on bucolic lanes between the wars, was restricted to faculty and administrators. When death put a property back on the market, it could only be sold to another eligible buyer. Stanford showed surprising—maybe even uncharacteristic—solicitude in not evicting surviving spouses.

I walked past rusting wrought-iron furniture on the brick porch, and knocked. A broad-shouldered, rawboned woman opened the door.

"You are Mr. Michaels?" she asked, running her eyes from the thinning hair on my crown to my loafer-encased feet.

"Yes. Glad to meet you, Lady Vansittart." Her silver hair was worn with bangs in a bouncy pageboy.

My courtesy was greeted with a horse's whinny of a laugh. When we were installed in her living room, she said, with only vestiges of an English accent, "Americans are so enthralled by titles. And you got it exactly right. Thanks to an accident of birth, I was once called Lady Penelope. I became Lady Vansittart when Claude was knighted. If you really get a kick out of the title, keep on using it, but otherwise, I'd prefer Penny. I've lived in California for more than fifty years, and I've taken to the informality."

"Okay. And please call me Ian."

"Ah, my mother's father's name. Are you Scottish, too?"

"Only by way of the baby name book my mother used."

She reached over to the teapot resting on the small round table in front of her.

"Is Earl Grey satisfactory, Ian?"

"Yes, please."

She poured us each a cup.

"Milk?"

"Yes, please." She passed me the cup and saucer.

"Biscuit?" she asked, extending a plate of shortbread.

No matter how much butter was used in the baking, I didn't think one cookie was enough to clog my arteries. I just wouldn't tell Rowena.

I looked around the room. With the chintz on the furniture and the portraits on the wall, we might as well have been back in her father the earl's family seat.

She sipped and then I did. She looked at me over her half-spectacles. "Isobel Marter?"

"Right," I said.

"A tragedy when she died. Claude said she was one of the most brilliant physicists he'd ever known. But so tough for a woman back then."

"How do you mean?"

"Claude had to referee. She and Tompkins did not get along at all. He was the fair-haired boy and made her into the wicked witch."

"How did he do that?"

"Lots of ways. He'd play practical jokes on her."

"Such as?"

"Unwinding dozens of rolls of toilet paper in her office."

"How mature. And what did she do about it?"

"She cleaned it up."

"She didn't complain to your husband?"

"Never. That wasn't her style. She just focused more on her work. One of the boys, maybe Tompkins, hung a sign on her office door that said 'The Convent.'"

"Funny place for a Jewish woman to hang out."

"It wasn't meant to be anti-Semitic, just sexist." Lady Vansittart took a sip of tea, and I followed her lead. "You know about the famous experiment at SLAC where the existence of quarks was proven?"

"In August 1969."

"I'll take your word for the year. I do remember the month. Why do you think in August?"

"Because they were ready?"

"Not really. It was because both Isobel and my husband were on vacation. We were at a conference in Denver when Claude found out what they were up to. So he got back in time. But Isobel was in Yosemite. This was before cell phones. She couldn't be reached."

"Whose idea was it to do the experiment while they were out of town?"

"Tompkins. Even though it was all based on Isobel's work. But Claude got even, didn't he?" Again the equine laugh. "He told the *Times* reporter about Isobel and didn't mention Tompkins or Solenski."

As I'd seen. "Served them right?"

She gave one quick vertical snap of her head. "Yes, it did. Well, at least it served Tompkins right. Solenski was just along for the ride. Anyway, I thought Tompkins might have an apoplectic seizure when that story came out."

"I'm sure the Nobel Prize provided a certain degree of solace."

TWENTY

As I PULLED INTO the Accelenet parking lot twenty-five minutes after leaving Penny Vansittart, I saw the Intel automatons march out the front door. Just inside I ran into Ron, who was watching them through the smoke-colored glass. Despite my nudging, he refused to guess on the odds of an offer coming from the colossus of the semiconductor world.

It was after five—my favorite time at the office. At the end of the day, employees were a little more relaxed and greeted me with weary smiles. I asked the engineers how the tweaking of the latest TurboCom board was going, the sales reps what I could do to help them close their big deals, and the bean counters how much work was left to close the books for the latest quarter. What I heard from them was unfiltered by the vice presidents who reported to me. Leon had taught me that I could ask any employee anything, but could only tell my direct reports what to do. Managing the others was—who'd've thunk it?—the job of their managers. As I popped into offices or cubicles, I was following in the footsteps of the

Founding Fathers of Silicon Valley, Bill Hewlett and Dave Packard, who advocated MBWA—management by walking around.

Although we tried to keep the Intel visit quiet, everyone seemed to know where the three engineers who'd spent a day-and-a-half with us hailed from. No one would have come to me if I'd stayed in my office with the door shut. Wild rumors would abound. When employees asked me about Intel, I told them it was good news. "Think about it," I said. "What we've got is so hot that Intel is interested." In response to the inevitable next question, I reported that we were not in discussions to sell Accelenet to Intel, just seeing if there was common ground for a deal. They'd nod and thank me for the update.

Around eight, I hopped in the car to go home. As I passed the Shoreline turnoff on 101, my iPhone beeped and wiggled in my pocket. A text message from Rowena. She wouldn't be home till after ten. Go ahead and eat. She'd grab a bite at the office.

At home I opened the refrigerator door and looked into a frigid wasteland. We really hadn't done any grocery shopping since getting back from her parents' place in Del Mar. Down below in the beverage compartment were a couple of loose beer bottles. I levered the cap off a Gordon Biersch Blonde. After all, what was beer but grain, yeast, and water? Liquid bread.

Ah well. Chug and think. Think and chug. After what I thought of as two loaves, I sat down in the den and pushed the "2" key. It was answered on the first ring.

"I thought you would call tonight," she said.

"How's it going down there, Mom?"

"Your sister has called twice today."

"Of course, she has. She knows she's your favorite and wants to stay that way."

Giving my last comment that attention it deserved, Mom moved on. "It's not so bad. Caroline is sad, so sad, but she's functioning."

"What have you two been doing?"

"Talking. I've talked about your father, and she's talked about Rowena's."

"You two are just sitting in the living room all day talking?" That did not sound like the perpetual motion machine that had given me birth.

"No. We talk while we're walking to and from morning minyan at the synagogue."

"You are going to synagogue every morning?"

It was hard enough to get her there on Yom Kippur.

"Caroline wants to go for *kaddish*."

"What time does the service start?"

"Eight. It's a couple of miles each way."

That was more like it. "You'll be at services more in a week than you usually go in a year, maybe a decade."

"Rabbi Kahn is there. It's a nice way to start the day. Gets you thinking."

My sister had done it long ago, Rowena was working on me, and now my mother, the one-time socialist, the member of the Free Speech Movement at Berkeley during college, was going to turn to religion?

"What else?"

"One friend or another of Caroline's drops by in the afternoon bearing a casserole or roasted chicken."

"You're not starving then?"

"Hardly. Her refrigerator could cure hunger in a small African country. After they leave, we take another walk."

"Anything else?"

"Have you been doing anything about Aunt Isobel?" she asked, wresting control of the conversation.

"Yes," I said, in the same tone I had once used to report that I had indeed practiced the piano after school. "Who would have guessed it? It sounds melodramatic, but she really did help unlock secrets of the universe."

"So?"

"So, I've met with Tompkins, Solenski, and Vansittart's widow."

"What about the lab notebooks?"

"Lab notebooks?"

"Rowena didn't give them to you?"

"No, just the letters."

"Oh. Maybe I forgot to put them back on the dining room table. Where did I leave them?"

"I'll go over to your place and find them," I said.

"Lots of formulas—wait is it 'formulae'?"

"Probably depends on whether you live in ancient Rome or twenty-first century California."

"Well, whichever it is, the notebooks are filled with them. I couldn't figure much out."

"I'm sure I won't either. I think the linear accelerator center has archives. Maybe all Isobel's letters and notes should go there."

"Maybe," she said. "You're on it, then?"

"Yes, Mother."

"I'll want a full report when I get back."

"Okay." She paused. "Tell me about Rowena's trial."

I filled her in on the highlights, minus Nolan's threat and my subsequent outburst.

"Anything else new?"

"Nothing too important." No sense mentioning the financial tightrope I was walking at the office either. "Is Caroline around?" I asked.

"She's gone to bed."

"It's just after nine."

"Well, I don't think she's really asleep. She likes having me here, but I think she needs time alone, too."

"You're leaving the day after tomorrow? Will Caroline be all right?"

"Well, I wish she'd let me stay, but she will be fine. She's tough."

"Good. You'll have a terrific time in Israel, Mom."

"Maybe we should cancel the trip? I could stay with Caroline and then we could reschedule for a time when you and Rowena could come, too."

"Caroline would never allow you to postpone it."

"I guess you're right." The immovable force and the irresistible object. "Will I talk to you before I leave?"

"I'll say have a good trip now, just in case we don't."

I awoke Wednesday morning in the same paisley armchair where I'd drunk my dinner and talked on the phone. Even after extricating myself from the chair, I remained bent over in an ape-man's crouch. Maybe a surgeon had snuck in during the night and fused my spine? I stumbled into the kitchen and spotted the note taped to the table.

"Had to get going for early morning meeting. Find glass fresh-squeezed OJ in fridge. Love, R."

This was embarrassing. Rowena had gotten home after me and arisen before me.

After letting the shower's hot water pound on my back for twenty minutes, I managed to stand upright. A few minutes later I headed out to the office to rejoin the battle and try to save Accelenet.

TWENTY-ONE

WEDNESDAY AFTERNOON JULIANA DIDN'T lean around the doorway into my office as she usually did when delivering a short message. She strode in and stood before me.

"Barclay Corwin's on the phone."

"Okay. Shut the door, would you please?"

I picked up the receiver. "Hello, Barclay."

Juliana did close the door. With her on the inside. She looked at me and crossed her arms. I shrugged. Fine with me. She knew more about what went on in the office than anyone.

"No bullshit, okay?" Corwin asked.

"Sounds like a good ground rule to me."

"We're intrigued."

Funny, that mushy claim of interest sounded like bullshit to me. "Intrigued enough to make an offer by tomorrow?"

"Maybe."

More bullshit. "Why not yes?" I asked.

"What's the price to buy the whole enchilada?" he asked, abandoning coyness.

"I'm not saying we wouldn't sell, but I thought we were discussing an investment."

"Give me a price."

"Six hundred twenty-five million dollars." A premium in valuation for the whole kit and caboodle. Only two-and-a-half times Frankson's fire sale offer.

"I thought we said no bullshit."

"That's not bullshit. I haven't spoken to the board. It could end up higher. How about we go back to the fifty million for ten percent of the company we discussed Monday? Lowers your risk."

"Okay. We might be able to do that with a couple extra provisions."

"Shoot."

"We're your foundry."

Made sense that they would want to manufacture the Turbo-Com chip. "We'll need a second source, but we'll start working with you six months before anyone else."

"I think we can work something out along those lines."

"And what else?"

"You."

"Me?"

"Yes. We don't want to sign a deal and have you walk away. We want you to sign a contract with the company for at least two years, but I also want you to tell me that you're committed. Man to man. Leon says you won't bullshit me."

That bullshit word again. "I'll commit," I said. A hostage still.

"I'll get a term sheet drawn up," Corwin said.

"Bryce Smithwick will get you one tonight," I said. In any deal it was always better to have control of drafting the document.

"Okay," he said.

"We need to have it signed by tomorrow night," I said. "As you said, no time for bullshit."

"Okay," he said again.

I hung up and looked at Juliana. She took a couple of steps around my desk and towered above me. She bent at the waist and planted a kiss smack-dab on the middle of my forehead.

"You did it," she said.

"It's not done till it's done."

"You saved us just like you did when Paul disappeared."

"Let's make sure. Get the board here tomorrow for a meeting between eleven and one. Please. I'll call Bryce."

Juliana pulled a tissue out of the box on my desk and took a swipe at my forehead. I saw the carmine smear on the Kleenex. "You did it," she said again as she opened the door.

———

Drinking dinner two nights in a row? Not a good idea. On the way home this Wednesday evening, I picked up a smoked turkey on wheat and a cup of fruit salad at Piazza's. Then I stopped at my mother's and found a pile of five black and red lab notebooks on an ottoman in her living room—right where she'd left them.

I drove the two hundred yards from my mother's to our house. I fetched the mail, too and reported to my mother that I'd found the notebooks. Then I took the newly delivered *Economist* with me to the kitchen table and read about entrepreneurship in China, while munching on the sandwich and washing it down with the last beer in the house.

The final drop of the brew was trickling down my throat when I heard the garage door creaking open. Rowena stomped into the house, her face flushed. She hit her right fist into her left palm.

"I think we got her," she said. Her teeth flashed in a smile of achievement. "Her goose is cooked."

"Her goose is cooked?" I repeated. "Such strong language."

She moved her face so close to mine that our noses almost touched. "For the first time since I got this assignment, I'm convinced we're going to send this woman away for the rest of her life. It's what Daisy Nolan deserves and what she's going to get."

A faint scent of cinnamon meant she'd been chomping on Dentyne, her habitual way of dissipating nervous energy.

"How did you do it?" I asked.

"You remember that the CEO's admin had shown Daisy an email the day before the murder."

"Right. So Daisy knew she wasn't going to get the VP slot at the time of the murder."

She nodded. "Daisy's attorney tried to undermine that testimony. Guerrero was getting nowhere, when the defendant leaped up and started calling the witness a liar and cussing her out. I guess this trial could set a record for courtroom outbursts." She raised an eyebrow.

I ignored the jab. "So what happened?" I asked.

"As calm as could be, our witness said, 'Daisy, you know I'm not lying.'"

"And how did Daisy react?"

"Like she'd been kicked in the head by a mule. She just sat down without another word. I looked at the jury box. It made an impression."

What I thought was it sounded more like show business than a trial before twelve persons "good and true," but what I said was, "Terrific!" So long as justice was served.

She put her arms around me. Her chest squeezed against mine. I could feel her heart pounding against her ribcage. I rubbed a hand over the back of her head.

She pulled away. "I have some papers to go through. What time is it?"

"Ten-thirty."

"I'll be ready for bed in an hour," she said.

That sounded like an invitation. Finally. After her father's death, the anger at my courtroom outburst, the overall pressure of the trial.

"Me, too," I said. "I'll meet you there."

She gave me a peck on the cheek and headed upstairs.

I opened up my laptop right at the kitchen table. While I was scrolling through email, a new one came in. Corwin said the term sheet looked good from a business point of view, and he'd turn it over to Intel's lawyers for a review. They were standing by. Huh. Intel lawyers probably pulled all-nighters about as often as dermatologists made house calls.

I turned off the lights and locked the front door. When I walked into our bedroom, there before me, illuminated by her bedside lamp, lay Rowena. She wore a flimsy, filmy nightgown I hadn't seen since our honeymoon. She'd meant to get my blood boiling and succeeded. Only one trouble. The legal briefs on her chest rose up and down with her breathing. Her eyes were closed. She was asleep.

TWENTY-TWO

WHAT COULD I DO? I gathered the papers off her chest with purposeful clumsiness, but Rowena's breathing remained metronomically steady. I thought about crawling into bed myself, but I knew I wouldn't sleep. Anticipation had melted away fatigue. I turned out the light and crept back downstairs and hefted the pile of lab notebooks. Lust was not going to be sated tonight. Maybe curiosity would be.

Tucked inside the first book lay a couple of postcards with aerial pictures of SLAC. It looked like a leaf rake with the two-mile length of the above-ground gallery forming the handle and buildings and parking lots splayed in a fan shape at the end. Next came a staff directory that included photos of five dozen experimental and theoretical physicists. The streak of her eyebrows made my great aunt easy to find. As did the fact she was the only woman. A thin pamphlet called "An Informal History of SLAC" recapped the chronology from the Varian brothers' first successful Klystrons in 1937 to the first successful electron beams being fired thirty years later.

All three black notebooks had contrasting yellow tape on the spines and a card glued on the cover with Isobel's name, phone number, and the dates covered. I opened the one that started on August 27, 1968. Inside was not the expected lined paper, but graph-style pages made up of little boxes. Out of a fountain pen had flowed notes, equations, and sketches. As legible as the blue ink letters and numbers were, I still did not understand all that much, even after having read Professor Randall's book. I cursed myself once again for not having taken a couple of physics classes in college.

In the middle of a page dated March 6, 1969, was a sketch of two balls, one labeled with a big capital "N" and the other with a "P"—despite the paucity of my physics knowledge, I reckoned they represented a neutron and proton. Each ball was divided into three pie-shaped wedges, each labeled "quirk" with either a +2/3 or -1/3 where the crust should be. My hands shook. Tompkins, Solenski, and Vansittart won the Nobel Prize for discovering that neutrons and protons were not indivisible, but were made up of quarks with a charge of either +2/3 or -1/3.

Springing up the stairs, still holding the lab book, I wasn't as quiet as I should have been.

"Is that you, Ian?" came Rowena's drowsy voice from the bedroom.

"Sorry. Go back to sleep."

"What time is it?"

I glanced at my watch. "Two-fifteen."

"You need to sleep."

"I'll be there soon."

I went into my office and pulled Tomkins' *Small Matter* off the bookshelf and started riffling through the pages. There it was.

"Late on the night of April 27 I sketched my theory of quarks on the chalkboard for Ivan and the next day for the director of SLAC, Claude Vansittart. The way his polka-dotted bowtie began bouncing up and down with excitement confirmed we'd made the kind of discovery every scientist dreams of."

No, Billy-boy, you weren't describing your theory. You were stealing Isobel's. The lab book I held in my hand was akin to a scrap of paper from 1905 where Einstein had first scrawled $E=MC^2$.

TWENTY-THREE

ON THE WAY BACK in from our morning run, I reached down and picked up the three newspapers delivered to our doorstep each morning. I had managed a few hours of sleep before the alarm. Rowena was focused on her case, so we didn't talk much as we galloped through the fog along the Bay. We'd agreed to talk more about Aunt Isobel over the weekend.

Once home, she headed upstairs for her shower. I put a kettle on the stove.

Slipping the blue plastic off the papers, I spread them out on the kitchen table. The Warriors had won their basketball game with the Lakers last night. Somehow, after two decades as a cellar-dwelling laughingstock, they'd become competitive. Somewhere, I knew, my old boss Paul Berk was getting the same charge reading about last night's victory as I was.

Among denizens of Silicon Valley, reading the latest news on an iPhone or Blackberry or Kindle was standard operating procedure (SOP). Not for me. A creature of habit even while living in the capital of Silicon Valley, I read the papers the same way and in the same order I had since high school. First, the *San Jose Mercury News*, then the *Times*, and, lastly *The Wall Street Journal*. In the *Merc*, sports first, then business, then news. In February the sports didn't take long, nor did an emaciated business section, which had never recovered from the bursting of the Internet bubble. In fact, the paper as a whole was suffering from journalistic anorexia. The revenue from classified ads that had supported the paper's news bureaus was being siphoned away by Craigslist and Google.

The kettle started to whistle, and I poured the boiling water into an oversized mug for my tea and into a French press for Rowena's coffee. I brought my tea back to the table and settled back to read the front page.

Holy shit! I knocked over the tea and grabbed the sopping *Merc*.

I was running up the stairs calling Rowena's name. She must be in the shower. I threw open the bathroom door and yelled "Rowena" one more time.

"Damn," came the voice from behind the shower curtain. I threw it open. Bent over, she held a razor in her hand. One leg was fully covered with soap, the other had two long swipes of suds missing and a streak shedding red tears into the tub.

She turned her head and looked at me. "You scared me."

"Did you see this?" I held up the newspaper that was dripping tea at about the same rate as Rowena's shin dripped blood.

"Oh," she said, as she brought a hand to her mouth. "I didn't think it was that big a deal."

"When you said the defendant started yelling during your witness's testimony, you said it was good news. You didn't say she was threatening to have you killed again."

"Oh, c'mon, Ian. It is good news. It makes her look guilty. What're you going to do? Beat her up for me?"

In reply, I waved the paper, and then said, "Look what the headline says—'Defendant Threatens Rookie DA.'"

"I'm not a rookie D.A., just a rookie homicide prosecutor. I've been there in the office almost four years." She leaned back down and started shaving her other leg. I watched the muscles ripple across her glistening back.

"Don't worry. She's going away for a long time. And it wasn't just me. She threatened the witness, too."

Rowena's tongue peeked out of the side of her mouth as she swept the razor up her legs. I watched as she let the water wash away the shaving cream.

She held out a hand. "May I see the article?" I hesitated. "I know my hands are wet," she said as she stood up, "but it doesn't look as though that much matters."

I handed the tea-soaked paper over. After half a minute, she turned to the carryover page.

"Ah, look here," she said. "Your little outburst gets mentioned at the end of the article."

The Merc had laid off so much of its newsroom that it didn't have a reporter in court last week, but I guess they had yesterday. "Oh. I didn't make it that far."

She turned back to the front page. "What do you think of that funny expression on my face? Not the best picture of me ever, is it?" she asked as she stood wet, bleeding and naked in the tub.

TWENTY-FOUR

WAS SOMETHING A MIRACLE if it was performed routinely? Juliana had managed to round up the overbooked, preoccupied, and egocentric members of the Accelenet board on a day's notice for our meeting to review the Intel offer. It was eleven in the morning in Silicon Valley and eight in the evening in Aix, whence Darwin Yancey's voice began its transatlantic journey to the Polycom speaker on the table. "Are you willing to sign up for another two years?" he was asking me.

"Yes."

"Just 'yes'?" Darwin asked. "You left four years ago."

It was almost Zen. Since Accelenet meant less to me now than it did four years ago, it was easier to agree. If I didn't get everything I wanted, I could still stay on. Success at Accelenet had meant so much more four years ago that I couldn't stay when I didn't get what I wanted. When Paul wouldn't give me the promotion I thought I deserved, I resigned. Now it was different. I had Rowena. We'd been talking about children. Of course, I couldn't forget about the company—four hundred people counted on me to protect their livelihood. But in all, because it was not the most important thing in my life, I could promise to stay.

"Just yes," I said.

"Bryce, what happens if Ian changes his mind?" Margot asked.

"If it's before the deal closes, the deal doesn't close. If Ian leaves voluntarily after it does close, Intel has an option to buy another forty million shares of stock at a dime a share."

"Which means?" Margot asked.

"They'll pick up another quarter of the company for just about nothing," Smithwick said.

"You ever seen anything like this?" Margot asked.

"I tried to talk them out of it, but Intel thinks this protects their investment."

"The answer to my question, please?" Margot asked again.

Smithwick showed no sign of irritation at Margot's peremptory inquisition. "Not exactly."

"So it all hinges on Ian?" Margot asked.

"I'm thirsty," I said. "I'll be back in ten."

"There's iced tea and water on the table," said Tim Yee.

"I feel like a Diet Dr. Pepper," I said.

"And it will take ten minutes to drink that?" Yee asked.

I waved on my way out.

"Everything okay?" Juliana asked when I walked by her desk.

"I think so."

"They're talking about you?"

"Yes."

She nodded, accustomed to my leaving the room during discussion of my performance or salary, and looked back down at her computer screen.

It was time to prepare my escape to another decade. I went into my office and dialed Ivan Solenski.

He answered his own phone. "Professor, this is Ian Michaels. I'm going to be in the neighborhood late this afternoon and had one more question."

We arranged to meet in his office at five. I headed back toward the boardroom and then remembered what I was supposed to be doing on my break. After a little rooting around the kitchen refrigerator, I turned up one lonely can of Diet Dr. Pepper amidst the dozens of Mountain Dews, Cokes, and Pepsis.

When I opened the door to the boardroom, it was as though I'd caught the lot of them *in flagrante delicto*. Both Leon and Smithwick were leaning forward and looking at Margot. Yee's chair was behind Margot's right shoulder, but he was looking at her, too. Aided by her flawless ivory complexion and chiseled expression, Margot herself was doing a pretty good impression of Venus de Milo.

Slipping back in my chair at the head of the table, I took a swig from my can.

"Ten minutes wasn't enough to finish your soda?" Leon asked, leaning against the backrest of his chair.

"I wanted to savor every drop," I said. "May I have a motion to accept the terms Intel's offered?"

"So moved," said Leon.

"Discussion?" I asked.

"I think we'll want a backup plan," Margot said. Yee nodded.

"Good point," I said. "We don't want to piss off Ricky and Torii any more than we have to."

"They are not going to wait around while we're making googoo eyes at Intel," Margot said. Yee nodded again.

"What do you want us to do, Margot? Intel's deal values us at twice what Torii does. We've got upside, too, since we remain independent. We can figure on a public offering, even."

"There's a big downside if we're not cashflow positive before running out of the fifty million."

"Yes," I said. "Thank you for making that point, too. Any other discussion?"

"I move we accept the Intel terms," said Darwin's disembodied voice.

"Ayes, please?"

Smithwick, Leon, Darwin, and I called out "aye."

"Nays?" Margot and Yee remained mum.

"Motion carried."

———

I'd left plenty of time to make it to SLAC to see Solenski by five, but I was moving down 101 in fits and starts, averaging no more than five miles per hour. I turned off at the Rengstorff exit, figuring I could still make it on time if I took surface streets.

My iPhone started shaking against my chest. With the Intel deal pending, Juliana had extracted a Boy Scout's-honor pledge that I would stay accessible. I came damn close to hitting a Prius, the Model T of Silicon Valley, while doing the contortions required to get the phone out of my jacket pocket. I looked at the screen. "Blocked ID."

"Is that you, Michaels?" said the voice emanating from my phone.

"Hello, Ricky." I'd left my headset in the office. I pulled over to the side of the road in front of a hydrant so I could pay attention.

This way, too, I would not be indulging in one of my frequent violations of the California law that required a hands-free device when driving.

"Do you think Intel is really going to do a deal with you?"

"Ricky, I'm not really at liberty to discuss that right now."

"I am. It is not going to happen. Do you hear me? It will be stopped."

"How will you do that, Ricky?"

No answer. Once more he'd indulged his disconcerting habit of hanging up without saying goodbye.

TWENTY-FIVE

"How are you?" I asked Solenski from across his desk.

"Cannot complain," he said. "I woke up this morning, a good thing. And the bed was dry."

I laughed at the old age humor. Worrying about waking up and soiling your sheets. Something to look forward to.

"So what can I do for you?" Solenski asked.

I'd made a copy of the page with the two pies divided in thirds and handed it across his desk to the professor.

He leaned down and stared at it, leaving me to watch the top of his head, an eggshell surrounded by that fluffy ruffle of white hair.

After two minutes, I said, "You know what this is."

He nodded. "Where did you get it?"

"From Isobel Marter's lab book."

"I know that. Where was it?"

"Her niece had it." He nodded. "When did you first see the drawing?" I asked.

"Tompkins had just joined the lab. You know he was only twenty-three. He came to us from Caltech. His references called him the smartest student they'd ever enrolled. I was showing him around, and we saw one of Izzy's..."

"Call her Isobel, would you? She didn't like being called Izzy."

He considered the request with his head tilted to one side. "That so? Okay. Anyway, what I started to say was we saw her notebook, Isobel's, lying on the counter."

"Closed?"

"Well, yes. But..."

"But what?"

"Well, I was showing Bill around. He just picked up the book and leafed through it. He was just that way. Still is. No shame."

"The drawing of the protons and neutrons there is awfully close to the picture in his book."

"He did a lot of work on quarks. There was a lot of skepticism and only when we—Tompkins and I—found evidence of the gluons that held the quarks together in a neutron or proton did everything fall into place."

"But it was Isobel's work that put him on the right course."

"Yes, but so what? We were supposed to be a team."

"You feel no guilt?"

"Why? She would have won a share of the Nobel if she'd lived. The day I heard I won the Nobel Prize I wrote two equations on my blackboard, "First, smart equals Bill, Claude, and Izzy. Second, Ivan equals lucky."

"Did Isobel ever find out that Tompkins had seen her sketch?"

"I didn't tell her. Maybe Bill did."

Yeah, right, I thought. I asked Solenski, "Why didn't Isobel go public with her idea of quirks? She seemed to have had the basics down."

He sighed. "You didn't know the woman. It wasn't in her nature. She wouldn't show anything till it was perfect, till she had an answer for any objection. She thought Bill was reckless when he went to Vansittart."

"Not much of a team member, huh?"

"No," he shook his head. "A loner."

"She didn't realize where Tompkins had got the idea?"

"He'd been working on the problem, too. He was going down the same path as she was."

"Just a few steps behind," I said.

"He did put together a grid that's still the essence of the Standard Model of particle physics."

"But she wanted to wait and get proof of quirks' existence from the accelerator?"

"I think so," he said. "You know, I haven't heard them called quirks in forty years."

"Whose idea was it to run the experiment while she was on vacation?"

He looked down at his desktop.

"Tompkins?" I asked.

He nodded once.

"I'm going over to the campus to talk to him." I got up from my chair.

"I'll call him and tell him you're coming," he called after me.

"Do what you want," I said without turning around.

I heard Solenski saying hello to someone on the phone even before the office door shut behind me.

After twenty minutes of crawling along Sand Hill Road and a five-minute run from the parking lot, I threw Tompkins' office door open. Empty. Solenski must have told him I was on my way, and he'd rabbitted.

Grabbing an eraser, I wiped a panel of equations off his blackboard. In foot-high, yellow-chalk letters, I wrote, "Tompkins, call me," and scribbled my name and cellphone number below that.

TWENTY-SIX

Rowena hadn't been home before ten all week, but now on Thursday at seven, there she stood, back to me, in front of the stove. An apron over her courtroom chalk stripes, she flipped two thick pieces of fish that were hissing on the griddle. The noise of the stove's hood masked my entry.

I leaned over and whispered into her right ear. "Looks good."

This time she did not even turn around. "Whew, I took a chance that you'd get here in time. This tuna is best right out of the pan."

"What are you doing home already?"

Now she twisted her head around with a smile.

"The trial can't be over," I asked. "You must have rested your case, but then you'd be getting ready for cross-examination tomorrow. Maybe the judge wants a three-day weekend? Enough of my babbling. Spill it."

"We did rest. The defense caught us in the hallway before we could even get in the elevator. They're ready to accept a life sentence."

"In return for your dropping the death penalty?"

"Right."

"They offered this before they even presented the defense?"

"Yes."

"Her goose really *must* be cooked."

"To a cinder, especially after those courtroom tantrums. Daisy needs to be locked up. In her mind anyone who stands between her and what she wants deserves to, well, die. She may have no regard for human life, but the People ought to."

"So you're going to accept the offer?"

"We need to discuss it with the D.A. tomorrow morning," she said. "But that's a formality. Sally will say yes. You should be happy." Rowena knew I was no fan of capital punishment.

"And we're going to eat well in the meantime?" I asked.

"Starting with grilled sashimi-grade tuna."

Most wives would want to go out. Rowena, though, found cooking therapeutic, and I never found reason to complain about this idiosyncrasy. Along with the fish, we ate long white spears of asparagus, pear and arugula salad decorated with walnuts, and a giant cigar-shaped Acme Bakery sourdough baguette. Philistine that I was, I swigged from a bottle of Speakeasy Ale she'd picked up, while she sipped at her Aussie merlot.

We were eating in the dining room by candlelight rather than at the kitchen table under fluorescent lamps. She was celebrating, and I was happy to help. There's no English equivalent to the Yiddish word *kvell*. It represents the feeling you get when a loved one makes you proud, makes you thankful to be alive to see such a thing. Rowena had won her first homicide case, and I was *kvelling*.

She cut me a piece of the berry tart she'd conjured up. The fact she was ignoring the cholesterol implication to me of the stick of butter in the crust meant she was really celebrating. This was not hardship duty.

"Now you've heard enough about the case," she said as her fork delivered the last piece of dessert to her mouth. "What about you? Is Intel going to come through?"

"I think so."

"They're going to snatch fair Accelenet off the tracks just before the onrushing train."

She raised her crystal goblet, and I clinked my schooner of coppery ale against it.

"To escaping the clutches of Snidely Whiplash," she said.

"To justice," I said.

We drank.

"One more thing," I said after finishing off the beer.

"Does there *have* to be one thing?"

"Isobel's notebooks make interesting reading. It turns out she was the one who figured out quarks, not Tompkins or Solenski."

"They stole everything from her, didn't they? She was dead. goddamn grave robbers."

Cheeks that had been pink with wine flushed scarlet with fury. Rowena slammed her wineglass down on the table. I watched it shatter and then saw the wine spread across the tablecloth like a spot of ink on a blotter.

"Let me see your hand," I said. She still held the bowl of the glass, but a shard from the stem protruded from the meaty part of her palm. I plucked it out. A small gusher of blood spurted forth.

"Your leg this morning and your hand tonight. We need to keep you away from sharp objects." She squeezed a napkin against the hole in her palm.

"You're going to do right by Aunt Isobel, aren't you?"

"Yes, but I don't know what good it's going to do her."

"You just offered a toast to justice."

"A little late for Aunt Isobel."

"You're so full of it," she said. "I know you feel the urgency, too. You're making the time to work on Aunt Isobel now, even with everything else going on. You can play the cynic if you want to, but you're after justice, no matter what you say."

"Schoolchildren should know her name."

"Starting this weekend, I'll help. Together we can move even faster."

When I came to bed that night, Rowena lay atop the comforter with her hand propping up her head. She was naked—naked except for bandages on her shin and hand.

"Speaking of physics," she said. "Do you know why Richard Feynman..." She queried with an upraised eyebrow.

"Yeah, the physicist," I said. "Solenski just mentioned him."

"Right. Anyway, do you know why he said physics and sex were alike?"

I tried to think, but not for long. With Rowena looking up at me like an odalisque in a nineteenth-century French painting, I'm not sure I could have come up with the square root of four. "No clue."

"He said, 'Physics is like sex in that it may give some practical results, but that's not why we do it.'"

I laughed and she smiled. "Turn over," I told her. I used my thumbs to knead her shoulders. I headed south, spending extra time

131

on her legs. I found the long muscles of her thighs and calves underneath the sleek skin. When I worked my fingers into the arches of her feet, her toes curled.

"Come back up here," she said.

I lay on top of her, and we kissed. When I entered her minutes later, she arched her back and moaned. Nails dug into my shoulders. My eyes closed and I was being sucked into a vortex. I heard an "ahh" coming out of her throat and felt her hips shimmy. I knew what that meant. I exploded inside her.

A few minutes later, Rowena was sliding her hands up and down my back as my breathing began to slow.

She laughed.

"What?" I asked.

"Maybe absence does make the heart grow fonder."

"Definitely worth waiting for."

"Ah, so this is all it takes to put a smile back on your face?"

"I do love you," I told her.

"And I you," she said. "Now hush."

Still inside her, I put my head down on her chest. The steady thump-thump of her heart filled my brain, leaving no room for thoughts of upcoming pay periods or subatomic particles.

Five minutes later, after my own chest had stopped heaving, Rowena's started to move in silent sobs. Was she crying because she was happy? I didn't ask.

TWENTY-SEVEN

I EXTRICATED MYSELF FROM Rowena's snaking arm. By the time the alarm went off, I had my running togs on.

"What time is it?" she said, her mouth filled with a cotton ball of sleep.

"Five."

She dropped her head back to the pillow. "I don't want to run today. Come back to bed."

"I'm up already, but go ahead and stay under the covers. I'll wake you up at six-thirty or so after I get back."

She sat up, and the comforter fell away from the silhouette of her torso. My willpower started to melt away. Climbing back into bed might be a better plan.

"No, no, I'll come, too," she said and swung her legs onto the floor.

Fifteen minutes later we ran out into the wisps of fog that encased the house. She turned right toward Stanford, not left to the Baylands as I expected. Rowena ran because, like a wild horse, she was born to. So effortless was her stride as we traversed the deserted streets of Palo Alto that she didn't appear to be moving all that fast, but the poor slob who was trying to keep up could bear witness to the pace she was setting. She could run in her sleep—as she was proving.

PART II

TWENTY-EIGHT

THE WHINE OF THE siren ceased as we pulled up to the emergency entrance to Stanford Hospital. They whisked the gurney out. Still able to walk, I followed. Adrenaline had to be working in my favor. Without looking down, I knew a sharp edge of gray-white bone had driven through the skin about ten inches below my right knee. I took off my sweatshirt and tied it around my waist to hide the wound. Then I tried to keep up with the paramedics conveying my wife through the hallway. I was gaining when I found a meaty paw on my shoulder. I swatted at it. The paw closed.

A guy with a stubble heavier than Richard Nixon's at dinner-time was smiling at me. "May I help you?" he asked.

"Yeah, that was my wife who just passed by."

"They're going to do a CAT scan on her."

"And I want to be there when they do." I tried to move again. The paw turned into a vise.

"The dispatcher said there were two injuries coming in. One head injury and a compound leg break."

I twisted around and saw his hospital badge. Patrick Leary, R.N.

"I want to be with my wife."

His free hand reached down to untie the sweatshirt. "You will, but first let's have someone look at that leg."

"What are you, the E.R. bouncer? How about I go with my wife and then we'll worry about the leg?" I tried to shrug off the hand on my shoulder. Instead of falling away, it twisted, and I found myself being guided by this brute of a nurse. He installed me in an examining room while he filled the doorway.

"There's no way you get to go into the exam room with your wife," he said. "Sorry. That's just the way it works."

"Where is she now?"

"Well, having that CAT scan."

"Already?"

"Probably. She came in unconscious. She'll be top priority."

"Okay. I want to call my doctor." I took my iPhone out of its pocket in my running shorts.

"No cell phones in the hospital," Nurse Leary said.

"I want to call our doctor and get him over here."

"If you promise not to move, I'll go out and call him for you."

"It's Frank Dubitzky. Please tell him that Rowena and Ian Michaels are both here."

"Okay," he said and left.

I looked down at what I held in my right hand. The prohibition on cell phone use didn't much matter—my two-month-old iPhone was ready for the recycling bin. I'd have to root around desk drawers to find the original model I still had at home.

Nurses and doctors scurried by the open door, but Leary did not return. After five minutes, I stood up. I took a first step and then another one. My leg had stiffened. I walked with an old man's swivel and each pace hurt, but I was ambulatory. How this could be with a cracked leg, I didn't know.

On TV the emergency room is filled with doctors and nurses scurrying to save the lives of the injured. From what I saw out the doorway, Stanford Hospital's emergency practice consisted primarily of juggling the available exam rooms among the infirm whose ailments ranged from common cold to heart attack.

After twenty-five minutes of waiting, I figured my promise had expired. I tottered out to the main desk where a whirlpool of doctors, nurses, and EMTs was circulating.

"Where is Rowena Goldberg, please?" I asked the one seated woman.

She did not look up.

"Excuse me?" No reaction. Another hand settled on my shoulder. This time I knocked it off and whirled around, ready to slug Leary.

"Frank," I said. There before me stood the tall, spare figure of Dr. Frank Dubitzky, an atavism in a blazer and red-and-blue striped repp tie. Leary had remembered to call after all. He'd just forgotten to pass the word back to me.

"Whoa, boy. Let's go find a place to talk."

Back in the exam room, Dubitzky said, "Sit down. I doubt it's good for you to be standing." After I obeyed, he continued. "She got quite a conk. The car that hit her must have sent her flying."

"No car hit her. I pushed her out of the way, and she ended up hitting her head against a tree trunk. It was my fault." I covered my face with my hands, and my head started shaking.

"Better a push from you than from a speeding automobile would be my guess."

I dropped my hands away and opened my mouth to argue, but Dubitzky cut me off. "No matter. What does matter is that she has an epidural hematoma."

"Which means?" I had a hard time taking a breath.

"Slow down. No need to panic. What it means is that she has bleeding in her head. There's no room there for the blood because…"

"Because it's already filled with her brains?"

"That about sums it up. Pressure builds up in the skull, which makes it harder for the heart to pump oxygenated blood up to the brain."

When I nodded, the pools of tears along my lower lids overflowed. I could taste the wet saltiness on my lips.

"So what we've got to do is get the blood out of there."

"And how do we do that?"

"By opening a tiny window in her skull, pumping the blood out, and then closing the window."

"They're going to saw out a piece of her skull?"

"Yes."

"And when is this going to happen?"

"Soon. They're getting an operating room ready."

"Who is the neurosurgeon?"

"The best. Dr. Harold Griffith." Dubitzky put his arm on my shoulder. "If it were my wife, that's who I'd want."

"And what does this all mean for the long run?"

"The hope is that she'll be good as new, but it will take time to heal."

"The hope?" I exhaled. "Has she awakened? Is she conscious?"

"No."

"I still want to see her."

"You should be in a wheelchair. It can't be good for you to walk."

"You think I give a goddamn?"

"You wait here then. I'll find out where she is."

He left. What to do? What to do? After five minutes of waiting, of being left with my thoughts of terror and blame, I just started saying "Please, God, help Rowena" over and over. After a few minutes I stopped, skeptical about how much good it would do.

"Ian?" I opened my eyes. "Let's go." Dr. Dubitzky was more reliable than the nurse.

We caught up with Rowena outside the elevator. Eyes still closed, she was lying in a bed on wheels. Her temporary caretaker pushed her in the elevator car, and Dubitzky and I followed. The doors closed.

As the aide pushed the bed, I took her hand and held it. We came to swinging doors.

"You need to stop here, sir," he said to me.

I looked at Dubitzky for support.

He shook his head. "You can't come, but I'll be there."

I leaned down, kissed her forehead, and whispered, "I'll be waiting."

The doors swung open wide. I watched her being rolled down the corridor. Then the doors swung shut, leaving me standing alone.

TWENTY-NINE

ACROSS THE CORRIDOR FROM the swinging doors was a nook that a placard proclaimed "Surgery Family Waiting Area." A gray-haired volunteer in a candy-striped apron sat behind a desk. Most of the three dozen or so seats were occupied by families huddled together and murmuring in Spanish. With my first step came the searing pain below my right knee, but I made it across to an unoccupied coffee-colored armchair. I sat there without seeing, without thinking, reasoning faculties frozen with fear.

I was roused from my fugue by a round-faced cocoa-skinned woman in her fifties. She held a half-unwrapped foil package two feet from my face. A cheese and bean burrito.

People were good, they wanted to help. We had to stick together in the fight against life's unending procession of desolation, despair, and death. "No, thank you," I told her. "*No, gracias.*" I shook my head and then I smiled. Saltwater pools started forming again in my eyes.

She understood what I said, but still stuck the package under my nose. As I began to shake my head again, the double doors swung open and Dubitzky stepped through.

"Frank," I called. The woman returned to her husband, and I pushed my arms against the chair to stand up.

Dubitzky was wearing blue-green scrubs. "Sit down."

I sat, and he towered over me. Then he crouched and looked at me straight in the eye. I was not breathing.

"An artery was bleeding. We stopped it. Griffith evacuated the blood that was raising the pressure in her skull."

"Will she be okay?"

"I expect so, but she's still in a coma."

"Expect so or hope so?" I asked.

"Both. I told you. Dr. Griffith is the best we have, the best I know. And it doesn't hurt that Rowena is a marathoner in great shape."

"When can I see her?"

"She's in post-op. Once they get her settled in the ICU, you can go in. That'll take an hour or so. Let's go downstairs in the meantime. We'll clean up your leg, get some X-rays, and see what else we need to do."

"I don't have time to wait down in the emergency room. I'd die of old age before I got out of that place. I want to be back here in an hour to see Rowena."

"I'll get you back here by then. What about a wheelchair now?"

"Please, Frank, no. I can walk." I didn't want to be an invalid. I needed to suffer.

Dubitzky helped me up, and I hobbled along with him to the elevator.

"How much does it hurt?"

"Less than I would have thought. How come I *can* walk?" I asked.

"You've broken your fibula, not your tibia. We'll get you on antibiotics and after a couple of days of bed rest..."

"No bed rest, Frank. I have work to do."

"If you walk around too much and put weight on that leg, healing could be slower."

"I'll deal with it."

"You could end up with a limp."

"And will walking on it now make any difference?"

"Maybe, but probably not."

"I'm going to walk then." A bad leg seemed inconsequential next to a hole in the skull.

"Well, no sense fighting yet. We'll have to look at the X-rays and see what they tell us."

As we walked by, I smiled at the woman who had tried to feed me. "*Gracias. Vaya con dios,*" I said to her.

She gave me a solemn nod in return.

———

We were back in a small room in emergency. On a flat LCD screen, Frank was peering at the dark outline of a crack in my fibula.

"It's a mid-shaft fracture. Your main risk is infection. All we need to do is clean it out, sew it closed, and bandage it up. You'll have to take antibiotics, too. If it were your tibia or up higher on your fibula, we'd be doing surgery to insert hardware..."

"Hardware like metal plates and pins?"

"Right. If you'll allow me a doctor's joke, you got a lucky break."

He got down to work without checking to see if I smiled. I hadn't. Frank's gnarled and liver-spotted hands took care of business. The speed with which he moved the needle and thread in and out would have daunted a Garment District dressmaker.

Five minutes later, when he'd finished wrapping up the wound, I asked, "Don't you have other appointments?"

"I just had routine physicals this morning. Nothing that couldn't be rescheduled."

"May I use your cell phone?" I asked him.

"You know they're not supposed to be used in here."

"There are no vital signs monitors in this room to foul up. It's just like on planes. They tell you not to use cell phones, not because they're dangerous, but because they can. If using cell phones in the air was really dangerous, planes would be filled with terrorists dialing away. Institutions can't resist treating people like sheep."

Dubitzky handed me his phone. I called the D.A.'s office. Once she heard who it was, her admin handed me over to Huang before I could say anything.

"I don't care if she's got a cold or the Ebola virus, get your wife in here," the D.A. barked. "She's supposed to be in my office right now so we can decide how to deal with her murder."

I was about to yell back at her when I remembered my courtroom outburst. After a quick pant, I said in a tone as calm as I could make it, "Her murder? Not far from the mark. I'm at Stanford Hospital. She's just had brain surgery."

"Oh, my God. She had a stroke?"

"No. A car tried to run her over."

"Are you saying someone tried to kill her?"

"Wasn't she threatened in court again just the day before yesterday?"

"Holy shit. An accomplice of Nolan's came after her?"

"Who knows? Something to think about, though," I said. "I'm going to the ICU to see her now." I pressed the end button on the good doctor's phone.

THIRTY

HEAD HALF-SHAVED, EYE SOCKETS circled with dark shadows, left arm tattooed with purple bruises, Rowena looked like a punk Sleeping Beauty. Her chest rose and fell, but her eyes remained shut. I gave her a kiss on the cheek, but she awakened not. I was no prince.

"How is she doing?" came a voice from behind me.

"Huh?" I'd been thinking how much Rowena looked like my great aunt. Turning around, I saw Sergeant Susan Fletcher of the Palo Alto Police.

I started to get up, but didn't make it. Damn leg. She held out a hand. A short and cylindrical kewpie, the good sergeant did not lack in towing power. A fluid pull of her right arm and I was on my feet. She kept right on tugging until I was close enough for her to wrap her arms around me. My arms pinned to my sides, her cheek against my chest, I kissed the top of her head, hoping it would unlock the bear hug. It did.

"I hung up on the D.A. less than half an hour ago," I said. "You got here quick."

"Yeah, that's me. Janey on the spot."

"Glad it's you."

"Instead of…"

"Anyone." Four years before, the powers-that-be had figured me for the killer of my sister-in-law. Fletcher stood alone among the law enforcement crowd in counting me innocent. The sergeant's stripes had come as her reward for being right.

"So here we are at Stanford Hospital again," she said.

"Yeah, here we are." Four years before we'd chased through these same corridors to confront Gwendolyn's killer.

"How is Rowena doing? What happened?" she asked, looking from Rowena's bandage-turbaned head to my filthy T-shirt and then down to my bandaged leg.

"Let's step outside."

In the corridor she asked again, "What happened?"

"What do you know?"

"That a defendant threatened her in court Wednesday, and someone tried to run her down this morning."

"That's about all there is. Goddammit, Susan, they should have had her under guard."

"A uniformed officer is on his way. We'll take no more chances." I snorted.

She said, "We'll find out who did this, but, Ian, if it's a murder-for-hire, there's no room for amateurs."

"That's what you think of me as, an amateur?"

"No room for avenging angels either."

———

"You may not go in." The police officer stood in the doorway to the ICU room and blocked the way of a blonde who looked more Rockette than assassin.

I came out.

"Officer Baroojian, this is a colleague of mine."

I took my admin Juliana by the arm and walked out to the corridor.

"Ian, what is going on?" she asked.

"How did you find me?"

"I called Rowena's office when you went MIA. They told me you'd be here. How is she doing?"

"She's sleeping. They say she'll be okay."

Juliana flung her arms around me. "Poor, Ian." She started patting my back as if I were a colicky baby. I looked over her shoulder at the police officer whose expression was hard to read—envy maybe.

When we separated, Juliana started with an "um," followed by an "er."

"Spit it out," I said.

"I hate to bother—to bother you at a time like this, but Intel has signed the term sheet. You need to, too."

"Bryce has given it a last once-over?"

She gave me a hurt look. "Of course."

The document was only three pages long. As best I could, I proofread it myself. How could I promise to focus on the company, to stay there for two years, when Rowena lay unconscious in the next room? What choice did I have? I initialed the bottom of the first two pages, then signed and dated the third.

"Do you need anything else?" Juliana asked.

"Could you get my old iPhone reactivated?" I asked.

"That's all?"

I nodded. Access time to the Net would suck, but voice and email would be fine.

After Juliana left, I couldn't put it off any longer. Four years ago Caroline Goldberg had lost a daughter. Two weeks ago a husband. Her remaining daughter was in line to be next. I went outside and called Caroline from a pay phone.

———

"I tell you, Nolan could not have arranged it," Huang said. "She's talked to no one, not even a phone call."

It was nine o'clock Saturday morning. The Santa Clara District Attorney had stopped in to see her incapacitated employee. We sat in the hospital chapel, the closest empty room to Rowena's. If you didn't get in the way, the understanding nurses didn't enforce visiting hours for close relatives. I'd spent the night on a chair next to Rowena's bed and was bristly in both senses of the word—my face needed a shave, my orneriness a target.

"She threatened Rowena in open court," I said. "Someone could have heard. Even if she didn't have anyone in the gallery, the front page of *The Mercury* sure let any confederate know what she wanted. Or her lawyer could have carried a message to someone."

"Guerrero? I've known him for a long time. I don't think so. Doesn't matter though. The Palo Alto police, the San Jose police, and the investigators in my office are working on this incident."

"Incident? Incident? What, you think it was just an accident?"

"I don't know."

"I was there. It was not an accident. It was attempted murder."

"How can you be sure?" she asked.

I'd gone over the same ground with Fletcher half a dozen times.

"We both wore white. We had lights around our arms and reflective tape on the back of our shoes. The car sped up as it came closer, and then swerved at us."

"Suggestive but not conclusive."

"Are you going to question Nolan about this?"

"Sure, but we'll get nowhere. She's going down on a murder rap. We know she didn't issue orders herself beyond what she said in court."

I whirled around and started to walk away.

She grabbed my arm with slender fingers. "Listen. I have no higher priority than this. It's not good for the legal system to have a deputy D.A. attacked."

I shook her hand off. "Right now, I don't give a shit about your legal system. I want to find the guy driving that car. And I want my wife back."

———

A few minutes later when I returned to Rowena's room, her mother was there, back to the door. I could hear Caroline Goldberg murmuring prayers. She hadn't needed me to testify to her bona fides to get by the guard.

I wanted to tell her that it does no good. That I had tried every prayer I could think of and Rowena still did not wake up.

THIRTY-ONE

THE DOORBELL RANG.

My mother-in-law had convinced me that I could go home to clean up and take a nap. Dr. Griffith was stopping by every morning and afternoon, the nurses were looking in every hour, and Caroline sat by the bed squeezing Rowena's hand every minute.

Walking toward my front door to answer, I thought of families with sons and daughters in military service for whom such a knell could mean death. I quickened my step and swung the door open with a pull that sent it banging into its stop.

No uniformed representative at the door. Instead, smiling with concern stood the second-richest man in California. I could see a blue Bentley at the curb, the burly bodyguard in the front passenger's seat.

"Hello, Ian. I am so sorry about your wife."

"Thank you, Ricky. Thank you for coming by. Very much appreciated."

I started to shut the door on the avatar of all those billions.

Like a shy suitor, Frankson whisked a bouquet of flowers from behind his back. "These are for your wife."

I stopped the door before it swung shut on his wrist and reached my hand out.

"Thank you. I appreciate your concern."

"I know this is no time to discuss business."

"Thank you. I appreciate your consideration."

He'd already used the flowers to deter me from closing the door. So this time he used his right hand to push against the knob.

"It's tragic about your wife. Would have been even worse if you'd been hit, too."

"What do you mean? I'd trade places with her in an instant."

"Of course, you would. I just meant that if you were incapacitated, the Intel deal would be over."

"Go to hell, Ricky."

If he'd had slower reflexes, the push I gave the door might have broken his arm.

I leaned my back against the three inches of maple, as though barricading the entrance against another assault by Frankson. What an asshole. I heard the smooth thrum of an engine and then the screech of tires.

A few deep breaths and my mind kicked back in gear. Margot had snitched again. I *really* might as well start inviting Frankson to the board meetings.

I went upstairs to the bathroom and turned on the water for the shower. I reached for the shaving cream. After staring at the orange and black can for a few seconds, I put it back down. While a narrow reading of the Jewish rule against shaving during the shiva period would not apply to me—I was a son-in-law, not a son—I still hadn't taken a razor to my face for the seven days after

Rowena's father died. If I wouldn't shave in deference to my dead father-in-law, how much more important to show that I cared about my living and breathing wife? Superstition maybe, but no razor was touching my face until Rowena woke up.

I left my bad leg outside the tub and turned on the shower. A little awkward, but it would work. I opened a bottle of Rowena's shampoo. The whiff of roses worked like Proust's madeleine, and we were back on our honeymoon on Bora Bora. What I remembered best about that Polynesian idyll was the lovemaking. After sex, Rowena and I would just lie naked side by side and laugh. Not that anything was funny. No, we were happy—happy as Adam and Eve before the snake butted in. I was depleted, drained, each time we were done making love. More sex didn't seem possible. Yet, later that day or the next morning, we would do it again. The palm-thatched cottage we stayed in, called a *faré*, was suspended over the lagoon on poles. We kept the windows open and listened to the waves while coupled on the grass mat in the living room. One night we lay on the beach, pretending we were Burt Lancaster and Deborah Kerr in *From Here to Eternity*. On our fourth day there, walking back to the *faré* after dinner, I reached under her skirt and pulled down her panties.

"What are you doing?" she whispered in mock protest while making certain we were alone on the dark pathway. She lifted one leg and then the other to facilitate completion of my goal.

"I just don't know when the moment will be right, and I want us to be ready," I said as I stuffed her underwear into my pants pocket. We didn't even make it back to the *faré*. We made love under the stars, her skirt pushed up, her back resting on a curving palm trunk.

"Shit." Loud banging on the front door—audible even over the hiss of streaming water—had interrupted my reverie. Did I care? Let Frankson pummel till he broke every bone in both hands.

Even a couple minutes later when drying myself off, the door-pounding had not stopped. Should I call the police to stop this harassment? I wrapped myself in a bath towels and headed downstairs. Jerking the door open, I began to yell. "What the hell..."

I stopped. No need to call the police. They were here.

Fletcher stood in front, but the shaggy blond head of her longtime partner towered over her.

"Yeah, it's us," Officer John Mikulski said.

"Don't you guys believe in telephones?" I asked.

"We knocked," Mikulski said.

"Better than battering the door down with guns drawn, I guess. Thanks."

"John, why don't we give Ian a chance to get dressed?" Fletcher asked. Then she turned to me, gaze directed first up at my face, then down at my feet and sideways at my door frame—anywhere but at my bare chest. "Sorry, Ian. We've got questions."

A few minutes later, I'd pulled on a T-shirt and jeans, and we were sitting in the living room.

"Why do you think someone was trying to run down Rowena?" Mikulski asked in a skeptical tone.

"You know, I went through this with Sergeant Fletcher yesterday." I emphasized her rank. When I'd spoken to the two of them four years ago, Mikulski was the senior member of the duo. What I observed back then was that Fletcher knew the obvious answer was not always the correct one. In contrast, Mikulski eschewed subtlety and relied on brawn more than brains. Now Fletcher outranked her partner. It doesn't happen as often as it should, but occasionally merit is rewarded.

"Humor us," Mikulski said. Fletcher smiled and nodded.

"Okay." I went through the facts again. It didn't take long.

"Can you describe the car?"

"Dark. Black or navy maybe."

"The make?"

"I had the impression it was German. A BMW maybe."

"The grille was split like a BMW's?"

"I think so. It looked like an open mouth about to swallow us whole. The sound more than anything said BMW to me. You know, that whiny purr? But if you told me it was a Lexus or a Mercedes, I wouldn't be too surprised."

"A good-sized car then?"

"Yeah. If it was a BMW, not a 3-series."

"How far were you from the road?"

"Well, there was no sidewalk, but we were running on a dirt path a foot or two from the asphalt."

"She was in front and you were behind?"

"That's right."

"There are three possibilities," he said and counted them off on the fingers of his right hand. "Someone was trying to kill your wife, trying to kill you, or the whole thing was a complete accident."

"One more, at least in theory," I said. "What about trying to kill us both?"

His eyes narrowed. He didn't much care for being corrected. "At least in theory," he conceded. Maybe he had a certain sympathy for anyone who'd decided to do away with me.

"But a defendant on trial for murder threatened to kill my wife. That was your first option."

"So far we haven't come up with anyone who would do this for Nolan," Fletcher said. "If she were a gang member or a drug dealer, it would make more sense."

"So who *was* driving that car then?" I asked.

"It could have been some anonymous drunk, too," Mikulski said. "On his way home. Not everyone at five-thirty in the morning is just starting their day."

"Drunks don't turn the wheel to aim at people."

"Not on purpose anyway."

"Does this mean you're not going to do anything to find out who put my wife in a coma?"

"No. We're looking for the car and driver, accident or not. We're even pulling in gang members. Or rather *we're* not pulling them in—not the Palo Alto police—but the San Jose department is. They just want to feel they're doing something. It's not good for business if people in law enforcement—which includes deputy D.A.'s—are targeted."

"Yeah, that's what the D.A. herself told me. I guess it's supposed to make me feel better."

"Ian." Fletcher was speaking so softly that I leaned forward. "We can't ignore any of the possibilities—there are four of them, remember—if we're going to do a good job."

"What do you mean?"

"Is there anyone who would want to kill you?"

"You think this is some Agatha Christie mystery with a clever plot twist at the end? A woman on trial for murder said she was going to get my wife. Two days later Rowena's almost killed. You need to find out how she got word to someone and who that someone is. Just because Nolan is the most obvious answer, doesn't mean it's wrong."

THIRTY-TWO

AFTER MIKULSKI AND FLETCHER left, I sat back down in the paisley armchair. They hadn't needed smart-ass me to point out that, as a rule, the most straightforward solution was probably the correct one. William of Occam had that one pegged in the fourteenth century. Fletcher had probably insisted they go through other possibilities just for the sake of completeness. Or maybe Mikulski figured someone as obnoxious as me would naturally engender homicidal attacks.

The old iPhone I was using rang in the bedroom, and I made it up the stairs as fast as I could with a leg and a half to pick it up. I looked down at the screen and recognized Barclay Corwin's number.

"Hello?"

"Barclay here. You okay?"

"Yes, fine. Why do you ask?"

"I heard there was an accident yesterday."

"Was there something in the paper?" The D.A. had told me they would try to keep things out of the paper. If any enterprising reporter asked, it was going to be an accident. I didn't know how long that would last. Sex, betrayal, and murder had attracted the reporter from the *Mercury News* to Nolan's trial. She'd heard the threat, too.

"No, no, my boss told me."

"Where did he hear about it?"

"Don't know. The CEO tom-tom circuit, I guess." He hesitated. "Is your wife okay?"

"I hope so."

"I hate bothering you now, but word of our deal is starting to leak. Therese Poletti from MarketWatch just called me about the term sheet."

This was Silicon Valley. It was back to what really counted—the deal. Be angry with Corwin himself for bothering me? How could I? That's just how the Valley worked. If I didn't like it, I could move to a farm in North Dakota.

"Too many people knew for it to stay secret," I said.

"Yeah, I thought we'd have a couple of days, but we need to get something out by five-thirty Monday morning, you know, before the market opens. You should already have a draft press release in your inbox."

"The mail must get through," I said.

"I beg your pardon?"

"We'll get back to you with comments by the end of the day," I said.

"Thank you."

At a red light on the way back to the hospital, I forwarded the press release from my iPhone to Juliana and asked her to get Bryce and my staff to review it.

———

Caroline might as well have been in suspended animation. She had not moved in the two hours I'd been gone. She still sat immobile, holding her daughter's hand. Her lips were moving, appealing a verdict to a judge she could not see.

She barely nodded as I pulled up a chair to the other side of the bed and leaned over its guardrail to take Rowena's other hand.

About ten minutes later Caroline looked up. "Are you going to call your mother?"

"No."

"You sure?"

"Yes." I loved my mother, but having a maternal dynamo around now would be more hindrance than help. Let her stay ten thousand miles away while I tried to cope with what had happened.

Caroline went back to praying.

I don't know how long I'd been sitting, staring at Rowena, when I heard a noise behind me. Looking back at the doorway, I saw the guard inserting his bulk between a tall woman and the room.

"Justin," I said. "It's okay. It's our rabbi."

He was unwilling to trust me and asked for her I.D. Rabbi Shulamit Frankel held up the hospital badge she had on a chain around her neck.

She stepped into the room, a tall angular woman, clad in a navy pants suit, plain white blouse, and low-heeled shoes suited for walking through long corridors. Her kinky coppery hair formed an inverted vee over her head. The rabbi held out her hand, not to be shaken but to be grasped in the old-fashioned manner.

"How did you know Rowena was here?" I asked.

"You must have listed her religion as Jewish when she was admitted."

"Okay." They'd asked lots of questions on the ambulance ride.

"Well then. The Jewish chaplain gets a computer list of all Jewish patients every day. He's a member of Beth El. He called me."

"I appreciate your coming." Did the call violate some medical privacy laws? It didn't matter. I wasn't going to sue.

"But?"

"This must be tough for you," I said.

"Because?"

"It's a tough job to have to make excuses for what God does."

"Do you blame God for this?" she asked.

"No, not really. I blame a person. But if God is hanging out, looking for something to do, why not make the pressure on her brain go back down to 20 where the doctor says it should be?"

"We should pray for that then," said the rabbi.

"Why? I'd like to believe in prayer, but it's kind of like presidential campaign promises. Once you've been disappointed so many times, it's just tough to get your hopes up."

"Ian," my mother-in-law said in horror, not so much at what I was saying, but to whom I was saying it.

"No, it's okay," the rabbi said, still grasping my hand. "But what harm can it do?"

I thought for a moment. "You're right. What harm can it do?"

The rabbi had the three of us hold hands and say a *mishebei-rach,* a prayer asking God to grant Rowena *refuah sh'leimah,* complete healing.

Before we'd let go of each other's hands, Rowena's eyes flittered. I stopped breathing.

"Ian, you're here," my wife said, eyes all the way open now and her head turned to me.

"I'm here. So are your mother and the rabbi."

She gave no sign of hearing. "Have you got Aunt Isobel her recognition yet, the recognition she deserves?" Rowena asked in a clear and deliberate tone.

"Right after you're better," I said. "First things first."

"Aunt Isobel is a first thing," she said.

"But…" I stopped. She wasn't listening. Her eyes flittered again and then closed.

Caroline, the rabbi, and I were still holding hands and looking down at the bed. Rowena was breathing more smoothly now.

The rabbi volunteered to look for the doctor. Four long strides carried her out of the room.

"Do you think Rowena's back?" I asked. "Is she just sleeping now?"

"She knew it was you," Caroline said. "She knew what she was saying."

"So she's lying in a hospital bed and thinking, not about herself, not about who put her here, but about my great aunt, someone she never met?"

———

Five minutes later the rabbi returned with Dr. Griffith. He told us that Rowena's awakening, brief as it was, counted as a good sign.

"Does this mean she's out of her coma?" I asked.

"I didn't say that. But it's progress. What she needs is rest."

Once the surgeon left the room, the rabbi asked who Aunt Isobel was.

I explained.

"So what are you going to do?" the rabbi asked.

"What do you mean?"

"Are you going to do what Rowena asked?"

"Right now? Go chasing after the truth of what happened to Aunt Isobel?"

"Maybe."

"Why should it matter to a woman who's been dead for years?" I asked the rabbi.

"The Torah says, 'Justice, justice shalt thou pursue.' It doesn't say to just pursue justice for the living. Perhaps obtaining justice for the dead makes a better world for the living."

"Shouldn't pursuing justice mean finding who put Rowena in here?"

"Aren't the police doing that?" the rabbi asked.

"So I should leave my wife here and start pursuing justice for Aunt Isobel now?"

"Rabbi Hillel did ask, 'If not now, when?'"

"What difference does it make whether it's sooner or later?"

"I don't know. Maybe none. Maybe a lot."

"Do you mean that getting Aunt Isobel the credit she deserves can help with Rowena's recovery?"

"Possibly. I don't know."

Caroline interrupted. "Maybe what Rowena was saying is what God wants."

"Is that what you think, Rabbi?"

The rabbi shrugged, not quite as confident in God's intercession in the affairs of us mortals as Caroline. "I am sure that I don't understand the way this world of ours works, but for someone like you, doing may be better than sitting. Or at least some doing may be better than all sitting." She then resorted again to an argument that had worked a few minutes ago. "It can't hurt."

The three of us sat in silence for another half an hour watching Rowena's chest rise up and down.

If there was a chance, no matter how minute, that justice for Aunt Isobel would help bring Rowena back to me, I had to do something, didn't I? I kissed Rowena. Her forehead felt neither clammy nor feverish. I looked down at her. Often when we were in bed, I watched her sleep, but then there were no bandages or bruises. I told her I loved her, got no reaction, and then shook the rabbi's hand and hugged Caroline.

"I'll be back later," I said.

"Don't worry," Caroline replied. "We can manage here. I promise to call if there's any change at all."

So I limped down the corridor, still hearing the echo of my wife's last words and trying to figure out what to do about them.

THIRTY-THREE

I RIPPED UP THE Stanford parking ticket I found on my windshield and threw the pieces in the air. A preternatural calm had come over Caroline after her daughter awoke. Not me. I feared hope. My father used to tell me of his grandmother, born in Poland, who never even said "good morning" without saying *keinahora* and spitting three times to avoid tempting the Evil Eye. Superstitious for sure, but I knew what she meant. Hopes raised led too often to hopes dashed—whether by the Evil Eye, God, or happenstance. What I really wanted was to put my hands around the neck of the driver of that car and squeeze. I watched the scraps of the ticket swirl across the asphalt.

Approaching the intersection of Palm and Campus Drive, I pulled, without thinking, into the left turn lane as if heading home. Then I looked in my rearview mirror. No one coming. I turned right across two lanes. A minute later, I parked my Acura near the Quad below a sign that said places were reserved for permit holders. I grabbed a paper off the passenger seat, folded it, and put it in my shirt pocket.

My wife was lying in a hospital bed. And what was I doing? Marching off to see a professor.

I limped toward the Varian Building. I should have brought my sunglasses. Last year, on this kind of February day, I'd posted a Facebook message to let everyone I knew on the East Coast that it was in the sixties and sunny in Palo Alto. *Schadenfreude* is what it was. My enjoyment at the frozen misery of my friends.

Mid-afternoon on a Saturday, Tompkins must have figured he was safe. I found him sitting at his desk in his office writing in longhand on a yellow legal pad. His lips would pucker as he sucked on a white stick that protruded from his lips.

"A sequel to *Small Matter*?" I asked.

He dropped his fountain pen and jerked his head up. He smiled when he saw me and removed what was a round purple lollipop from his mouth. "You, Ian, are like a lepton. You randomly appear and disappear."

"Let me try to play the same game. Doesn't quantum theory say two particles that have once been in contact continue to influence each other no matter how far apart they move? That's how I think of you and Professor Marter. She's still influencing you."

He pointed at me with the lollipop stick. "Not bad, not bad. You have been reading up on physics, haven't you? But to answer your original question, yes, I am working on a second volume of memoirs. Now please answer mine. Why are you so obsessed with Izzy Marter?"

I reached into my pocket and pulled out a paper. I unfolded it and smoothed it out on Tompkins' desk. "I found this."

He stared at it for some seconds. "Where is it from?"

"One of Professor Marter's lab books."

"Yes, this is what we were discussing in the spring of 1969."

"Who is we?"

"Me, along with Solenski, Vansittart, and Izzy."

"This drawing is pretty close to what you described to Vansittart in April 1969. Only one problem. The date of the entry in Professor Marter's lab book is March 6, 1969."

He took a lick of his grape lollipop whose color matched his shirt. "As I said, we were all working on the problem together."

"Then why wasn't she in the meeting with Vansittart?"

"You want me to remember why Solenski's assistant wasn't in a meeting four decades ago?"

"She wasn't an assistant to Solenski. Back then she was an assistant professor of physics, just like you were."

"Whatever," he said with a wave of his lollipop-laden hand.

"You set up the experiments at the linear accelerator in August, Professor Tompkins. Why then?"

"Your wife works in the district attorney's office, doesn't she?"

I put my palms on the desk and leaned across. "How do you know that?"

"From the reception," he answered. "I bet when she's hot on the scent, she doesn't wait. Neither did we."

"But Isobel and Vansittart weren't there."

"That was no reason to wait."

"Even if Isobel was the one who designed the experiment?"

"I told you it was a team effort. Still, as I said in my book, I was the one who consolidated what we learned and put it into a model."

I just stared at him.

"Listen, we are talking about events from forty years ago," he continued. "Your impulses are commendable. You are here as the champion of a woman you never knew, even if she was a relative. I'm all for naming a lab after her, even if she was a snotty bitch." Now Tompkins leaned across the desk and waved his lollipop stick like a conductor's baton. "But if you start imputing that there was anything amiss about my behavior in discovering quarks, well, I'd consult with your wife the attorney on the laws of defamation. I have a considerable reputation. It's hard-earned and worth defending."

"I am no lawyer, Professor. It's my understanding, though, that truth is a defense to any suit for defamation."

THIRTY-FOUR

WHEN I GOT BACK to my car, I was greeted by another parking ticket on the windshield. I ripped this one up, too, and was about to throw the pieces in the air when I noticed a couple of passing undergraduates staring at me. I stuffed the pieces in my pocket and started home.

From the car, I called Bharat Gupta, our CFO, and told him to start coordinating the due diligence for Monday. Just because we had a term sheet didn't mean the deal with Intel was done. Like locusts approaching a wheat field, a plague of accountants, engineers, and product managers was going to descend on Accelenet to ensure that I hadn't misled Corwin concerning our business. Exaggeration to prospective investors was not an unknown phenomenon in Silicon Valley.

"Goodbye then, Bharat."

"Um, Ian? Before you hang up, we're all worried about Rowena..."

Bharat was asking me something personal? "You've spoken to Juliana?"

"Of course. Don't get mad at her. She had to tell us what was going on. You had disappeared."

"Thank you for asking. She's getting better. I spoke to her this morning." I knew I sounded stilted.

"That is good news," Bharat said in the quasi-English accent of an Indian who'd attended one of his country's top prep schools.

I pulled into the driveway and tapped the screen of my phone to call Rowena's room.

"Ian, I told you I'd call if there was any news," Caroline said.

"Can't help it."

"Of course not. She's still sleeping. There's nothing more to report."

Four hours later I was back at the hospital. I sent Caroline to our house and spent Saturday night in Rowena's room myself, sitting on one cheap vinyl guest chair with my legs propped up by another. I'd doze off for a few minutes, but then I'd move and the pain in my bad leg would bring me back to life. Still, I couldn't very well complain about the boarding arrangement in the ICU since I was breaking the rules by being there.

The resident who came by told me to be patient, to be grateful that healing was going on, but I thought it was peculiar that Rowena would awaken for a short minute and then go back to sleep for what was now another twenty-four hours.

I didn't pray over Rowena like her mother did. Instead I read aloud her favorite book, *Pride and Prejudice*, from beginning to end, from "It is a truth universally acknowledged" to "the means of uniting them." Her face was calm, serene even. Who knows if the words penetrated the fog that enshrouded her brain.

Sunday morning, Caroline came in bearing a baker's dozen of Izzy's Bagels. I didn't much feel like eating, but managed to chew and swallow half of a poppy seed while she was watching. When she was looking down at the bed, I broke the remainder in two and stashed one piece in each of my jacket pockets. The other twelve bagels went to the nurses' station and thence to the staff break room.

We resumed our habitual positions on either side of the hospital bed, each of us holding one of Rowena's hands.

After we'd spent the next fifteen or twenty minutes watching Rowena's face for any sign of consciousness, I realized Caroline was speaking.

"I beg your pardon?"

"Have you and Rowena talked about having children?"

In normal circumstances I'd figure this was something for her to discuss with her daughter or with both of us, not me alone. But with her oldest daughter and husband dead, and Rowena lying in a coma, I could understand why generational continuity was on her mind.

"Yes. She's firmed up her position on the homicide unit now. She said she was ready to start trying. Um, I guess you'd like a grandchild?"

What an inane question to ask a Jewish mother in her early sixties. She didn't seem to notice and just nodded. Then, for the first time I saw her cry. I reached over and put my arms around her. Squeezing her harder didn't stanch the sobbing. Things were running backwards. Our roles had been reversed—I was playing the parent and she the little girl.

———

After calming down, Caroline had sent me home to take a nap. Outside the hospital, I checked my phone. One voicemail message—from a familiar number, but not one I'd programmed into my contact list.

I listened. "Ian, Susan Fletcher here. Call me."

I called the number she left, but was told by an Officer Gonzales she was on the phone. She and Mikulski had dropped by on me unannounced. I decided to do the same to them.

Police headquarters sat on the back side of City Hall, a white stone eyesore from the 1970s that fit in downtown Palo Alto about as well as Scarlett O'Hara's Tara would have in Times Square. At the front desk, I asked the dispatcher for Fletcher. An air of somnolence hung over the place. Apparently, in Palo Alto criminals took the weekend off.

Fletcher brought me back to her office.

"Being here bring back memories?" she asked.

"You mean like vomiting in a cell?" I'd been a guest of the city when a suspect for the murder of Rowena's sister.

"Wasn't it only for one night?"

"Right." Even on the weekend, Paul had found a judge to set bail and a banker to certify his check for a quarter million dollars. He'd got me out of there.

"Back to now. You're here because of my call?"

"Yeah. No partner around?"

"We split up our tasks. He's out."

"And the news?"

"We trust each other, you and I?" she asked.

"I trust you," I said. "But the damn police department you work for and the D.A.'s office my wife works for, no. They tried to railroad me into a murder conviction four years ago. They're looking for easy answers now. They're too bureaucratic, too interested in covering their asses. So yeah, I trust you, but not them."

"At least you're honest. I figure I'd rather have you inside the tent pissing out, than outside the tent pissing in."

"Meaning?"

"If I don't tell you what's going on, you'll start meddling like you did last time."

"It turned out okay, didn't it?"

"If I keep you in the loop, you won't interfere?"

"Do you trust *me*? I'll do my best not to interfere."

"And you'll try to behave rationally?"

"I'll try."

"I guess that's about as good as I'll get." She took a deep breath. "Nolan has a boyfriend."

I stood up. "Who went after Rowena?"

"Sit down," she said. I did. "Don't make me sorry I'm telling you this. Nolan's beau's name is Carlos Edwards."

"Yes."

"He's a sales rep for Genzene, the biotech firm. He's traveling."

"On a slow boat to China?"

"Close. He's on his way to Thailand. Flying."

"Peculiar that he'd be out of town with his girlfriend on trial for murder. That's not too supportive."

"We've left him a voicemail and email asking him to get in touch. No answer yet."

"Has he flown the coop?"

"He was at work on Friday. Left from SFO Friday night."

"So he was in town Friday morning?"

"Yes."

"And what kind of car does he drive?"

"A BMW 535."

THIRTY-FIVE

FLETCHER DIDN'T KNOW WHETHER they had the probable cause needed to search Edwards' condo. Tomorrow morning she and Mikulski were going to meet with the D.A. herself to discuss getting a warrant.

Back home, I sat down at my computer and typed the phrase "Carlos Edwards" into Google. You'd think the combination of a Spanish first name with an Anglo-Saxon family name would be rare enough to make Nolan's boyfriend the only person to show up. Wrong. Two seconds after I hit the enter key, Google sprang back with more than sixty thousand hits. Who knew that Carlos Edwards was the name of a Trinidadian soccer player? I added "Genzene" to the search. Nada.

Fletcher hadn't told me where he lived, and I hadn't asked for fear of arousing suspicion of what I would do with the information. I did know Genzene was in Menlo Park. If he were single, he'd live in San Francisco with the other trendies, like his squeeze Daisy Nolan. When I was a boy in Palo Alto, my father and thousands of commuters had driven or taken the train each morning to downtown San Francisco. Now the commute patterns had reversed. Tens of thousands of San Franciscans in their twenties and thirties formed a daily traffic jam as they commuted south on 101 to the icons of the Valley: Oracle, Torii, Cisco, Intel, and Apple, and the oodles of start-ups that aspired to the same status. The City had become the suburb.

I added San Francisco to the search and came up with an entry in the Alcatraz Triathlon which told me that someone with that name had an "L" as a middle initial. Putting in "Carlos L. Edwards" into Google turned up a construction permit on Zoe Street in San Francisco, south of Market where old warehouses had been transmogrified into lofts for affluent singles and young marrieds. Bingo! I'd found the X on the virtual treasure map.

If Fletcher and Mikulski tried to get into Edwards' place without a warrant, any evidence they found would be tainted as "the fruit of a poisonous tree" and inadmissible in court. And they'd lose their jobs, too. They were police officers sworn to uphold the law and the Constitution, which, last time I looked, prohibited government agents from conducting unreasonable searches and seizures. I was not a government agent. So, reflecting on my conversation with Fletcher, I resolved it was rational for me to take action now, even if it wasn't for her and her partner.

I hadn't done a résumé in years, but on my last one, I remember listing mergers and acquisitions among my areas of expertise. Not breaking and entering. I wanted to get into Edwards' place now, during daylight on a Sunday. Doing justice sure as hell included finding out who tried to run us down. Pulling on an old Red Sox cap and a pair of sunglasses, I jumped into my old Acura. Twenty minutes later I sat in Juliana's chair at Accelenet. Our IT guys required that we change computer passwords every month.

Juliana and I struck a deal. Ours would be the same save for the last digit where hers was three more than mine. I opened her machine and set to work.

I arrived outside Edwards' place by one. I'd had it pretty well pegged. A rectangular red brick fortress with snazzy rubbed bronze doors where the "The Lighting Factory" was spelled out in rubbed gold letters. I headed to a liquor store down the street and bought a pack of Marlboros.

In New York, the default condition was to distrust everybody. That's why there was a doorman in every building where tenants could afford one. In San Francisco human nature received the benefit of the doubt. After ten minutes in front of the building, smoking—but like our forty-second president, not inhaling—the door swung open. I flicked my butt into the gutter. A woman was trying to hold the front door and manipulate a stroller through. I was trying to impersonate a gentleman, so I held the door for her.

"Wife won't let you smoke inside?" she asked.

I gave her what I hoped was a sheepish smile.

"Me? I stopped when I got pregnant with Nathan. It's tough. Good luck. Thanks for your help with the door."

I walked in. No doorman, no guard. Less cynical than the New Yorkers, and more naïve, too. On the list of tenants, I saw Edwards was on the third floor.

Whoever had renovated the building had done an especially nice job on the elevators. Their polished brass and black wrought iron doors looked like the antiques that required passengers to pull them open by hand. Luckily for Nathan's mother, though, they did move apart automatically.

On the mat outside Edwards' front door a Sunday *Chronicle* awaited the return of the subscriber. He'd left in a hurry then. No time to cancel the paper, but his plane was on Friday. Where was Saturday's paper?

I went to the door across the hall and rang the bell. No answer. Then I tried the one on the same side of the hall to the left. A disheveled man in his early thirties opened the door. A tattoo of a snake coiled up from beneath his Grateful Dead sleeveless sweatshirt, and opened its mouth to reveal fangs and a forked tongue on his neck. The pungent scent of marijuana drifted into the hall. That's San Francisco. A condo that had to be worth close to a million dollars occupied by a pothead. Probably a web designer or software geek from South Park.

"Hey, man, what can I do you for?"

He held the front section of yesterday's *Chronicle* in his hand.

"Do you know my brother? Carlos Edwards?" I asked.

"Sure, but he's gone."

"Yeah, I know. He's in Thailand. He was supposed to leave his key under the mat."

"He didn't mention you coming by to me."

I put out my hands palm up in a way that was meant to convey "What do you expect?" Then I asked whether there was a building manager or anyone I could talk to.

"I've got a key, man, but I can't let you in without ID or something."

I handed him a laminated card, the one I'd just made at Juliana's desk. A photo ID for Pablo Edwards, Accelenet sales rep.

"Your mom insisted on the Spanish first name for you, too, huh?"

"Si."

He laughed and then held out his hand. "Maverick Smith." Somehow I doubted *his* mother had saddled him with that name.

We shook and then he said, "Just a mo, Pablo." He giggled at his poetic flair. Twenty seconds later I was walking back to Edwards' condo with a key on a chain dangling from my right index finger. It was better to be lucky than good.

THIRTY-SIX

I PUT THE KEY in the lock and swung open the door without touching anything with my hands. Once inside I reached in my parka pocket and pulled out the pair of leather gloves I'd found in back of a closet at home.

On a laminated fiberboard desk, I saw disconnected cables and wires where Edwards' laptop would ordinarily reside. To the right of the serpentine cords, a head shot of a windblown Daisy Nolan smiled out at me from a sterling frame. Blonde with a cherub's face, she looked more like an over-aged child actress than a woman who would murder to get what she wanted. In thick black ink, across the bottom of the photo was scrawled, "Forever yours, Daisy." Did she have delusions of movie stardom?

Well, I had inveigled my way into the right condo, anyway. Whatever his taste in women, Edwards did okay as an interior decorator. Ikea did seem to be the main source of his furnishings, but the condo's kilim rugs, natural wood tables, and gray upholstery all seemed to work together. It was easy to see what he and his neighbor Maverick had in common—over the sofa hung a poster for a 1992 Grateful Dead concert that featured a skeleton wielding a baseball bat. Underneath the fifty-inch flat screen TV suspended from the wall were pirated CDs with the band's name and date handwritten on the case. The Dead was there, too, along with Smashing Pumpkins and White Stripes.

I found a clean coffee cup on a hook under a cupboard and used it to water the fern in the living room. What was I doing? I started looking through drawers. Apparently, Daisy was not on the pill because inside the nightstand was a blue and black box containing lubricated Trojan Triple-X rubbers. Nothing incriminating about that. In the desk drawer I found a claim check from Dan's Auto Laundry for a full detailing of the 535. He'd brought it in Friday morning, and it would be ready at the end of the day.

I took the glove off my right hand and felt under the desk drawer. And I pulled an index card away from the tape that held to the drawer bottom. Edwards's passwords to his Amazon account, Facebook page, in-home network, and Gmail account. Tsk, tsk. Shame on you, Carlos. You do not follow secure procedures. I wrote down the passwords on a piece of paper I slipped out of the inkjet printer, then pressed the card back to where I'd found it.

A knock came on the door. Shit. I looked through the spyhole and got a fisheye view of Maverick Smith weaving back and forth as if on the deck of a ship. I exhaled. Not Fletcher, not Mikulski, not a police officer at all. Tucking the gloves into my pocket and putting my sunglasses back on, I twisted the door knob open with my palm.

"Hey," I said with a smile.

"Hey, man, I was supposed to water the fern."

"I took care of it. I brought in this morning's paper, too."

"Why did you need to get into Carlos' place again?"

"I just flew in from Boston and was going to crash here at my brother's tonight. I'm going out now to get my luggage from the rental car. I'll be leaving early in the morning. Can I leave the key for you in the mailbox?"

"Sure, man," he said with a nod. Too bad he hadn't taken a few more tokes this afternoon.

We let the door slam behind us, and I twisted the key in its hole.

"You don't have to double-lock it if you'll be right back up."

I wagged a finger. "Can't be too careful."

He nodded, and we walked toward his door and the elevators.

"Cool tattoo," I said. "It reminds me of the snake on those old flags that said, 'Don't tread on me.'"

"That's cool. Don't tread on me. I'll remember that. Thanks, man." He held up his right hand, and I slapped it. Maybe he had taken those extra tokes.

On the way out I dropped the key through the slot that said M. Smith. No mail on Sunday.

On the way home, I called Fletcher. When she answered, I said, "Hey, I had an idea."

"Which is?"

"What would you do to your car if you'd hit someone?"

"Drive it off Highway 1 into the Pacific?"

"A little obvious."

"Take it somewhere off the books to get bodywork done?"

"Good idea. Worth checking. What if the damage wasn't serious?" I asked.

"Get it detailed?"

"Bingo."

"That is a good idea. We'll check out where Edwards might get detailing done."

"Try to finish your checking before discussing probable cause with the D.A. tomorrow morning."

THIRTY-SEVEN

FINDING A STARBUCKS IN a yuppie neighborhood like Edwards' should have been as easy as finding French fries at McDonald's. Not quite. I had to drive three whole blocks heading toward AT&T Park before I saw one. I ordered myself a green tea, pulled up a bar stool, and used my sluggish first-generation iPhone to get onto the Internet. First Facebook. That was easy. I saw from his birth date that Edwards was twenty-nine. He had over three hundred photos, most of himself, in nine different albums. They were not accessible by anyone on Facebook but him. And now me. Edwards' looks contrasted with his girlfriend's. While she was blonde and round, he was dark and lean. His stubbly face probably helped convince his Deadhead neighbor of our common blood, since I hadn't been shaving the last couple of days myself. I clicked on the album labeled "Trip to Martinique." He stood beside his girlfriend in front of a pool, one hand wrapped around her hip, the other around a tropical drink. Like her face, Daisy Nolan's body was made of circles. The balloons of her chest were connected by inverted parentheses to the larger balloon of her hips. Her top strained under its load. I could see the shadows of erect nipples under her skimpy bikini. A lush body. A body worth killing for?

Next I checked the Amazon account. To log in, I needed the account name as well as the password. Most people on Amazon used their email address. Carlos.edwards@gmail.com. Nope. Carlosedwards@gmail.com. Nope. Carlos.l.Edwards@gmail.com. Bingo! I looked through his account activity. He was no fiction reader. Every couple months, he ordered a business book on how to sell more product or how to make more money. If he'd followed the advice of 2004's *Become a Real Estate Millionaire* and bought property in Sunbelt cities like Las Vegas and Miami, his bank account would have been on a crash diet over the last few years.

I'd saved the most promising vein of online ore to mine last. From within Gmail, I did a find on "Nolan" to get all the Daisy-Carlos correspondence. Last July there'd been a flurry of messages. She'd expected a promotion and big, fat raise. She asked Edwards if he could get away. Damn them. They'd been planning a trip to Bora Bora. It would have been obscene for the two of them to vacation where Rowena and I had gone on our honeymoon. I could feel a vein thumping on the right side of my neck.

Once my pulse sank back below ninety, I glanced through the rest of the emails. Nothing incriminating. I went to the Genzene website and tried to log in as an employee. I guessed Edwards' account name first try—Carlos.L.Edwards@Genzene.com—and, like most of us mortals, he used the same password on multiple accounts. I sifted through his work emails. Carlos was doing pretty well, making close to 200K a year as a sales rep. No emails from Nolan in his business account. Nothing incriminating there either. Had he done it? I was far from certain. All I had after committing a felony was the fact of the detailing job on Friday. Not exactly proof beyond a reasonable doubt.

I took the untouched paper cup of tea for refreshment on my trip south on 101. Not much traffic on a Sunday. Somewhere around Millbrae I hit a bump as I sipped, and tea cascaded out of the cup. Fortunate that the tea had cooled. I peeked down. It looked like I'd pissed in my pants.

THIRTY-EIGHT

THE NURSE COMING IN to the hospital room awakened me a little after six on Monday morning. Too bad Rowena didn't wake up, too. Her chest rose and fell with the steady respiration of someone sleeping, but it had been more than forty hours since she spoke. Why hadn't she come back to me? By eight Caroline had returned to her station after spending the night at our house again. On my way out, I looked back and saw her leaning over Rowena, lips moving.

As I unlocked the door at home, the scent of fresh baking accosted my nostrils. I had no appetite and knew I wouldn't till Rowena woke up. Still, I swallowed one of eleven still-warm muffins that Caroline had left on a plate on the kitchen counter. Only on the way up to the shower, licking some crumbs off my lips, did I realize the muffins were orange pecan, my favorite.

I rotated the showerhead so it shot miniature liquid daggers. I turned the knobs to get full pressure. Damn restricted flow. I made the water as hot as I could endure and stood under it for five minutes, bad leg on the other side of the shower curtain. What I was trying to scald away, I don't know. When I was toweling myself off, I saw that my trunk glowed pink.

I'd forgotten to turn the ringer back on my iPhone after I left the hospital, but saw it shaking on my dresser like a hyperkinetic Mexican jumping bean.

"Yeah?"

"You have a Red Sox cap?" It was Fletcher.

"Am I under suspicion for something?"

"Burglary?"

"Burglary?" I repeated.

"Yes, the crime of breaking and entering with the intent to steal."

I was better off than I thought. I hadn't taken a thing.

"It's early on a Monday morning," I said enunciating each word. "I'm moving slowly. Could we start at the beginning?"

"The boyfriend's car *was* detailed on Friday near where he lives. What a lucky guess you made, huh?"

"Clairvoyant. Any evidence from the car?"

"We'll see. The lab guys are going to look it over, but I doubt they'll find anything. There was a dent on the right of the front fender."

"Isn't that good?"

"And a dent in the middle and on the right and on the driver's door and passenger's door. The car's fenders and sides are dinged all over. That's what you get parking on the street in the City."

"Too bad."

"You wondering why I haven't thanked you yet for the idea of checking out the detailers?"

"Okay, tell me."

"A guy came by Edwards' condo yesterday. He wore a Red Sox cap."

"Yeah?"

"Told a neighbor he was Edwards' brother.

"Uh-huh."

"One problem. As best we can tell, Edwards has only one sibling."

"A sister?" I asked.

"Yup. So do you have a Red Sox cap?"

"You know I went to college back in Boston. Do you want me to see if I can find it?"

"Do you want to go up to the City and meet the neighbor?"

I shrugged. "Don't know what for, but, sure, I'll go if you'd like."

She sighed. "Like hell, you don't know. But it's not necessary."

"Whatever you say."

"Well, thanks. There's no doubt we'll get a warrant to go into the condo now that we tracked down the car at the detailer."

"What more are you doing to get hold of Edwards?"

"The Thai police are supposed to make sure he gets in touch. We'll get hold of his boss at work this morning and pass along a message through him, too."

"Thanks for keeping me in the loop."

"Do better staying out of mischief, Ian. I mean it. That was our deal."

Not exactly. In any case I didn't know if she *really* meant it, but I was going to do what I had to do.

In order to show the flag, I drove to Accelenet. The place was roiling with excitement. The MarketWatch story of the potential investment from Intel had hit the wires. I checked with Ron and

Bharat on how Intel's due diligence was going. I saw the list of information they required. Everything but the brand of toothpaste our junior engineers used.

"Let's do our best and see where we are on Wednesday," I told Bharat. "I'll call Corwin then and ask for relief if we need it."

"Makes sense."

"And their engineers?"

"Yeah, they're back."

"We're going over more test results and more potential chip layouts," Ron said.

"What sense are you getting?"

"They're not trying to hide their excitement like they did before."

"Good."

I stopped by and checked in with Juliana on my way out.

"Reporters are calling about the Intel deal."

"Have them talk to Intel's PR people."

She ran her eyes up and down. "You look like shit," she said. "At a time like this, you need to take care of yourself. Rowena needs you to be strong. So do we."

I guess Juliana was not a fan of the four-day stubble look. Promising her to keep my iPhone on, I headed back toward Stanford and the hospital.

I heard the beep of a text message coming in on the phone. Grabbing it off the passenger seat, I held it atop the steering wheel and squinted to read from the screen.

A horn blared. A car swerved. I swung my Acura back on to the right side of Palm Drive. Killing myself this way wouldn't help Rowena.

In the hospital parking lot, I picked up the iPhone from the floor mat where I'd dropped it.

"How's C? All fine in the H L. Mom wants to know the latest on A I. Luv, Allison."

Rowena had awakened from a coma to tell me to find out about Aunt Isobel. Now my mother was having my sister nag me from Israel—the Holy Land—about her. I took it as a sign. SLAC was just two miles from the hospital.

The guard with the thing for John Irving stepped out of his shack with a paperback copy of *The Cider House Rules* in his hand. He just waved me through this time. That meant Solenski must be here.

"I am sorry to be such a pain," I said when seated in my now familiar position on the opposite side of the desk from Solenski. "I want to talk more about the discovery of quarks."

"It's always fun to reminisce about the glory days."

"Yes. The way it was. Not the way Tompkins wrote about it."

"Ah, there's a difference you think?"

"Oh, no. It was just a mistake when he won the National Book Award for biography. He should have won it for fiction." Solenski rubbed his upper lip in an effort to hide his smile. "Did you all have the sense that the quark experiment would win you the Nobel Prize?"

"Oh, we knew. Not instantly, but that's because the data took a long time to analyze. We didn't have everything computerized like today. We even still had bubble chambers …"

"That's like a cloud chamber?"

"No difference really. In one, particles left a contrail in a glass box filled with smoke and in the other they left a track of bubbles through a box filled with liquid. No matter, by 1969 we were using computers. They were just slow. When we got the results back, we all celebrated. Vansittart even brought out some champagne."

"Was Isobel back from Yosemite?"

"I think so. Yes, yes, she was. We were laughing and pouring bubbly on each other. When Tompkins came close to Izzy, er, Isobel, with a bottle, she gave him a stare that froze him in place about three feet away from her."

"Two of them didn't like each other too much?"

"Especially then. Isobel was no idiot. She knew Tompkins had scheduled the experiments for when she was out of town. He wanted glory and did not want to share it with her."

"And how about you? You won the Nobel, too."

"I was no competition. Bill knew he was brighter than me. I told you before that I knew it too."

"And Vansittart?"

"He was the big boss. Bill needed to impress him. And Vansittart needed Bill—or someone like him—to make the breakthroughs that would make SLAC famous."

"But Vansittart supported Isobel, too."

"Why not? He didn't care which of his minions made the discoveries. Vansittart would be happy to play Pierre Curie to Isobel's Marie."

"They were having an affair?"

"No, no, that's not what I meant. All you young people think of is sex. I meant the part of an older, wiser mentor."

"I see."

"So what are you going to do with all this information you're gathering." He nodded toward the black notebook where I was keeping notes of our conversation.

The question had been called. And I knew the response. "I'm going to write a book. I want to get Isobel Marter the credit she deserved."

"What good will that do? Let sleeping logs die."

"You mean let sleeping dogs lie."

"Whatever."

I continued, "I want to tell the real story, not the story Tompkins told in *Small Matter*." I paused. "How about this for a title? *A Small Matter of Stolen Glory*."

"Is it your intention to try to tell the truth or to awaken the ferocious temper of my old colleague?" Solenski asked. "No one will thank you either way."

THIRTY-NINE

I'D BEEN SITTING FOR four hours by Rowena's bedside. I thought about getting started on the biography of my great aunt. I thought about how Intel was going to keep Accelenet from becoming one more tasty morsel swallowed by Ricky Frankson. I thought about the police fetching the person back from Thailand who'd probably put Rowena here. All would be well if she'd just wake up. Right. "Other than that, Mrs. Lincoln, how was the play?" I wondered what Rowena was thinking about.

Her mother sat across the bed from me, eyes squeezed shut. Like a cold in the head or the madness of crowds, asking for help from the deity must have been contagious. I didn't know the prescribed Hebrew words like Caroline did. I winged it. "Please, please, let her be well. Wake up my wife. Give her back to me."

I felt a tap on the shoulder and looked up expecting to see a doctor or nurse. Instead, Juliana. The guard must have recognized her and let her through.

"May I talk to you?" she asked.

Caroline opened her eyes.

"I'll be right back," I told her.

In the hallway, Juliana started apologizing for bothering me. "I didn't know what else to do. I'm sorry." And she began to cry.

I put an arm around her shoulder and guided her into the chapel. No one there.

"What's going on?"

"The Intel engineers left two hours ago with no explanation. Bharat went over to their headquarters for a meeting and was told it had been canceled."

"And did he call anyone?"

"Sure. He left voicemails and emails and no one is getting back to him."

"I'll call Corwin right now."

"I've gotten friendly with his admin. I called her."

"And?"

"She doesn't know why, but she says the deal is off."

"What did they find in their due diligence?"

"Of course, I asked Ron and Bharat that. They thought everything was going great."

"When you talked to his admin, was Corwin in his office?"

"She was whispering like she didn't want someone to hear."

"Okay. I'm off to Intel."

"Do you want me to come along?"

I should have brought Juliana to ride with me. Then we could legally traveled in the carpool lane on the way to Intel headquarters. Instead, I became a scofflaw and went into the far left lane even with an empty passenger seat. First littering with scraps of parking tickets, then trespassing into Edwards' condo, now a traffic violator. I wondered what would be next on the road to a life of crime.

Thirty minutes later, I walked into a building named after Robert Noyce, one of the "traitorous eight" whose departure from Shockley Semiconductor loomed as large in Valley history as the exodus from Egypt did in the Bible. One of the founders of both Fairchild Semiconductor and Intel, Noyce was the co-inventor of the microprocessor, the electronic brain that ran everything from cell phones to server farms. I went up to the receptionist and asked for Barclay Corwin.

She asked who I was. After I told her, she dialed a number.

"He'll be down," she reported. She must have spoken to the admin Juliana knew.

A few minutes later, Corwin and I were shaking hands. When I started to move back toward the elevators, he pulled my arm the other way. "Okay if we take a walk?"

Corwin didn't want me up on Executive Row.

We were heading back toward the parking lot. He was going to hustle me out.

"You parked out this way?"

"Yes."

"I figured I'd hear from you," Corwin's said in his smooth voice. "I just didn't figure on a personal visit."

"What's going on?"

"Just between me and you? I'll tell you for Leon's sake."

"This is my car." We stopped. "Okay, just between us."

"The word came from our CEO. There was going to be trouble with the board on this deal. No go."

"I thought you didn't need board approval for a deal our size."

"Don't usually," he said, "but that doesn't mean my boss can ignore a board member. Our deal was a nice-to-have, not a have-to-have."

Duh. I was a little slow on the uptake. "Someone got to a director to quash our deal? Do you know which one?"

He folded his arms and said nothing.

"Who could pick up the phone, speak to a board member, and be listened to?"

Silence again. I knew what that meant.

"That question was rhetorical. I appreciate your talking to me."

As I opened the car door, he said, "You'll not pass on what I told you?"

"Told me what?"

"Your wife is getting better?" Corwin asked.

"Yes," I said. "Thank you for asking." I slammed the door and pulled out. In my rearview mirror, I could see Corwin's pinstriped figure standing motionless, arms still crossed. I was now *persona non grata* at Intel, and he was making damn sure I got out of there.

FORTY

I DIDN'T LEAVE THE hospital right away. I stayed with Rowena for a couple more hours. Then at five I went out to the car, ripped up another parking ticket, and set out for Torii.

"Is he expecting you?" the security guard on the ground floor of the ten-story golden cylinder asked me, looking down at my business card.

"Yes."

He clicked a couple of keys on a console. "You're not listed."

"I didn't have an appointment."

He looked at me through his black plastic-framed glasses. "He was expecting you, but you didn't have an appointment?"

"You got it. He knew I'd show up sooner or later."

The guard looked at me and then hesitated before saying, "Just a second." He hit a button and started talking through his headset.

"He's not in the office right now. I've told them upstairs to leave a message that you stopped by."

As I walked back to the car, I wondered if Frankson was in his tower redoubt. No. I just couldn't picture him cowering up there in fear of me.

In for a dime, in for a dollar. I knew just where Frankson lived. In putting together a twelve-acre parcel in Woodside, he'd bought the house and property of my old boss at McKinsey. From gossip in the press and blogosphere, I knew Frankson was in the process of moving a Japanese stone castle piece by piece from outside Kyoto to his property. In the meantime, the poor fellow was making do in a fifteen-thousand-square-foot place designed by Julia Morgan, who'd also used her architectural muscles on San Simeon, two hundred miles to the south.

What was good enough for William Randolph Hearst was apparently not good enough for Frankson. He called the Morgan house unfit for habitation and wanted to pull it down once his Japanese castle was erected. About a year ago, the town's planning commission had refused him a demolition permit. Their decision maintained that if the house was indeed unfit for habitation, it was because Frankson himself had not maintained it. The town council voted five to two to uphold the planners' decision.

Frankson took a don't-get-mad-get-even approach to the problem. The autocrat turned to democracy. He supported three candidates for the council who ran on a platform of "homeowner sovereignty." The bitter contest was between the horsy set of old Woodside and the new money of Silicon Valley. Only one of his three candidates made it on to the council. Chalk one up for the equestrians.

Behind the wheel, I reckoned it was best to avoid 101 this time of day. I took surface streets to El Camino, then headed up to the town in Silicon Valley where the local members of the Forbes Four

Hundred roosted. I took a left on a road that was marked "Private." About a quarter mile from Woodside Road, I came to a steel-reinforced gate with a buzzer on an aluminum stalk. I pushed the button and heard the whirring of a video camera which I spotted on a stone pillar.

"Yes?" came a disembodied voice.

"I'm Ian Michaels, here to see Mr. Frankson."

"He is not expecting you."

"Would you check with him, please?"

"Please make an appointment."

"He won't want me turned away."

The line went dead. Maybe Frankson had given his staff lessons on telephone etiquette.

Two minutes later the gate slid open. I drove past a hill of white stones and a covey of Caterpillar tractors and earthmovers poised on the edge of a gaping hole a hundred yards across and twenty deep. In another quarter mile I came to the U-shaped driveway by the front door.

The door opened before I knocked. I was greeted by a slight woman in a blue patterned kimono, who wore sandals and white socks. She bowed and said something in Japanese. I followed the little red pillow belted to the hollow of her back as she walked with affected delicacy. At the end of a tiled hallway, she opened a door, bowed, and moved aside.

Entering the room transported me across the Pacific. At the opposite end, twenty feet away, were glass doors that looked out on a garden of stones and bonsai. The left wall was painted gray; along the right one covered in slate, water dropped in a continuous sheet. A tatami mat covered the floor. In the middle of that mat, on a black pillow facing the cascade wall knelt Ricky Frankson in a *keiko gi*, the loose-fitting white garment worn by students of karate. His eyes were closed, his hands resting on the tops of his thighs. Whether this was all for show or not, I did not know. I just bit my lower lip and waited. And waited.

"You need patience."

I looked up. Frankson had caught me looking at my watch. But I wasn't being impatient, I was checking on the results of a wager I'd made with myself. I lost. I'd bet he'd keep me waiting at least ten minutes, and it was only six.

"Thank you for seeing me."

"What choice did I have with you storming my gates? Do you want to sit down?"

"No, thank you. I prefer to stand."

He stayed on his haunches. "Oh, yes, your leg injury."

"You are remarkably well informed and also used to getting your way, aren't you?"

"Oh, yes."

"And you scotched our deal with Intel?"

"Listen. I will get your company. Isn't it better for you and the employees if it's a friendly takeover? Quite frankly, I am impressed with your little Intel stratagem. Impressed enough that I will not lower the price I offered two weeks ago for another week."

"Friendly? It seems little better than a smash and grab."

"And I am a smasher and grabber?" He paused for my response, but I said nothing. "Deals like this are best done quickly."

I recited, "'There is no instance of a country having benefited from prolonged warfare.'"

"Ah. You impress me again. You know *The Art of War*. Then you know what I intend. As Sun Tzu says, 'The best thing of all is to take the enemy's country whole and intact; to shatter and destroy it is not so good.' You accused me of smash and grab. I am trying to do the very opposite."

"What about prolonged warfare?"

"I do not think so. You do not have the resources or the support. In fact, we are both fortunate. If the car that hit you had been going a couple of miles an hour faster, you would be out of the picture."

"What do you know about that car?" I leaned down, closer to him.

He waited a beat or two before answering with the calmness of a Buddhist monk. "Are you accusing me of something?"

"Listen. My wife is in the hospital because of some maniac driver. And thanks to the same guy, I need to buy ibuprofen by the barrel. If you're asking if I'm touchy when it comes to that car, the answer is 'Fuck, yes.'"

Frankson folded his arms. "I was saying we were both fortunate, you to be alive, me because I want you working at Torii. You have till Friday to get back to me."

I fought down the impulse to grab him. Even with two good legs, I'd have as little chance of winning a physical contest against this ninth-level black belt as I did of keeping Accelenet out of his clutches.

FORTY-ONE

A TRIP DOWN FRANKSON's driveway was longer than some of my friends' commute. I called Bharat.

"How are calls going with potential investors?"

"Even when it looked like we had a deal with Intel, I didn't stop looking."

"Good man."

"No, not a good man," he said. "I haven't come up with diddly."

Bharat might speak with an Anglo-Indian accent, but he had the Silicon Valley vocabulary down.

"Keep trying," I told him.

"You really don't want to have to do a deal with Torii, do you?"

"What I want isn't what's important. We have investors, employees, and customers we need to do right by."

"Got it. I'll keep trying."

"Thanks." I appreciated him not asking about Rowena this time.

———

When I got back to the hospital, Rowena's room was empty. A yawning chasm opened in my gut. I scrambled out to the nurse's station.

"Where's my wife?"

"Ah, Mr. Michaels. She's gone for a CAT scan. She'll be back shortly."

"What's the matter?"

"Just precautionary."

I could not ask more. My throat had constricted. Then I felt a hand on my shoulder. I whirled around and saw Dr. Griffith. Caroline was behind him, face white, but standing and dry-eyed.

"Let's go in the room," Griffith said.

He led. Caroline took my hand and squeezed.

"This may be hard to believe, but what I have to say is good news," the neurosurgeon said.

I found my voice and blurted out, "Why hasn't she awakened for good?"

Griffith nodded. "We've been concerned. When we did the operation on Friday to remove the epidural hematoma, we placed a monitor in her head to make sure that the pressure we'd relieved stayed down. All through Saturday, the pressure stayed where we wanted, but then it began to climb. We tried Mannitol to bring it down, but it's not working, at least not well enough. We're going to try something else."

"She needs another operation?" Caroline asked.

"No, that's the good news. We got the clot last time, and the CAT scans show that it hasn't come back. So we don't have to surgically intervene. We think we can bring down the pressure with drugs."

"You said you tried that," I said.

"We're going to try something else. She's going to stay on a drip of Phenobarbital for a couple of days."

"Which means?" I asked.

"That she will be in an induced coma to bring down the swelling."

"And that is the good news?" I asked.

"I'm just a doctor, not God, but, yes, I think so. We've had good luck with phenobarbital in cases like this."

"Okay" is all Caroline said.

When the doctor started to leave the room, I said, "Let me walk with you."

In the hallway, I asked Griffith, "What does good luck mean?"

"At least an even chance."

"My wife's life is a coin flip?"

He turned and looked at me. "We like to think we're doing more here than tossing pennies."

Before I could apologize, a male nurse came around the corner pushing a gurney. On it lay Rowena, blue arteries visible through the translucent skin of her eyelids.

Griffith and I retraced our steps back to Rowena's room. We found a Filipina nurse standing next to Caroline.

"Let's get her started on the drugs," Griffith told her. "Wait outside, would you?"

Standing side-by-side in the corridor, my arm touched Caroline's. I could feel hers quaking.

In the midst of a black terror, my mind flew back to a freshman English class. From the back row in Burr Lecture Hall, I saw Professor Alford wheel out a large tower. He explained that when things were bleakest for the protagonist in a Greek tragedy, the gods performed miracles as required from the platform atop the contraption. *Deus ex machina*, god from the machine, it was called.

Come on, God, this was no play, it was real-life. We could use a little *deus ex machina* right about now. If not for my sake, then for this good woman next to me who's already lost a husband and a daughter.

FORTY-TWO

THERE WAS A LIMIT on how far we could stretch hospital rules. The nurses said only one of us could spend the night in the ICU. I sent Caroline home at midnight and sat holding Rowena's hand. Every few minutes, I got up to check the intercranial pressure on the monitor. It seemed stuck at 38 and Dr. Griffith wanted to see it go down to 20. I stared at it. I begged it. I cursed it. The monitor paid no attention.

After three hours, I left to go to the bathroom. I nodded at the police officer outside the door. Ten steps into the corridor, and I panicked. A supernova of dread exploded in my head: I'd left and she died. I turned around, dashed past the guard, and back to her bed. Her chest still rose and fell. I exhaled and then took Rowena's hand back into mine. She would not die, she could not die, so long as I did not let go.

Caroline checked in by phone at four. She hadn't slept. I told her the pressure monitor was down a notch to 37. She walked back into the room at nine with Rabbi Frankel and gave me a hug.

"Did you get any sleep?" I asked Caroline.

"A few hours." That slight decline in pressure must have offered a little hope.

Caroline said, "It doesn't look as though you did, though. Go. Go home and get some sleep."

"Call me if there's any change."

"I will."

"The moment it happens."

"I promise."

I nodded and kissed Rowena's forehead.

"Thank you for coming, Rabbi."

She tilted her head. She just looked at me, saying nothing. After thirty awkward seconds, she proffered her hand. It didn't matter much to me what she said or whether she said anything at all. What counted was showing up.

If members of her congregation complained about Rabbi Frankel, it was that she was stand-offish or even stuck up. She didn't fit the stereotype of those who chose a pastoral life because they're good at providing comfort. A Princeton graduate at twenty, she'd been the comments editor on the law review at Harvard. After clerking for a judge on the D.C. Circuit for a year, she'd enrolled in the rabbinic program at Hebrew Union College in Cincinnati. Her book displayed, not the touchy-feely sentiments of most clergy-written manuals, but a rigorous Talmudic logic. Scratch the rabbinical shell and underneath you'd find an intellectual, albeit a shy one. Despite muttering, she was in no danger of losing her pulpit at Beth El. Intellectual brilliance was held in high esteem by a congregation filled with doctors, lawyers, professors, and entrepreneurs. I'd bet visiting the hospital and providing comfort was hard for someone who lived a life of the mind. Courage was doing the right thing even when it was hard.

"Go home and get some sleep," Caroline said again. The rabbi's nod seconded the suggestion.

When I turned in the doorway for one last look at Rowena, I could see her mother in what had become a familiar pose—leaning over her suffering daughter, lips moving in prayer. A Jewish *pietà*.

———

"You heard about the Nolan case?" The D.A. herself was calling me as I made my way back home.

"The plea bargain is all done?" I asked.

"The judge signed off on it yesterday. Your wife did a great job. How is she doing?"

I told her, then switched topics. "What about Carlos Edwards?"

"He's arriving at SFO today."

"You got the Thais to cough him up?"

"No. He's coming back voluntarily. He'll land in less than two hours. If he had anything to do with Rowena's injury, we'll nail him."

After we hung up, I called Juliana. "I want you to work backward, please. If I wanted to take a flight from Bangkok that brought me into SFO at..." I looked down at my watch. "...At eleven or so, when would I need to leave? What airline would I have taken?"

"Eleven in the morning?" Juliana was used to my off-the-wall requests.

"Right."

"Just a sec."

It wasn't one second. More like a hundred fifty before I heard her voice again.

"You'd leave Bangkok at six-fifty in the morning and fly to Tokyo. Then take United in from there. Flight 852 arrives at eleven-fifteen."

"And ETA today?"

"Forty minutes early."

"Thanks."

I pulled into my driveway and didn't even turn off the engine when I ran inside. Passport in hand, I jumped back in the Acura. Twenty-five minutes later I exited at the airport turn-off and left the car with valet parking.

I waited in line at the United ticket counter.

"I've just got a month off and want to buy a ticket for a travel lottery."

"Okay," said a skeptical blonde.

"Where can I go cheapest outside the U.S.?"

"Probably Vancouver."

That wouldn't work. Canadian flights left through the domestic terminal.

"In Europe or Asia. I want to leave today. A one-way ticket is okay."

She raised her eyebrows. I smiled and pushed over my AmEx Platinum, my United 100K Card, and my passport.

She examined all three. Then she looked up and smiled, reassured by documentation that I wasn't dangerous, even if a trifle eccentric. "You're sure, cheapest?" she asked.

"Yes, please."

She shrugged and began to flick her fingers over a keyboard. "Mr. Michaels, our flight 854 leaves for Heathrow at seven-twenty. That ticket is five hundred eighteen dollars."

"Perfect."

"Any luggage to check?" the woman asked me.

"No."

"I hope you find what you're looking for." She pushed a boarding pass over the counter.

"I know I will," I said.

Even though the flight didn't leave for more than eight hours, the boarding pass and passport took me through security in the international terminal. I scuttled down the G corridor past duty free shops, bookstores, fashion boutiques, and sushi bars, but past almost no people. A ghost terminal.

Finally, I came to Gate G-95. Seconds later, the agent opened the door for the disembarking passengers from Flight 852. A salmon swimming against the current, I pushed myself through the stream of people to a point just where the jetway met the solid floor of the terminal.

Like me, the passengers had slept in their clothes. Probably like me, too, they gave off a stale musty smell of dirty laundry and stale breath.

He must have been flying business class because it didn't take long for him to show up. After seeing all those photos on Facebook, I didn't have any trouble recognizing Carlos L. Edwards. During the car trip to the airport, I had rehearsed introducing myself and asking a few polite questions, but one look at him and I lost it.

I knocked into him and pushed his face against the wall and then grabbed his right arm and levered it up to his shoulder blade. With his arm pinned and my knee in the small of his back, he could squirm, but could not get away.

"What the fuck?"

"You tried to kill my wife."

"I tried to kill your wife? Who the hell is your wife? Are you out of your fucking mind?"

"Your girlfriend told you to kill my wife."

"Girlfriend? What the hell girlfriend you talking about?"

I made no effort to rein my temper in. I lifted his arm an inch and answered his question. "Daisy Nolan."

"Daisy?" I don't know if Edwards' voice usually had a high pitch, but it did now.

"Yeah, Daisy."

"We broke up."

"Yeah, right." I pushed his arm up another two inches against his back.

"Shit, that hurts."

I let it back down a little.

"There's no way in the universe I'd kill someone for Daisy," he gasped.

No way in the universe. It all came back to physics, didn't it? But, as it happened, I had only seconds to speculate on how the cosmos worked before my wrist was encased in a strong grip that jerked my arm down and pulled me backward.

"I told you to butt out. You are under arrest for assault and interfering with an investigation."

Mikulski. Next to him, not quite coming up to his shoulder, stood Fletcher. "Let him go, John," she said. After I released Edwards' arm, Mikulski twisted my wrist one more time for good luck.

"Go home, Ian," Fletcher told me. "You're meddling. This is our job, not yours."

As I trekked back through the international terminal, my pulse slowed. I should have learned from the scene in the courtroom. My self-image was of a rational man. I'd gone to college and business school. When a crisis hit at Accelenet, I was the guy people turned to, the one they expected to keep a level head. But with Edwards, I sure as hell hadn't had the kind of cool, collected conversation I'd intended to. Instead, I'd lost it. Inside me dwelt something primitive. Rowena had seen it in that confrontation with Nolan. She'd said I turned into a movie monster. But goddam, this wasn't the movies.

FORTY-THREE

When I came out of Rowena's room that afternoon, I went into the hospital courtyard and turned on my iPhone. It started shaking in my hand a second later. The call was from a Stanford extension.

"Hello?"

"*Allo.* This is Françoise Roux. Did we have an appointment today? Or did I write it down wrong?"

Damn. I'd set up this appointment before the accident to discuss Aunt Isobel. It was four-thirty. I was half an hour late.

"It was I who made a calendar mistake. I can make it to your office in fifteen minutes."

"*Ça va bien.*"

Trying to play detective at the airport hadn't done much to help Rowena. Back to the irrational but irresistible alternative of working on Aunt Isobel.

Roux was on the same floor as Tompkins, but on the other side of the building and, named chair or no, her office was half the size of his. Well, he did have a Nobel Prize.

Chic in a blue knit dress and Hermès scarf, the professor waved away my apologies with a slender arm. Living proof that French women really do not get fat, she might have tipped the scales at 115 if toting an unabridged copy of *Les Misérables*.

"Do you mind if I smoke?" she asked me.

Mind? It gave me a splitting headache, but it was her office. "Of course not," I said.

She reached over to a pack of Gauloises on her desk and then stood up and closed the door. She lit up and inhaled deeply. "I could not be a professor without smoking. I cannot think without nicotine. Please accept my desolation. At Stanford it is preferred to be addicted to cocaine rather than tobacco."

I asked how she was getting along.

"People wonder what I'm doing here."

"They wonder what a professor is doing at a university?"

"Fifty years ago Felix Bloch came from Stanford to set up CERN. Now the child has surpassed the parent. Most particle physicists want to be in Europe."

"CERN?"

"The European physics consortium, the one operating the Large Hadron Collider."

"The huge new atom smasher outside Geneva?"

Her lips pursed in a Gallic moue. "Yes. Your government no longer seems interested in pure science, but happily, the Europeans and Japanese do."

"So why be at Stanford?"

"Maybe I am a contrarian by nature. And, President Ono and I agree that American students need to be shown that science is more than sitting in front of a PC screen."

"Weren't you here for graduate school, too?"

213

"Yes. In the late 1970s. I love it here, even if it seems that the only way for a Stanford professor to win prestige is to start a successful company."

"Americans may not be interested in how the universe is made. I can tell you, though, in Silicon Valley they definitely do want to know how money is made."

"Ah, Silicon Valley. It owes much to my world."

"How so?"

"A researcher at CERN wanted to share information with other physicists. He invented a language to send it around and we ended up with the World Wide Web."

"Ah, Tim Berners-Lee came up with HTML. He *was* a physicist, wasn't he?"

She moved her hands together in a pantomime of applause and then tilted her head. "Of course you would know of our wonderful Sir Tim." She nodded. A teacher by temperament, she couldn't resist a mini-lecture. "The computer nerds at SLAC in the early 1970s hosted meetings of what they called the Homebrew Computer Club. Steve Jobs and Steve Wozniak came." She jerked her chin as if tossing me the conversational ball.

"And from that came Apple Computer and the whole PC industry. So you're saying Silicon Valley wouldn't be much without the physicists?"

"*Peut-être.* Now I can't promise that anything wonderful is going to come from my work."

"But if you could prove there is another dimension where much of the gravitational force is hiding?"

She smiled. "Yes, who knows where it could lead? The new collider should be able to confirm or deny whether we are correct."

My iPhone started to quake in my shirt pocket. "Excuse me." When I saw that it was not the hospital or Caroline, I hit a button to still the device. "Sorry. You were here too late to meet Professor Marter yourself?"

"Yes, unhappily. But I heard much about her. If she had lived, she would have been one of the winners of the Nobel Prize for discovering quarks."

"It is a shame that it took the prize committee so long to award it."

"I was here in 1982 when the announcement came that Tompkins, Solenski, and Vansittart had won. The rumor was that there were so many people involved, it took the committee a dozen years to decide to whom it should go. That was the controversy. There was little doubt that the discovery would win the prize."

"I wonder how many people were involved."

"There were ten. No, eleven."

"How would you know if you weren't here?"

"Ten went to the Nobel Prize ceremony. Isobel Marter was the eleventh. It shows how physics has changed. Eleven staffers on the team that discovered quarks. For smashing together particles at CERN, there are two thousand staff members. Physics is getting bigger and far more expensive."

"Do you know who did what here at Stanford?"

"My understanding is that your great aunt laid down the theoretical basis for quarks and then designed an experiment to find them. Tompkins ran the experiment and, based on the results, built the model of what protons and neutrons really consisted of. Solenski designed and implemented the experiment's detector apparatus."

"The detectors?"

"Yes, the pieces of doped plastic that caught the ricocheting electrons and the computers that found and measured them."

"And Vansittart?"

"Being English he would not like the comparison, but to me he was the Napoléon of the lab, an emperor in a bowtie. He directed everything, he was everywhere, tireless. Without his strategy for attacking the problem and his tactical corrections, no one would have found anything. Without his ability to extract money from the university and Congress, we would have had no resources for our experiments."

"Stanford must have had resources in the old days if it paid for all those people to go to Stockholm."

"No. Tompkins himself paid for seven people to come."

"Tompkins paid?"

"Even the techs. It is a legend. You doubt, because he is an egotist?"

"Yes."

"You are correct. But he is generous, too. People are very loyal to him. How do you say it? He is a team player."

"So long as he is captain," I said.

She clapped her hands and laughed. "*Capitaine? Exactement.*"

FORTY-FOUR

ROBERT FROST SAID HE could sum up everything he knew about life in three words—*it goes on*. While Rowena lay unconscious, ignorant of her courtroom victory, while my great aunt lay moldering, deprived by death of her Nobel Prize, life proceeded. A look at my iPhone with over sixty unread emails and fourteen unheard voicemails proved the poet's point in a quotidian way.

As I walked back across campus toward the hospital, I listened to the voicemail that came in during my meeting with Professor Roux.

"Hello, Ian," I heard Margot Fulbright say. "I admire your hard work on the behalf of the shareholders. I would like a better offer for the company as much as anyone, but with the Intel alternative dead, I think it is time to face reality. We need to get a deal done with Torii before we run out of money. Call me, please."

I started looking down the list for other calls. I pressed to listen to Leon Henderson.

"Ian, I have Juliana out looking for you. I don't want to meet behind your back, but Margot's coming by my office at one. Let me know if you can make it, too."

I looked at the time on the PDA's screen. Seven till one. Turning around, I popped a couple of ibuprofen and headed toward Leon's office at the business school.

Ten minutes later I took a step into Leon's office, a room so vast that I almost needed binoculars to pick out the two Accelenet board members against the far wall. They sat in maroon leather chairs, their heads tilted forward, nearly touching over a glass coffee table.

"Hello, team," I called out.

"Hey, Ian," Leon answered. Turning to Margot, he said, "I told Ian he could come by if he was in the neighborhood."

"Of course," Margot said in the warm tones of a cobra greeting a mongoose.

"We were just discussing alternatives," Leon said. "Come take a seat."

I sat at the end of the table. Through the glass top, I saw the swirling ivory, blue, and red of an antique Shiraz rug. Surveying the office, I caught sight of a new photo over the desk, Leon's grizzled head flanked by two earnest student types.

He followed my eyes. "Another sign of my vanity. Sergey Brin and Larry Page developed their search algorithm as Stanford grad students and, of course, started their company to exploit it. Stanford got shares in the venture in return for any ownership of intellectual property."

"And how many millions did that piece of Google add to the university coffers?" I asked.

"Three hundred thirty-six," Leon said.

"Not too shabby," Margot said. "Accelenet could use some of that money, couldn't we?"

"She says, bringing us back to reality," Leon said.

"I called Ricky and told him to get us a term sheet," Margot informed us.

She'd overstepped her bounds, but it made no sense to get too antagonistic. So I smiled before I said, "You're just one board member, Margot."

"I requested it. I didn't sign it. I just told him to get it ready and send it over. He told me you two had been talking anyway. Do you have an alternative?" She did not return my smile.

"You know what happened to the Intel deal?" They shook their heads. "I'm pretty sure Ricky threatened Intel with the loss of Torii's business."

"We could sue," Leon said.

"Oh, I am certain that any threats were implicit. They could never be proven in court. And anyway the main point is that Accelenet is about to run out of money."

"So?" Margot asked.

"So, we *do not* have an alternative, and I don't think there's much chance of finding one. I'll be looking for that Torii offer sheet."

Now Margot smiled. "I know this is not what we hoped for, but two hundred fifty million is a good outcome."

After she left, Leon looked at me. "Easy for Margot to say it's a good outcome. She doesn't have to work for Ricky for the next two years."

I shrugged. "I'm not giving up, I *want* to do better." I took a deep breath. "But it's sure looking like the Torii offer is the best we can do. Damn. I hate this."

"It's better than bankruptcy. Jobs will be saved. Investors and employees will make some money. The technology will be introduced to the market. Not a terrible outcome. You shouldn't let your ego get in the way."

"Margot has sold what, twelve companies to Torii?" I asked. "And how many more in her portfolio does she hope to sell to them?"

"Yeah, she's made her career as a VC being a start-up scout for Ricky and can't afford to piss him off over one company."

"Screw the other companies," I said. "She owes a fiduciary duty to Accelenet."

"Of course, she does. And she's probably convinced herself that she's doing what's best for Accelenet, too. Maybe she is." I heard a sandpapery rasp as Leon rubbed his chin. From experience I knew some philosophizing was on its way. "It is funny how often venture capitalists find that their duty to one company matches up with what's best for their entire investment portfolio."

"I am not laughing."

FORTY-FIVE

AFTER SPENDING TWO MORE hours in the ICU holding Rowena's hand and staring at the red numeral 32 on the ICP monitor, I drove back to Accelenet. I walked around the office so employees could see me, see that I was still with them. But the die was cast, wasn't it? Paul, the founder of the company, had disappeared and his dream of building a Fortune 500 company out of delivering video and other data streams faster and better was about to do the same.

Now sitting at my desk, I called Bryce to see if he had received a term sheet from Torii. No, he hadn't. I asked him to call Torii's general counsel, a former partner of his, and determine its ETA.

Drumming my nails against the desktop amused me for about twenty seconds after I hung up. I thought about my Aunt Isobel for another third of a minute. Then I picked up the phone and called Peter Reynard at FBS, the gigantic Federated Bank of Switzerland. Pete had helped us raise some money years ago, and he was always sniffing around for more business.

"Hey, Ian." Well, he obviously had caller ID.

"Pete, how are you?"

"Why are you calling me on my cell?"

"Because it's eight o'clock in New York."

"You think I keep bankers' hours? I'm still in the office."

"Shall I call you on another line then?"

"No, this works. Listen, I told Bharat I thought we could find the money you are looking for. It wouldn't be easy, and we sure as hell couldn't do it in a week."

"I know. He told me. If the stars lined up just so, how long?"

"I hate answering questions like that, because the stars *never* line up. Let's go through the process. We'd have to put together the pitch, send you to New York, London, and Geneva to meet our bankers, and then out on the road to those same three cities again, plus Edinburgh, Tokyo, and Shanghai. The next step after finding a couple of interested parties will be follow-up meetings and due diligence. It's like planning for a mini D-Day. Two months would be a miracle. Four months would be average."

"Success guaranteed?" I asked.

"C'mon. In banking you can't count on anything. When I started in this business, we used to say 'sound as the dollar.' Now with the exchange rate fluctuating all over the place ..."

"Okay. I get it. It's what I figured." This pass was going to fall incomplete. "I really called for a completely different reason. I have two favors to ask you."

"Before I say anything, let me hear what they are."

"You speak with an American accent, but you really are just a cautious Swiss banker, aren't you? My great aunt was killed in a car accident in Geneva."

"Oh, I am so sorry."

"Thank you, but it was long ago. I was wondering if you could have your office in Geneva get me two things relating to her death."

"Wait, wait, let me get a pencil and paper. What was her name? What was the exact date?"

"She was Isobel Marter, a Stanford professor, killed on October 11, 1971. First, I'd like to see a contemporary newspaper story of the accident. I'd think *La Suisse* is the best bet. I know it went under a few years ago, but there must be archives somewhere."

"Possibly," said my careful colleague. "It stopped publishing in 1994. That's more than a few years ago."

"And then I'd like to see any official reports on the accident. A police report or an autopsy maybe."

"I don't know about that. To have a prayer, sign and then fax me a notarized statement that you are asking for these documents as a surviving relative."

"I'll have it to you in ten minutes. And thanks, Pete. I owe you."

According to the statement I whipped up, Ian Michaels was the great nephew and heir of Isobel Marter. Juliana notarized the paper and into the maw of the fax machine it went.

FORTY-SIX

"How are you doing?" the voice on the phone asked.

"Recovering from police brutality," I said.

Caroline had taken the night's first shift at the hospital. I was home sitting in my paisley chair.

"You are very lucky that Mikulski didn't arrest you," Fletcher said.

"Can he do that outside of Palo Alto city limits?"

"He's a California peace officer."

"Next time I meddle, it will be in Nevada."

"That would suit both of us better," she said.

"Susan, I love talking to you, but it's ten-thirty at night. I have a feeling this is not a social call."

"Do you have a DVD player at home?"

"I've been known to vote Democratic, but I'm still an American patriot. Of course."

"Can I come by and show you something?"

"I'll put on a pot of coffee."

Even without sirens blaring, Fletcher drove from police head-quarters to my place in less than ten minutes. I handed her a mug as she walked into the front hallway.

She had her right index finger poking through the hole in a sil-ver disk. We settled on the family room couch and got ready for whatever video entertainment she had in mind.

"Push pause," she said as the DVD loaded. "If you tell anyone I showed you this, I could get fired."

"And I could be doing you a favor. Police work is not the most lucrative career."

"I still trust you, but I'm not sure why. Mikulski thinks you're unhinged."

"Maybe you're both right."

"Start 'er up."

I wasn't much of a TV watcher, but somehow Rowena and I had ended up with an oversized plasma screen hanging from the family room wall.

While no Blu-ray disc, the video was of surprisingly good qual-ity. On one side of a polished wood table sat Carlos Edwards. Co-starring with him was my late-night guest, whose square face looked a little washed out in the lighting.

Fletcher asked, "Mr. Edwards, are you here of your own voli-tion?"

"Yes," Edwards replied, "I can have a lawyer if I want?"

"You may have a lawyer, but, don't worry, you are not under arrest. I just have some questions for you. Let's get them over with, okay?"

"Okay."

"Do you know Daisy Nolan?"

"Yes. She was my girlfriend."

"She's accused of murder."

"I know that. Daisy works long hours and when she isn't at the office, I can't stop her from talking about her job. Normal around the Valley, don't you think? When she was indicted, I went nuts. You don't want to think you've, um, you've…"

"Been intimate?"

"Yeah. You don't want to think you've been intimate with someone who could kill."

"Why do you think she could kill?"

"I don't. Not really. She's just got this temper."

"Did you visit her in jail?"

I pushed the pause button on the remote. "You could check that, couldn't you?" I asked Susan.

"Yeah, we did. He tells the truth."

I pushed the start button and the figures on the screen awakened from suspended animation.

"Yeah, I did," Edwards was saying. "At Christmas she said she needed to focus on her upcoming trial. She said she had no energy for anything else."

"And what did you do?"

"I told her I wanted to stand by her, but she sent me away."

"So was she still your girlfriend?"

"I don't know. I want to be loyal, but I really haven't spoken to her in two months. I tried to visit her in jail twice, but she wouldn't see me."

"And since you didn't know if she was guilty, you were a little relieved?"

Edwards nodded.

"Were you in the courtroom when she threatened to have the prosecutor killed?" Fletcher asked.

"Yeah." He shook his head. "Daisy, she's got a temper."

"Did you talk to her after she said it?"

"How could I?"

"Did you do anything about what she said?"

"Is that what that crazy asshole at the airport was talking about?"

"Mr. Edwards, did you do anything about Daisy's threat?"

"No."

"Why would you leave just as the trial was beginning?"

"Well, Daisy spotted me there in court that first day. She'd told me before to leave her alone. And then there I was. She gave me a look. I knew not to come back."

"So you decided to leave town?"

"Well, if I couldn't be at the trial, there was no sense sitting around. I wanted to get outta Dodge."

"And you could decide to go to Thailand on the spur of the moment?"

"Yeah, they've been pestering me to come over for the last six months."

I pushed the pause button again. "Does that check out, too?" I asked Fletcher.

"According to his boss, yes." Back to the DVD.

"Why did you take your car to Don's Auto Laundry last week?" the on-screen Fletcher asked.

"Why are you asking me this?"

"It's best if you just tell the truth."

"Well, I always leave my car there to get detailed when I go away. I can't really leave it on the street. Leaving it at Chuck's is a lot cheaper than airport parking."

"Mr. Edwards, how do you feel about Ms. Nolan now?"

"I don't know. She's the smartest and classiest woman I ever got involved with. I don't think she could be a murderer, but…" And then the big galoot started to cry.

Back in real life, Fletcher said to me, "You can stop it." She took a sip from the mug of coffee. "This is good. You should look into a career as a barista."

"Did a member of our board ask you to suggest that? No, never mind. You're showing me the interview because what he says checks out? You don't want me attacking him again?"

Another sip. "That about sums it up. He took a polygraph, too."

"And that indicated he was innocent, too?"

"We'll get the final results tomorrow, but the preliminary looks good for him."

"Don't you think it's a coincidence that Nolan threatens Rowena, Rowena is almost run off the road by a large BMW, and Nolan's beau has a large BMW?"

"Yes, but coincidences happen. His polygraph is going to come back clean."

"If it does, who did try to kill her?"

"Maybe you can help me here. Yeah, yeah, I know we've been over it, but just humor me. Who *else* could have done this? A random driver? Jogging in the dark can be dangerous. I'll bet you've had close calls before on predawn runs."

"Not like this. That car was waiting for us and when we ran by, it started its pursuit. It even speeded up for the kill. It was like a lion chasing down a gazelle."

"Okay, we'll keep looking," Fletcher said.

"If it's not Edwards, you don't even know where to look."

"No, we don't, but if we're spinning our wheels, we're spinning them as fast as we can."

She leaned over and, with an un-policewoman-like gesture ran the square-ended fingers of her right hand over my cheek. I didn't flinch. There was nothing sexual about the caress. Rowena, whose gay-dar was far more sensitive than mine, had once asked me whether Fletcher was a lesbian. No clue—I'd never seen her with a date or partner, man or woman.

"That's prickly. You're hiding behind a beard?" Fletcher asked.

"I guess so."

"How do you cope? Wait. That's a stupid question. I guess I saw some of the answer today at the airport."

"I appreciate your concern. It helps."

She wiped her eyes on her sleeve. "Some cop, huh?"

"Come on, I'll go out with you," I said. "I'm going to the hospital." We moved to the front door and then outside on an evening crisp and clear.

"She hasn't come to, has she?"

"No, not yet."

"You're just going to sit with her?"

Under the street lamp by her car, I nodded.

FORTY-SEVEN

THIS TIME I SAW Paul watching me through a window in Rowena's third-floor hospital room. I wanted to explain to him that I was trying to save her by doing justice for Aunt Isobel. I had to do something. Then I awoke and knew I had gone beyond rationality.

Eyes now open, I hobbled over to the window overlooking the hospital courtyard. A man in scrubs was walking toward the garage. No Paul, though.

I spent the next two hours back in the chair beside Rowena's hospital bed. My leg throbbed from the broken fibula, and my back ached from the way I'd slept. When Caroline came back on watch at six, the monitor read 32, and I went home to shower and change. It only took seventeen minutes—not shaving knocked three minutes off the twenty I was used to. The bathroom mirror told me I looked like shit, but that was still better than I felt. On the way to the office, I chewed on the three ibuprofen tablets that had replaced oatmeal as my breakfast of choice.

A couple minutes before seven I drove up to Accelenet. Two cockamamie software engineers—was that redundant?—who followed the circadian rhythms of Count Dracula were leaving the building as I walked in. There was already a hum in the building, thanks to the half-dozen telemarketers who covered the East Coast. Guarding the gates in front of my own office was my own Cerberus, the ever-vigilant Juliana.

"I left the faxes from Geneva on your desk," she said. I wondered if she could be an opening act for David Copperfield as a mind reader. She'd known I'd be in early to see them.

A scrawled note on the cover sheet asked me to call Reynard as soon as I received the four pages of the fax. I turned the page and came to an unclear, smudged PDF copy of a story from *La Suisse* headlined: *"Professeur américaine tuée par une voiture inconnue dans le Parc l'Ariana."* I ran my eyes down the article. My French would be good enough to translate the story with a little help from an online dictionary. Given the poor quality of the image, though, I'd probably need to borrow Juliana's magnifying glass to make out some of the words. Wait, no, I wouldn't. On the next page of the fax was a typewritten translation of the article. "American Professor Killed by Car Unknown at Ariana Park." Swiss efficiency.

Isobel had been attending a physics colloquium in Geneva. Well, I knew that. She'd been jogging in a park and was hit by a car at the park entrance at Avenue de la Paix at six in the morning. Goddamn. She'd struck her head against the ground, fractured her skull, and died. The article in *La Suisse* ran about two hundred fifty words in the original French. *C'est tout.* It quoted a police investigator as saying that it was a question of an *"accident au hasard."* If I hadn't been with her last Friday morning, last Saturday's *San Jose Mercury* could have run an updated version of the same story about her grandniece by marriage.

I went to the next page. By God, FBS had indeed managed to get a copy of Isobel Marter's autopsy. This time the copy was crystal clear, but the language was not. My French would need considerable help unless ... saved. A translation was supplied here, too.

The medical examiner had been meticulous. Aunt Isobel had an advanced case of ovarian cancer which had spread to her liver, lungs, and kidneys. She'd known it, too. The doctor noted she'd had a complete hysterectomy nine to twelve months before her death, presumably to excise an ovarian tumor. Dr. Rousell marveled that someone whose cancer had infiltrated so many vital organs could jog at all. With Swiss gloom he noted, "I would have expected to see the deceased on my table within a few months in any case." The person who'd run her over had deprived her of an end fraught with suffering and pain. It was practically euthanasia. I snorted at that thought. Too bad she'd died so quickly. She might have wanted to thank her killer.

The possibility she'd committed suicide popped into my brain, but after a few seconds of mental examination, I pushed it back out. This woman was tough. She held her own as the only woman in Stanford's physics department. A Nobel Prize was going to come her way. And in any case, why take the trouble to travel to Geneva to jump in front of a car?

Who had known of her condition? What difference did it make?

"Ian?"

My head jerked up. "Huh!"

"Sorry, I didn't mean to frighten you," Juliana said from the doorway. "Where were you?"

"In a park in Geneva in 1971."

"With Isobel Marter. Um, who was she?"

Of course, Juliana had read the fax. She wanted to know every-thing, but she passed along nothing. I could live with that. "My great aunt."

"And she was hit by a car while jogging, too?"

"What's up?" I asked, trying to be polite in asking why she'd in-terrupted me.

"I've got Peter Reynard on the phone."

"Oh yeah, he'd asked me to call him first thing."

I punched the blinking button on my phone.

"Peter, great job. I'm most appreciative."

"Well, you might want to get even more appreciative."

"You have more on Isobel Marter?"

"No, no. One of our Swiss bankers has an investor for Accele-net who can move quickly."

"Just like that?"

"Practically. It's so peculiar. I called my colleague Bruno Mueller to get his help on your requests. He went to work on them and then called me at home this morning and told me of the coincidence."

"That he was doing me a favor and then this offer came in?"

"Right. Here's the deal. It's thirty-six million euros for ten per-cent of the company."

"Who is the investor?"

"One of the funds the bank manages. The Locarno Fund."

"What's that?"

"A fund for rich people."

"And you can't tell me more?"

"Only that they think Accelenet is a good investment."

"Who are the rich people who've invested in the fund?"

"I work for a *Swiss* bank, Ian. I can't tell you. Jules Schweitzer is the manager of Locarno, and he's done a great job for his clients in the five or six funds he manages. One more thing though. With the investment would come an order for twenty million euros worth of your accelerator chips from Swiss Telecom."

"We've never even spoken to them." Swiss Telecom had a reputation for stodginess.

"I asked Bruno why they were interested. He told me ST wants to get itself on the cutting edge."

"Okay."

"And one last thing. If you'll let us, the bank itself would invest alongside Locarno for five million more euros."

"Listen. We're about to do a deal with someone else. If we're going to change horses, I need a signed term sheet from Monsieur Schweitzer by tomorrow and a purchase order from Swiss Telecom."

"The PO from ST can be contingent on the investment?"

"Yes. Then our board can decide which of the two offers is more attractive."

"Would the deal I've outlined put us in the running?"

"The PO from ST will help a lot."

"That must be what Bruno figured. I'll send you a draft term sheet before you wake up tomorrow morning."

FBS had connections all right. I said, "People in Geneva are going to be up late."

"Our people in New York are going to help, too."

"Great. Once I get the term sheet I'd like to talk to Schweitzer."

"As you said, it's late in Switzerland. I'll have my admin talk to Juliana and set up a call for tomorrow your time. It'll probably be early. Okay, Ian. I'm ringing off. I've got a lot to do."

"And thanks again for the material on Isobel Marter." As he'd remarked, he worked for a Swiss bank. He didn't ask why I wanted it.

I leaned back in my chair and replayed the conversation in my head, searching for the dark lining to this silver cloud. *Deus ex machina* might have made sense in ancient Greece, but not in twenty-first-century Silicon Valley.

FORTY-EIGHT

I GOT TO THE hospital a little after ten and walked, without being stopped, into Rowena's room in the ICU.

"Where did the guard go?" I asked Caroline after pecking her on the cheek.

"He told me he was being called back to the station. He said Rowena's in no danger."

"I wonder how the heck he decided that. How is she doing?" I asked.

She nodded over toward a forest of green screens.

I took a look. "Twenty-nine?"

"Yeah. It's going down, going down very slowly. The doctor should be by soon."

"Your prayers seem to be working," I said.

"There are plenty of things I've prayed for in my life that haven't happened. Who knows if they work?"

"So why bother?"

"Someone once said to pray as if all depends on God, but act as if all depends on you. That made sense to me."

"To me, too," I said.

"You're not happy about the guard being gone?" Caroline asked.

"No." I sat up straight and turned to her. "Why don't you go downstairs and get something to eat while I make a call? I'll be here awhile." I picked up the handset from the phone beside Rowena's bed.

Fletcher answered on the first ring. No chitchat. "What happened to the guard outside Rowena's room?" I asked.

"Edwards passed the polygraph with flying colors."

"Shit." I wasn't ready to let go of the idea that Edwards was the guy who'd tried to run us down. "It wasn't your decision to pull off the guard, was it?"

"Call the D.A. if you want."

Fletcher wouldn't say that she'd argued with the D.A. and lost, but I knew that's what happened. So I hung up and dialed again. A few minutes later the D.A. came on the line.

No preliminaries this time either. "You decided Rowena didn't need a guard?"

"We have no evidence that Nolan or Edwards had anything to do with your wife's accident."

"First of all, it was not an accident. It was attempted murder. Second, you of all people should know polygraph tests are fallible. Edwards had the right make of car, and he got it washed right after someone came after us."

"And I tell you that coincidences happen."

"This is a pretty big one, don't you think, Sally?"

"I've seen bigger, Ian. Last year we picked up a Harold Woodmansee for embezzling. He and his wife, Marilyn, lived in Sunnyvale."

"Wrong one?"

"Yup. We didn't figure it out till he'd spent a long weekend in the slammer. The right Mr. Woodmansee lived with *his* wife Marilyn, in Gilroy."

"An expensive mistake, I'll bet."

"Just listen to me. Four San Jose police detectives and five investigators from my office checked out the Nolan angle. Nada."

"Are you sure someone besides Edwards didn't carry out Nolan's bidding?" I asked.

"Time to get off it, Ian. Rowena works for me. I'm doing everything I can to find out who put her in that hospital room. Now, if you can show she's still at risk, I'll have the governor call up the National Guard to protect her, but it makes no sense to have guards against ghosts. You're barking up the wrong tree."

As I slammed the phone down, Caroline and Dr. Griffith came into the room together.

The surgeon picked up the charts, looked at the monitors, and raised each of Rowena's eyelids in turn. A frisson went up my spine. Her pupils had rolled up into her skull. They looked like hard-boiled eggs until Griffith pulled harder on the lids and a thin crescent of blue could be seen at the very top of the sclera. I didn't need that reminder of how close to death she'd come or maybe even was.

"The brain swelling is starting to subside," Griffith told us after he'd finished his exam.

I nodded at Caroline. We checked the gauges every five minutes. This was not news to us.

"And when will she regain consciousness, doctor?" I asked.

"We could start bringing her out of the coma tomorrow morning, but I want to play this safe. On current course and speed, we'll start Thursday morning."

"How long before she's conscious then?"

"Thursday evening or Friday morning."

"God willing," Caroline said.

Three days before I had my wife back. God willing.

———

Just watching Rowena's chest go up and down emptied my brain of all thought. I only came back to reality when Caroline came back at quarter past four. Three hours had just disappeared from my life. Perhaps I'd been visiting that other dimension Professor Roux was looking for.

"Go on home," my mother-in-law told me. "Or back to the office. I'll be here."

"I am not going anywhere."

"You're going to stay here till Thursday?"

"Yeah."

"Because the guard is gone?"

"Yeah."

"No one is going to try anything. I'll be here."

"Okay. I'll keep you company."

"I will only go to the bathroom when a nurse is here." Caroline folded her arms across her chest. "Go."

"I'll be back tonight."

She nodded. I hobbled out of the ICU. What if the D.A. was right and neither Nolan nor Edwards had anything to do with the car that hit Rowena? A random accident then?

When I got down to the car, I tore up another parking ticket.

FORTY-NINE

At two in the morning when Caroline returned to the ICU from a nap at our house, the pressure gauge was at 27.

"Do you know what this reminds me of?" Caroline asked

"No."

"Being pregnant. You wait nine months and then a new life appears. You count down the months and weeks and days. Here, with Rowena, it's automated. We just watch the gauge and when it's at 20, she will be reborn."

Half an hour after Caroline sent me home, I lay in bed looking at the ceiling. I saw the numerals on the clock radio change from 2:59 to 3:00, but must have dozed off because I didn't see the next hour change.

Around five-thirty I was up and checking email. FBS had come through. We had the term sheet and the contingent order from Swiss Telecom. I forwarded them off to Bryce for review, and then sent an email to Juliana asking her to get the board together for a meeting during the day.

I tripped over one of Rowena's running shoes on my way from the computer to the kitchen. By all rights, she should be lacing them up for a morning run, not lying unconscious on a hospital bed. I needed to run, too. It's when I did my best thinking. The continuous throb below my right knee reminded me that it would be months before I was back on the road. Muddleheaded, I toasted a whole wheat English muffin and washed it down with a cup of orange juice that had turned sour during its week in the refrigerator.

Before I made it up to the shower, Juliana called. Peter Reynard from FBS had left a message. In return she had called him to set up a call. The board meeting was set for one. That gave me time for an Aunt Isobel detour. It might help. Help what? My state of mind? Rowena? It couldn't hurt.

When it opened at nine, I was waiting on the third floor of the Varian Building at the doors of the Stanford Physics Library.

"Can I assist you?" asked the woman who unlocked the door. I followed her in past a life-size cutout of Albert Einstein.

"I hope so. There was a physics conference in Geneva in October 1971. I know Professor Isobel Marter was there. I wondered if Professor Tompkins gave any papers there, if he was there, too."

"That shouldn't be too hard." She walked behind the counter and sat down in front of a monitor. "If we just look at the online card catalog, we'd just see his books. I'll check SciSearch. That'll include all his articles, too. September, 1971, you said?"

"October."

"Okay, October, 1971. Here we go. 'Top, Bottom, Up, Down, Strange, Charmed: A Model of Quarks,' delivered to the C.E.R.N. Conference on Particle Physics on October 10, 1971."

The day before Isobel was killed.

"May I get a copy of the paper?"

"Of course." She didn't ask for a Stanford I.D. Why would she? What crazy person would be crashing a physics library? "Nice weather today," she said to make conversation. "My name is Tamara."

I took a closer look at her. Attractive, in her early thirties, with light brown hair gathered in a bun and glasses hanging from a chain around her neck—if she could sing, she was ready to star as Marian in "The Music Man." In return for her help, it only seemed fair that I play-act at being sociable.

"Many visitors here in the library?" I asked.

She laughed. "If Stanford were a prison, this would be its solitary confinement cell."

"I guess everything is available online nowadays."

"An awful lot. Most of what we have in here is bound journals."

I discovered she and Rowena had overlapped a year at UCLA, but, as the laws of probability dictated on a campus with over thirty thousand students, they had not known each other.

After a couple minutes chatting, I thanked her for the article and turned toward the door.

"Visit anytime," she called after me. "The company is welcome."

After a fifteen-minute walk, I was back in the ICU holding my wife's hand.

FIFTY

THE BOARDROOM DOOR BANGED open at quarter past one.

"I've been trying to reach you," Margot said as she stalked in. "What's this crap about competing term sheets?" She moved toward a seat with strides as long as the tight skirt of her suit allowed.

"Margot, my fault." I held my iPhone and pushed the power button. "I forgot to turn it back on."

"Shouldn't you have it on all the time?" Margot snapped.

Leon came to my aid. "Not in a hospital room."

If Leon had hoped to engender sympathy from Margot, he was disappointed. After a moment of silence, I said, "Margot, thanks for coming on such short notice. Bryce was just summarizing the differences between the two term sheets."

"Two?"

"Yes, FBS, the Swiss bank . . ."

"I know who FBS is," Margot snapped.

"Of course," I said. I reached down into the pocket of my khakis, fished out three ibuprofens, and tossed them down my gullet. "Yesterday we heard from Peter Reynard at FBS, and I talked to him again this morning on the way to the office. Locarno, a fund they manage, has given us a term sheet to purchase ten percent of the company for thirty-six million euros."

"That values the company around four hundred fifty million dollars," said Leon. "Torii wants to buy the whole thing for two hundred fifty."

"How many board seats do they want?" she asked.

"They didn't ask for any," Smithwick said. "It's very peculiar. They give Ian the right to vote their stock."

"The CEO can exercise their shares?"

"Not the CEO," Smithwick said. "Ian."

"That makes no goddam sense at all," Margot said.

"Never seen it before," Smithwick said. "It's as though Ian had come up with the money himself."

"So then with the FBS shares combined with his own and his position as the custodian for the Berks', Ian would control the company."

"If he could get the other employees to come along with him, that's true."

"Is Ian doing what's best for the company or what's best for him?" Margot asked.

She swung her head around and looked at Leon, Yee, and Smithwick. Her gaze was so fierce that when she turned it to the speakerphone, I imagined the wires carrying the heat to Yancey some six thousand miles away. He *was* the next to speak. "Careful, Margot. Let's not get carried away. Even the Torii offer requires Ian to stay. Ian didn't procure this offer. He'd never heard of Locarno. It came out of nowhere."

"Yeah, right," Margot snorted.

If only I did have the ability to conjure up big sums that she ascribed to me. Then Margot started in again. "Yeah, right. Let's not be hasty, though. The company won't be worth much without any orders. Samsung and Cisco have swung away from us. We could be in this room in a year after four quarters of low sales and not able to get anywhere near the two hundred fifty million Torii has offered."

"Oh, yeah," came Yancey's disembodied voice traveling from Southern France to us through the Polycom. "Margot, we haven't told you the best part of the deal. With it comes a purchase order from Swiss Telecom for twenty million euros."

"But I've told Ricky that we were going to take his offer," Margot said.

"That was premature, Margot," Smithwick said.

"I beg your pardon?" She was a partner in the Valley's third largest VC fund. She wasn't used to being reprimanded.

"You shouldn't have told him that," Smithwick said again. Margot was not going to deliver the company neatly wrapped up in Christmas paper and bows to Frankson.

Margot put her palms on the table and raised herself. "This all sounds too good to be true," she said.

"Margot, with the purchase order as part of the deal, the FBS offer is hard to say no to," Tim Yee said. It was one thing to follow Margot's lead, as Yee had always done before. It was another to follow her off a cliff. Without Yee, Margot stood alone.

Even as she was plummeting like the coyote in a roadrunner cartoon, she did not give up. "Perhaps we should give Ricky a chance to make a better offer?" she said.

"Let's do that right now," I said.

"I've got to go." The taut skin of Margot's face never revealed much. As she left this time, it looked like a waxen death mask.

"So let's call Torii and see what they'll do?" Smithwick said.

"They'll do? You mean, he'll do?" I said.

"Yeah. I've done a lot of deals with Ricky. He says he doesn't do bidding wars."

"We still have to call."

"Yeah, we do. Have to fulfill our duty to do best by the shareholders."

"Before you call, do you have any insights into why they're having Ian vote their stock?" Yee asked.

"Not beyond what they're saying. That they want to be a passive investor."

My iPhone rang. A blocked number. Could be news of Rowena. "Gotta take it."

I pushed the connect button. "Hello?"

"You have another offer?"

"Hello, Ricky. It does look that way." I put the phone into speaker mode so the other directors could listen in.

"They're paying too much," Frankson said. "The company's not worth it."

"A company is worth what someone will pay for it," I responded.

"In the end you'll be working for me."

"I must be one of the few in the networking world who's never had the pleasure. I'll look forward to it someday. But unless you're going to raise your offer by two-x, it's not this time."

"We'll see." He hung up. The man just didn't believe in those niceties of phone etiquette that included saying "Hello" and "Goodbye."

"Margot didn't waste any time reporting in to him," Smithwick said.

FIFTY-ONE

I DIDN'T REALLY TRUST my powers of observation, but, when I got back to the ICU, Rowena did look better. Before she left for a nap, Caroline told me Dr. Griffith had said Rowena was "on track." The pressure inside her skull had eased to 25 millimeters.

I held on to my wife's hand. They say one never knows how important something is until one loses it. In this case, *almost* losing something would be close enough. I fantasized that she could hear when I told her how much I loved her. It wasn't that I *couldn't* live if she died. I *could*, but I saw a lot fewer reasons to. The main one would be to help send the person who'd put her in this bed on the road to hell. Oh yeah, and do right by Aunt Isobel.

Six hours I sat there. When Caroline came back for her turn, she was fresh-scrubbed and fed. She didn't smile, but neither did her lips turn downward into the familiar worried frown. We'd both started to be infected by the virus of hope. Goddammit.

———

I was half-conscious in our bed at home and extended an arm to search for Rowena. Then I awakened the rest of the way. I felt the shock of her absence again, each time as bad as the first. No way was I going to be able to get back to sleep. The green numerals of the clock radio told me it was two minutes to three in the morning.

Padding downstairs to my office, which was on the other side of the house by the garage, I didn't even turn on the lights. I sat down in front of my home computer and began to log into email. I changed my mind and went to Picasa's online site where digital albums of photos from Rowena's and my wedding awaited viewing. I just stared at her in one of the posed shots. Who knows what the photographer had said to her, but she had her head tossed back and was laughing, mouth open, teeth white. Pure joy. God, I had been so lucky. It made the fall from happiness so much more painful. "'Tis better to have loved and lost than never to have loved at all?" I wondered if the Victorians really bought into Tennyson's romantic bullshit.

The beginning of a chime of the doorbell awakened me from the reverie. If the sound from the chime continued, I did not hear it.

Instead, my head was concussed by compressed air. My hands flew to my ears for protection against an exploding sonic boom. The chair I sat on was blown against the opposite wall. As though from miles away, I heard a rumbling and then the heehawing siren of the house's fire alarms. Oh, I needed to turn off the alarm or the security service would call the fire department, which charged two hundred dollars for a false alarm. Wait. What am I thinking? This one was real. I wanted them to come.

I got up, only to fall over. Damn leg. The explosion had done something to my balance as well. Using a bookshelf, I hauled myself up again. I was breathing fast—hyperventilating maybe—but after thirty seconds, I could stand up without support.

Dragging my right leg, I went out to the hallway. I don't know why I'd closed the door between the corridor leading to the back of the house and the foyer. Habit, I guess. God's hand maybe. The solid door had been blown off its hinges and I saw flames through the opening. And through the flames I saw the foyer filled with the oak floor, bed, dressers, and bookshelves from our bedroom. The front of the house had collapsed.

I went into the garage and pulled open an overhead door by hand. My iPhone was in the pocket of the running shorts I had on. 911. I reported the explosion.

"You're shouting," said the dispatcher. Was I? I was just trying to be heard over the sound of pulsating waves crashing in my head.

I lived a mile from the fire station, and the truck was already on its way. By the time I rang off, I heard the siren. Boy, the neighbors were going to hate me.

911 again. I got the police dispatcher. "Send Sergeant Susan Fletcher now. Tell her Ian Michaels was almost blown up."

I was leaning against a maple tree in front of the house when the fire truck got there. My closest neighbor, the former Giants relief pitcher with the shot rotator cuff, was trotting across his lawn toward me, too.

"What the hell happened?" a firefighter asked.

"Explosion," I told him.

"Sounds like natural gas."

They put a searchlight on the façade of my house, or rather what *had* been the façade. The house looked like an oversized dollhouse with the front cut away. Flames were coming up from the basement. One of the firefighters in the street was turning the gas off with a long wrench. Thirty seconds after the last rotation, the flames subsided. By that time a hose was attached to the hydrant and hundreds of gallons of water arced into the house.

The neighbor had been joined by his three pajama-clad boys aged four to eight. This was a show they would not forget.

"It's cold out," my neighbor said. "We'll get you something to wear."

I looked down. I was bare-chested, wearing only the pair of running shorts I slept in. I could see a white cloud form just in front of my face as I breathed, but I wasn't cold. A cottony barrier still separated me from external stimuli. Even the neighbor's generous suggestion seemed to be coming from another dimension.

"Yeah, thanks."

Next to join the party was Mikulski, who drove up in a yellow Corvette that I doubted was police-issue.

He greeted me with his customary friendliness. "You attract trouble like dogshit attracts flies," he said.

"Thanks, officer. Fletcher coming too?"

"Yeah."

Soon, I hoped, as I watched the growing swarm of neighbors buzzing about.

The eight-year-old from next door came out bearing an armload of clothes. First I pulled on a New Zealand All-Blacks rugby shirt. The sleeves were the right length, but Rowena and I could have both fit inside. The pants fit, but the boat moccasins were at least two sizes bigger than my elevens. I pulled on a red and yellow sweatshirt over the whole thing.

I looked down. "I'm not as big as your dad. Wearing this USC sweatshirt could make me a target for trouble around here."

"Trojans rule" was his reply.

Did God work in strange ways? Were we always too close to see the big picture? Was what looked like bad luck good fortune? Rowena was safer in the hospital than at home. If we'd both been sleeping in our bed, we'd be dead. If I'd taken night duty at the hospital and Caroline had been in the guestroom, she'd be dead.

Fletcher drove up in a black and white. A red car with "Chief" written on its side rolled up just behind her.

I walked out to greet them.

Fletcher grabbed my forearm. Her expression flashed first shock, then relief, then concern. I think she would have hugged me if Mikulski wasn't looking on.

"God, Ian. What is going on?"

"I was at my computer and kablooie!" I threw my arms upward and then teetered a second till I regained my balance.

"This is Chief Herrera," Fletcher said.

He nodded. "No warning before the explosion?"

"Y'know, I heard the doorbell begin to ring."

"Maybe a spark from the doorbell set off gas that was leaking in your basement."

"But you would need someone to push the doorbell to get the spark, wouldn't you?"

"Yeah, you would. Can you think of who might be calling on you this late?"

"If it wasn't the police, no clue." Mikulski and Fletcher shook their heads. "So … maybe not an accident?"

"We'll bring in the forensic guys, the arsonist squad, and see what we can find out," he said.

I turned to Fletcher and Mikulski. "In the meantime, can we take a ride? I've got an idea who could be behind this. Let's make a house call."

FIFTY-TWO

I CLIMBED INTO THE back seat of Fletcher's car. Sitting and watching my house suffer through the twin curses of death by fire and death by water wouldn't do much good. My life seemed to be a hot air balloon ready to float away. The tethers that bound me to my current existence were being sawed through, one by one. Rowena. Our home. My job.

Mikulski turned around to face me from the passenger's seat. "You're not going to say Edwards is behind this, are you?"

The words penetrated to my brain, but a quick quip wasn't forthcoming. Before I could formulate an answer, Fletcher spoke from behind the wheel. "No, he's not."

"And why not?" I asked.

"Because Edwards is on a plane back to Thailand," she said. "I watched him get on."

"Ah, so the Brainiac finally believes that Nolan and Edwards had nothing to do with things?" Mikulski asked.

"I guess not. I guess someone is targeting *me*," I said. "And doing a pretty good job of it. My bedroom is gone."

"Why weren't you in bed?" Mikulski asked.

"Couldn't sleep."

"You are a lucky bastard."

So long as Rowena lay unconscious in Stanford Hospital, I was not ready to count my blessings. I explained to the two officers what I had in mind.

"I hope you're right about this," Fletcher said. She'd figured out where I wanted to go and why far faster than her partner. She wore a pink ski parka over orange polyester pants. Maybe she didn't have fashion sense, but a sharp mind she did. She turned the key in the ignition.

Some sort of professional courtesy dictated having a local police officer along on the call we were making. The Town of Woodside contracted with San Mateo County to provide police services, so Fletcher radioed ahead, and we swung by a county sheriff's substation. When we arrived at the little building, a deputy sauntered over.

"Could you wait? Sheriff himself wants to come along. He'll be here in ten minutes. Do you want some coffee?"

Mikulski turned around and looked at me. "People are losing sleep over you, that's for sure."

"Hush up, John," Fletcher told him.

We went inside. No coffee drinker, I still accepted a foam cup filled with a muddy brown concoction. Maybe the caffeine would help stimulate my stunned synapses.

The county sheriff shambled in only five minutes later. He was a big guy, six-four, give or take an inch, with thinning brown hair and a concrete sack of a gut that protruded over his belt.

"Now why do you want to go bothering Mr. Frankson at four in the morning?"

As the senior of the Palo Alto Police duo, Fletcher answered. "He has been trying to buy Mr. Michaels' company."

"So what? He buys companies like my wife buys shoes," the sheriff said. I guessed he was being a little sexist to see if he could get Fletcher's goat. He couldn't.

"Another company has made a better bid for Mr. Michaels' company. Mr. Michaels here told us that Frankson said the deal wouldn't close."

The sheriff took a look at me. "A USC man, huh? I went to Berkeley."

"My neighbor's the Trojan. He loaned me the clothes."

Looking relieved, the sheriff asked, "You think Mr. Frankson would kill you to get hold of your company?"

"Finding out is worth waking him up," I said.

"How much did he offer?"

"Why is that relevant?" I asked.

"Answer him, Ian," Fletcher said.

"Two hundred fifty million."

"That's not much to someone with all his money," the sheriff said.

"Does he spread some of his wealth around in political contributions?" I asked.

"Ian," Fletcher said.

"What? Someone tried to blow me up tonight. My wife is in a coma. I don't have time to give a shit about disturbing Mr. Frankson."

"Someone tried to run down Mr. Michaels and his wife last Friday," Fletcher explained.

"Just a minute," the sheriff said as he hoisted up his two-hundred-fifty pounds and walked away from the table.

"We should not have brought him along," Mikulski said, nodding his head toward me and not giving a damn that I could hear.

"Four years ago he did okay in figuring out who killed his wife's sister," Fletcher told him. She turned to me. "Could you possibly make things a little easier for us here?"

I crossed my arms and said nothing.

Then the sheriff was back. "Let's go. You follow me."

We got up.

"You didn't call Frankson and warn him we're coming?" I asked.

The sheriff looked down at me. "No. I got hold of your chief of police and asked her what kind of officers she has running around."

"You woke her up?" Mikulski asked. "Oh, God."

Ten minutes later we were back at the gate guarding the driveway to Frankson's seven acres.

The sheriff in the lead car pushed the intercom. We couldn't hear what he said, but the gates started to swing open.

We made the long drive up to the horseshoe driveway just as I had on Monday.

There at the front door to greet us was the great Ricky himself, barefoot, clad again in a white *keiko gi*. As we approached, he gave us a bow as if ready to start a martial arts match.

"Sheriff," he said by way of greeting.

"Mr. Frankson," the sheriff responded. They knew each other.

"Please come in."

We settled in the living room. The Japanese woman who had let me in on my last visit brought out coffee and tea. Even with the choice, I opted for coffee as the richer source of caffeine. Fletcher flashed me a surprised look. As did Frankson.

"Mr. Frankson," the sheriff began, "we are sorry to disturb you." Looking at Frankson, clean-shaven, hair combed, I didn't believe he'd just awakened.

"Mr. Frankson, there was an explosion at Mr. Michaels' house this morning," Fletcher said.

Frankson turned his head to me. "Nobody hurt, I trust."

"No," I answered.

"And you think I might know something about this incident?" His tone was conversational, even amiable, as though he were discussing the appropriate wine to order with dinner.

"No, we don't. But we need to eliminate the possibility, no matter how small," Fletcher said.

"And my motive would be to get my hands on Mr. Michaels' piss-ant company?"

Fletcher ignored the question. "May we talk to other members of the household?"

"You wish me to have them awakened?"

"Yes, please."

Frankson went to the archway and called over the woman who'd brought us the hot drinks. He spoke to her in Japanese.

While he was occupied, I leaned over and whispered in Fletcher's ear.

"My wife's away, so there are four people in the house besides Haruka and me," Frankson said. "She is getting them for us."

"While they are gathering," Fletcher asked, "may we look at your garage?"

"Certainly."

The five of us went through a hallway embroidered with centuries-old Japanese woodblock prints and thence to a kitchen featuring a pair of stainless steel Brobdingnagian ranges all ready to roast a yoke of oxen. From there a door led to the garage.

Frankson flicked a switch and sodium vapor lamps whooshed on. The garage was bigger than my last house. Eight vehicles were parked, three each in the first two rows and two with a space between them in the third. I looked at Fletcher. She'd seen the black BMW M6.

"Very nice," Mikulski said and began to look at each car like a star-struck teenager. In addition to the BMW, Frankson's fleet included a Ferrari, twin Range Rovers, a Mercedes SLR convertible and S65 sedan, a pre-war Lincoln Continental, and a cherry 1957 Chevy in front of which Mikulski had parked himself.

I went over to the BMW and felt the hood. Cool to the touch. I checked the right fender. Factory smooth. Looking at Fletcher, I shook my head. She moved around the garage, laying hands on a couple of million dollars worth of automotive engineering.

"Don't you have a blue Bentley, too?" I asked Frankson.

"At the dealer for service," he said.

"Which dealer?" the sheriff asked.

Frankson told him. He smiled as if daring anyone to check on his veracity. The sheriff responded to the smile with one of his own.

The rest of the time we were at the house Fletcher and Mikulski questioned the household staff one-by-one. The sheriff and I listened. The bodyguard I'd seen with Frankson before told them he'd been awake in the control room where he watched video screens of the perimeter of the property. Nobody had been in or out of the property—other than us—since ten when Mr. Frankson and his driver had returned from the office.

When he showed us out, Frankson expressed his willingness to help in any way.

"We apologize for bothering you at this time of night," the sheriff told him.

"I understand," Frankson said to the sheriff. Then he looked at me. "Satisfied?"

FIFTY-THREE

"Could you drop me off at Stanford Hospital?" I asked as we followed the San Mateo County Sheriff down Frankson's driveway.

"Are we screwed? Is the chief going to come down on us?" Mikulski asked Fletcher.

"We did the right thing," Fletcher said. "If we're going to get in trouble, we'd just better take our licks like men."

"So what am I, a girly-man?" Mikulski asked. I don't think this aging surfer god cared for his five-foot-two kewpie doll of a partner taking a shot at his manhood.

Someone had just tried to kill me. I was aggravated and frustrated, ready to lash out at someone. Why not at the target on hand?

"Women stay out of jail, read more, and have higher SAT scores," I pointed out to Mikulski. "Maybe being a girly-man would be a step up."

Mikulski turned around. "Shut the fuck up," he said. Then he turned back to Fletcher. "Frankson's all alibi-ed up, isn't he?" he asked her.

I knew he wasn't talking to me this time either, but I answered anyway. Baiting Mikulski helped the time pass. "He is. Not that it matters much. I'm sure he could arrange for an accidental explosion to occur while he was in Timbuktu."

Mikulski turned around in his seat again and asked, "You think he did?"

Fletcher had pulled on to 280 now. That meant she *was* going to drop me off at the hospital.

"Some Frenchman wrote that behind every great fortune rests a crime," I said.

"Balzac," Fletcher said.

The woman continued to surprise me.

"I don't know what crime Frankson committed," I said. "Probably a lot more than one, but I just don't think we proved anything up there. Here's what's in his favor. If he wanted to blow me up, he'd do a better job. Same for the attempt while we were jogging. If he really wanted me dead, he would not have missed once, let alone twice."

"A Silicon Valley muckety-muck would kill over a business deal?" Mikulski asked.

I thought about Daisy Nolan. "It's not the business deal that's the motive. It's ambition, money, sex, greed. Plenty of *them* in the Valley."

"We need to keep looking," Fletcher said, eyes on the road.

"Yeah. I mean, I wouldn't give up on Frankson altogether, but I think he's a longshot," I said.

"And Edwards is out of the picture, too," she said.

"I guess we could construct some scenario where he couldn't get to Rowena any more so he came after me, but yeah, that's an even longer shot."

"We have some work to do," said Fletcher. "And I'll bet the Palo Alto Police are going to be on our own. Rowena's on the law enforcement team. If she's the target, we get help from the D.A.'s investigators and the San Jose police." She looked at me over her shoulder. "You, you're just a civilian."

"Right, and my wife is just collateral damage."

"Calm down, Ian. Listen, I'm saying it again. Don't go gallivanting around on your own."

"Because I'll mess up the investigation or because I need protection?"

"Yes," Fletcher said.

"I appreciate your concern, but I'll manage." The car pulled in front of the concrete facade with geometric cut-outs at the entrance to the hospital. I swung the door open. "Thanks for the buggy ride."

———

Still dressed like a USC sophomore, I sat at the head of the board table at Accelenet. At the hospital, to my hopeful eyes, it had appeared Rowena was continuing to improve, not by leaps and bounds but by twinges and twitches.

Just as gray pinstripes and power tie had been *de rigueur* for my father a generation ago, a button-down shirt and khakis were my everyday uniform. So my attire was bound to engender comment. And it did.

"You know how dangerous it is to wear USC clothing around here? It's like Bloods and Crips," Leon said.

"Oh, yeah, those Stanford undergrads are vicious," Smithwick said. "Maybe they'll teach the Trojans a lesson in an Ultimate Frisbee game."

Leon Henderson, Bryce Smithwick, Margot Fulbright, and I were present in the flesh. Darwin Yancey and Tim Lee were on the conference bridge.

"Bryce," came Yancey's voice. "Is there any reason not to sign the FBS offer?"

"The actual signatory is the Locarno Group, but the terms seem acceptable. I've spoken to Oxydrive and Singex where they have investments. They are completely passive."

"I've said it before and I'm saying it again. Watch out when something is too good to be true," Margot said. "I want to make sure we keep on good terms with Torii in case this falls through."

"That's going to be hard to do, Margot," I said. "Somehow Ricky knew all about the offer from FBS."

"You've spoken to him?" she asked.

"Last time only six hours ago."

"At four in the morning?"

"Why not? We were both awake."

"What were you doing up?" Margot asked.

"We had a gas leak at the house," I said. "You heard anything about that, Margot?" I paused to watch her open her hands in all innocence and then continued. "Can I have a motion on the offer from Locarno?"

Margot sat on her hands, but everyone else, even her acolyte Tim Lee, voted in favor of the deal.

Juliana brought in the term sheet, and Leon and Smithwick watched me sign it.

Darwin Yancey called out from the speakerphone. "This is going to be a great company, a great *independent* company. Terrific job, Ian."

"The money's not in the bank yet," I said. "Locarno still gets to do their due diligence. So do we."

Margot said, "You are one lucky SOB, Ian. This came from no-where."

The day was only ten-and-a-half hours old and I'd been deemed a lucky man of questionable parentage twice already. I just didn't feel that way. There were more important things than Accelenet.

FIFTY-FOUR

IN THE PELLUCID AIR of a crisp Palo Alto day, my house looked as though it belonged in a border town in Israel, target of a Hamas rocket.

"My God, Ian," Juliana said. "A problem with your natural gas line?" She'd offered to ferry me home.

"I'll be fine."

I showed my driver's license to the police officer who sat in his cruiser in front of the house.

"Are you protecting the crime scene or keeping looters out?" I asked him.

"I'm here because the lieutenant sent me here."

"Tanner?"

The officer's eyes widened. "Yeah."

"We were in high school together. Tell him I said hey."

Three men in overalls were sifting and digging like archeologists through the ruins.

"Fire investigators?" I asked.

"Yeah, from the county," the police officer said. We walked up the driveway to the back of the house where I hoisted open the garage door by hand. Before I could get to the car, the officer said, "Stop."

He called over one of the investigators. After a quick conversation, the two popped open the hood of my car. After pointing his flashlight around the engine block and tugging on wires and cables, the investigator slid under the car with a flashlight.

Five minutes later, satisfied that the Acura was not booby-trapped, I was behind the steering wheel. With a second's hesitation, I turned the ignition key. Still alive. No explosion. I was set now. I always carried a change of clothes and a toiletries bag in the trunk in case of an unexpected business trip.

I waved at the two men and drove away. Not far, though. I stopped a block away on Island Drive and just sat in the car. It took me ten or fifteen minutes to decide on what to do next. Then I took out my iPhone and called the Stanford operator. She switched me to the physics department admin, who in turn transferred me to Professor Roux.

"Ah, Mr. Michaels. So nice to hear from you." Of course, she had the good telephone manners of a Frenchwoman. "I just have a moment."

"Fine and I just have a very quick question, Professor."

"*D'accord.*"

"When we spoke last, you said it took the Nobel committee a long time to award the prize because it wasn't clear who should get it."

"Yes, that is what I heard."

"Why not just give it to everyone?"

"Oh, because a Nobel Prize cannot be split among more than three people."

"I see."

When I'd tried to figure out who killed Rowena's sister, I'd settled on the answer not through brilliant insight, but through the process of elimination. Sherlock Holmes had advised that when you eliminate the impossible, whatever's left, no matter how improbable, has to be the answer. And his track record was pretty good.

I headed over to Stanford. Dr. Griffith had told Caroline and me that Rowena could awaken anytime in the next two days. I wanted to be there when she did. Still, I had to make this stop. Maybe the karma would help wake her up.

There were no open metered spaces so I parked under a sign that warned a C sticker was required. Professor Leon Henderson was wrong. My USC sweatshirt didn't even merit a glance from passing students, let alone incite mayhem. I climbed up the stairs to the second floor of the Varian Building. Tompkins was not in. As I started to walk away from his office, a bespectacled man in his mid-twenties said in a Swedish accent, "He just went to lunch."

"You know where?"

"He usually eats at the Faculty Club."

"Thanks."

I cut through the Quad and White Plaza, dodging heedless cyclists the whole way. When I ate with Leon, we usually ate at Tresidder Union with its motley mixture of students and staff. I opened the front door of the Faculty Club and headed down the stairs.

"May I help you?" asked the man at the door to the dining room.

"I'm looking for Professor Tompkins."

"He's already seated at his usual table."

I walked in and surveyed the academic elite eating under a high planked ceiling spotted with round wrought-iron chandeliers. A picture window looked out onto a courtyard garden. All five dozen or so numbered tables were occupied. And there, at Table #11, Tompkins was sticking his fork into a tomato slice on his salad plate.

He kept talking to his luncheon companion about experiments at the Large Hadron Collider, even as I stood next to them like a waiter about to take an order.

It was the companion who looked up at me. Then Tompkins followed suit and blinked.

"Mr. Michaels. Surely, not again?"

Without standing up, he introduced me to Professor Constable from Imperial College.

"Professor Constable, would you excuse us? I have an urgent personal matter for Professor Tompkins."

"Of course," the Englishman said with far more polish than I would have shown in his place.

"No, no, Cecil. Sit down."

"Bill, I need to call home and say goodnight to the children. It's just the right time. I'll let you take care of your business and be back in ten." Off he went.

I eased myself into the still-warm chair across the table from Tompkins, this time his mismatched ensemble included a mustard jacket, paisley tie, and multi-colored striped shirt.

"This goes too far," he said. "This is unacceptable."

"Murder is unacceptable. This is merely rude."

"Murder?"

"Why did it take the prize committee thirteen years to award the Nobel for quarks? It's one of the two or three greatest physics discoveries of the last century."

"Well, thank you. A dozen of us worked on the experiment and…"

"I have heard you paid for everyone to go to the ceremony."

"Yes."

"Guilt money?"

"What are you talking about?"

"You are a competitive fellow, wouldn't you say?"

"Yes, and I think my competitive nature has served me pretty well. Served physics pretty well, too."

"And who was your foremost competitor, your nemesis even, in figuring out what neutrons and protons were made out of?"

"I figured it out. I put together the model."

"But who came up with the idea of quarks in the first place?"

"I…" He looked at me and stopped. "Well, Izzy and I…"

"In life she preferred to be called Isobel. Do her memory the courtesy of calling her that, would you please?"

"The ideas flew back and forth between us, between… between Isobel and me."

"I'm not sure the ideas were traveling roundtrip. More like one-way. You stole the concept for your model from her notebook."

"Did you ever check with your wife on the laws of defamation?"

"No."

"I recommend you do." He hesitated. "How could I have stolen it, anyway?"

"Solenski showed the notebook to you. It gave you the whole idea for your model."

"The common man's idea of a physics discovery is Isaac Newton watching an apple fall and, poof, in a flash of inspiration, he intuits gravity. That's not how it works. You have theories, you try them out, you run them by colleagues, they make suggestions."

"Right. That's how you worked with Vansittart. But not Isobel Marter. While she was alive, you kept trying to shut her out. Steal credit from her. Even after she died. In your book you called her an assistant to Solenski. That's bullshit. She was the brains of the outfit. Vansittart knew it. And so did you."

"That's not how it was."

"You even made sure that the experiments proving the existence of quarks happened when she was on vacation. You told her that you were doing something else and accidentally stumbled into a proof of quarks. Bullshit again. The sketch of hers told you what to look for. You are a thief."

"A thief? Let me tell you the way things worked. We fired the electron beams and whatever happened, happened. Why wait?"

"Because the person who conceptualized the experiment wasn't there?"

"She never minded. She ended up being part of the biggest breakthrough in particle physics since Rutherford discovered the nucleus."

"You've done what they did in the old Soviet Union. When someone fell from power, they just airbrushed him out of the photo of the Politburo."

He pretended to laugh. "I'm a communist now?"

"Isobel died not knowing you'd seen that drawing, didn't she?"

"Solenski must have told her."

"He did not. Why didn't you?"

"You just don't know what kind of person she was. Arrogant, abrasive."

"Oh, so you Photoshopped her out of the picture because of her personality? No credit for scientists you don't like? Is that why you killed her, so that someone you disliked wouldn't win a Nobel Prize?"

"Keep your voice down. What are you talking about?"

"You knew no more than three people could share a Nobel. If she was gone, you knew for sure you'd be one of the lucky trio."

"I was always going to win. That was my model. Who do you think came up with the whole idea of six types of quarks?"

"Would Isobel have shared the prize if she'd lived?"

"Why are you asking me?" I just stared at him until he lowered his eyes and focused them on his bowl of lobster bisque. He looked back. "Yes, I suppose so."

"You ran her down in Geneva to make sure you would get your Nobel Prize?"

"I wasn't even at the conference where she died."

I threw the paper from the Physics Library on the table. He looked down and then back up at me. First, he moved his knit brown tie to the side and then pulled out his tattersall checked shirt out of his trousers. He even pulled down a pair of striped boxers an inch or two. "Look," he said. "What do you see?"

What I saw was the hairless skin of a laboratory rat. Then he pointed with his finger.

There against the pink I could see a three-inch white streak. "A scar," I said.

"From an appendectomy. I never went to Geneva. On the day I was supposed to deliver this paper, I was recovering in the hospital. I am sure records of my operation still exist somewhere."

A woman with thinning white hair at a neighboring table stared as he tucked his shirt back in.

"You weren't in Geneva. You never gave the paper?"

"No. Solenski was going anyway, so he gave the paper in my place."

"God."

I knocked into the table as I leapt to my feet. Leaving behind a Nobel laureate dabbing up soup stains off his jacket, I ran as best I could with my bad leg through an obstacle course of tables and waiters. In front of the club, I galloped by Constable who was cooing to his bed-bound children.

"He's all yours now," I called over my shoulder.

The English academic looked back at me as if I were crazy—an analysis not far from the mark.

FIFTY-FIVE

THE JOHN IRVING SCHOLAR at the gatehouse had moved on to *Until I Find You*. I slowed and waved. He came out, and I said hello.

"You ever read any Irving?" he asked.

"Yes, when I was back in school." Lunchtime traffic between the campus and SLAC had been horrendous because of an accident between a van and a Town Car. I'd passed a man in a white painter's cap and overalls standing on the road yelling at a driver in a chauffeur's black cap and jacket. Two-and-a half miles in half an hour. I had no time for a literary chat and started to roll up the window.

"He's something, isn't he? Looks at the world from an unusual perspective."

I took my finger off the window switch. "I'm a bit late. I think I've still got copies of Irving around. I'll take a look, and we can discuss him next time I visit."

He got the message. "Shall I call ahead for you?"

"No, thank you."

He nodded and put his head back into the book. Being a regular at SLAC paid off. I wanted no call ahead on this visit.

I parked in the closest space to Solenski's office and hoped that no handicapped person would have to walk farther because I'd taken one outlined in blue. He was on the second floor of the Central Lab Annex and the only stairs up there zigzagged on the outside of the building. Physicists were peering through the doorways to see who would move down the hallway at a pace faster than a stroll. The days of modern-day Archimedes running through the street shouting "Eureka" were long gone at SLAC.

Solenski's office was empty. Damn.

Moving in a gimpy jog, I cut diagonally across a parking lot to the cafeteria. Not there either.

Over a thousand people worked on the campus. I didn't have the time to search each office, conference room, and lab.

"Excuse me. Excuse me." I was shouting from the entrance to the dining hall. The heads of those at the tables nearest to me turned. Then like a card trick in a football stadium, the rest rippled after them.

"I need to find Professor Solenski. Do any of you know where he went?"

A guy in his late fifties called out from a table where he sat with two colleagues. "We were eating with him when he got a call on his cell."

"How long ago?"

"About forty-five minutes. He said Professor Tompkins was reminding him to check on the set-up for an experiment in the linac."

I moved over to the table and saw that a fourth tray sat there with an untouched burger and fries. "Where?"

"Well, he'd probably be in End Station A. That's the building on the right at the end of the linear accelerator where the detection equipment is."

"Got it. Thanks."

"Anything I can do?"

"No, I just came from Professor Tompkins myself. I need a word with Professor Solenski."

From the cafeteria, I ran toward End Station A, cursing my right leg. I used my iPhone to call Fletcher. Fifty yards ahead, I spotted a shack with a security guard between me and where I wanted to go. If I stopped, the guard would need to call her manager, who'd have to call security who'd need to check with the director. No time for bureaucracy. Fuck my broken fibula.

I headed up a hillside and skirted around the shack. Through a window, I could see the back of the guard's head and the Starbucks cup in her upraised hand. I slipped on a patch of damp grass and a few pebbles trickled down to the road, but the guard didn't even look up from the computer game she was playing. Thanks to government budget cuts, End Station A was scarcely used anymore, and the guard was not exactly on high alert.

I skidded down the slope on my butt. Déjà vu. Like going down to get Rowena last week. At the bottom this time loomed End Station A, a concrete hangar badly in need of a paint job.

Then I saw that the façade stretching before me consisted of two sliding doors over thirty feet high. I grabbed a handle and heaved with all my strength, which fell far short of what was needed to move tons of concrete. Sidling along the front of the building, I came to an open doorway and slipped into a small vestibule.

After ten minutes in the bright February sun, I couldn't see anything for the first few seconds. Then I saw a screen with the words "No Access" lit in amber. I blinked and saw the other choices, "Controlled Access" and "Open Access."

I rattled the metal door.

A voice boomed from a loudspeaker. "This is the operating room. The linac is in operation in End Station A. There is no access. Please move back."

I looked up and spotted a small video camera.

"There is someone in there," I yelled.

"The linear accelerator is operational," the voice boomed. "We did a search sweep before turning it on. There can be no one in there."

"Professor Solenski is." I rattled the door again. "What happens if I open this door?"

"Do not do that, sir. The linac will automatically crash the variable voltage substations."

"He's in there. I know it."

I turned the handle on the door and kicked it open with my good leg.

FIFTY-SIX

EVEN OVER THE CLANGING alarm bells, I could hear the dying sigh of electric motors powering down. Once inside, my nostrils filled with the clean smell of a Midwestern farm after a thunderstorm. Ozone. The giant hangar was stuffed with wooden crates. The site of Isobel Marter's astonishing discovery was being used as a storage room.

There, there at the far right corner of the room sat Solenski on the top rung of a ladder. As I trotted over to him, the alarms went silent. He had used orange duct tape to bind himself to his perch three feet from the open end of a long gray metal tube. He'd wrapped more tape around his belly to secure a metal plate about two inches thick. Whatever had been shooting out of the tube was hitting the plate square on.

"You again," Solenski whispered. "The avenging angel. Thirty seconds more would have been enough."

"Enough for what?"

"To die." He moaned.

I climbed up the rungs of the ladder. "What are you doing?"

"I want to die here, where it all started." Where the experiment Isobel Marter designed proved the existence of quarks, where the very stuff of existence was shown to be far more complex and elegant than even Einstein imagined.

The dosimeter clipped to his shirt had turned black. "You're radioactive?" I asked.

"Not so much. Some trace elements in my body, copper maybe, might have picked something up. That's not what will kill me. I'm not dangerous."

Like hell he wasn't. "What is the plate for? To protect you from the beam?"

"No."

"Then what?"

He put his hand over the plate and closed his eyes. "This piece of lead splashes the beam all over my insides. Without it, the beam would pass right through me. I hope enough damage was done before the beam went off. I am ready to die. I'm an old man."

I got it. What he'd done turned the linear accelerator into a giant microwave and used it to cook his own innards. Once his internal temperature reached a hundred seven degrees or so, it would all be over.

I put my foot on the ladder's first rung.

"You killed Isobel Marter." It wasn't even a question—just a statement of fact. No answer. "You killed Isobel Marter to make sure you would be one of the three who won the Nobel Prize."

I climbed to the fourth rung to make certain I heard any reply, stopping only a foot from Solenski's face. "Was it worth it?"

"Yes. For thirty years I've lived as a Nobel laureate. I'm going to die as one, too. Yes."

"Even if you didn't deserve it?"

"But I *did* deserve it. What an idiotic rule to say that only three can win the prize. Without the detectors I set up, they wouldn't have found the quarks."

When Solenski rolled his eyes upward and paused to catch his breath, I leaned even closer, to within six inches of his face. That blood lust I'd felt during Daisy Nolan's outburst and again when I questioned Edwards began to rise in my chest. My hands began to float upward toward his throat. Wait. I jerked my hands back down. I had more questions. And choking him would be too quick a death. I needed him to *suffer*.

Solenksi looked back at me and started up again. "Every machine that smashes particles together uses the techniques I came up with. But Tompkins said I was just a technician with no imagination." His voice was faint, but bitter. He wasn't delirious yet.

"Why not kill Tompkins, then? Why Isobel?"

"She was in Geneva. He wasn't. I was in the car on the way to breakfast and saw her jogging. The wheel turned itself."

"The wheel turned itself?"

"I am sorry she died. I liked her. But it was necessary."

"Isobel Marter wrote in her diary that you did invaluable work no one else in the world could have done."

"She said that?"

"Did you know she was dying from cancer? You killed her for nothing."

"Oh, God. Oh."

I didn't know whether he was moaning with regret or pain. Or whether they were one and the same.

"Tompkins is right about one thing. It *did* show a lack of imagination to try to kill me the same way you killed Isobel."

"I couldn't let them take the Nobel away from me. I'd lived with that Nobel for so long … I always knew someone would come for me."

"My wife is lying in the hospital in a coma."

"I didn't mean to hurt her."

"Just me?" Somehow that was better.

"I'm going to die a Nobel Prize winner."

"And you *are* a technician, aren't you? Isobel said you could put together anything. So you rigged my house to blow up and made it look like an accident, like a gas explosion. If I'd been in my bed, no one would have known what you did."

He writhed. Red blotches were emerging on his forehead like stigmata. His jerry-built death ray demonstrated his technical acumen one last time. "Oh, forgive me."

Forgive him? His agony moved me little. Mild-mannered, charmingly accented, technically ingenious, he was a living exemplar of the banality of evil. His words of regret meant nothing. He'd shown he would kill anyone who stood in his way.

"I'm the wrong person to ask for mercy," I said.

Looking again at his throat, my fingers twitched.

"Ian?" came the voice from behind me.

I whirled. With the sun behind her, I saw only a silhouette.

"Is that you, Susan?"

"With Deputy Tran of the Stanford sheriff's patrol."

"Okay. Over in the corner is the person you're looking for. But don't get close to him. He could be dangerous."

Fletcher drew her gun. "Get out of the way."

"No, no. Not dangerous that way. Just a little radioactive maybe."

"He's the one who ran you down?" she asked.

"And the one who murdered Professor Isobel Marter."

"Who? What professor? What are you talking about?"

A whimper came from the far corner. Inside Solenski's body, the flames of hell were burning—as well they should have been.

FIFTY-SEVEN

I SPENT TWO MORE hours at SLAC. First, a hazardous waste team came and waved wands over me as though they were wizards. According to their high-tech Geiger counters, I was fine. Solenski died on the way to Stanford Hospital. He became the first casualty in the forty-plus years that the linear accelerator had been shooting out powerful beams of electrons at near the speed of light.

SLAC's head of security looked around and shook his head. "It's impossible for the beam to be on with someone in the room. You need a key to get in and if one is missing from the rack, the beam won't go on. We do a physical search of the room, too." Then he looked at me. "And if someone crashes through the door, the beam is shut down."

I pointed upward. Far above was a small open door.

"What is that? Who could know about that way in?"

"What are those pipes for?" I asked.

"They're what's left of the original detector."

"Which Solenski designed. Of course, he'd know about any door," I said.

"He climbed down those pipes?" the security head asked. "At his age? Must have been half mountain goat."

When I made a move toward my car, Fletcher took me by the arm. "You don't mind cluing us in on what's been going on, do you, Ian?"

Only ten feet from my Acura, I was tempted to bolt and make for a fast getaway, but Fletcher was just doing her job. Confronted by three armed representatives of law and order and slowed by a broken fibula, I had little choice anyway. I stood in the parking lot, explicating in the refulgent sunlight of the late afternoon.

Just as I finished a thirty-minute summary of what had happened, a black-and-white squad car skidded to a stop in a spray of gravel. The blonde-maned Mikulski popped out and joined our conversational circle. As usual, too little, too late.

"I've given you enough, haven't I?" I asked.

Fletcher squinted in the afternoon sun. "You know I'm glad we got there when we did," she said.

"Right. Just in time," I said.

"What do you mean?" the sheriff's deputy asked.

"We can talk more later," I said. "Right now though I need to get back to my wife at the hospital."

"We'll get you there," Fletcher said and looked at Mikulski.

I guess Susan had been infected by a touch of sadism, too.

Sitting in the back of Mikulski's police car, siren wailing, I watched the rush hour traffic pull to the side of Sand Hill Road. I could not see his face, but the back of his neck was red. He'd been relegated to being my driver. He didn't even turn around when I got out in front of the hospital entrance and said, "Thank you."

It was six then by the time I made it back to Rowena's room. Her eyes were closed, but Caroline was feeding her red gelatin from a spoon.

"The doc says the fact her swallowing reflex is back shows she's coming out of it."

I looked over at the pressure gauge. Twenty-three. "So when will we be able to talk to her?"

"Some of what she hears may be getting through. She's waking up, just very slowly. It's a process. Griffith says even after she's awake she'll have memory deficits and need some rehab."

"It looks like it will be awhile then. I'll hold down the fort here. Go back to my mother's."

"Why there?" Caroline asked.

"A gas leak at our place. It's being tended to."

"Go change clothes, take a nap. If anything happens, I'll call." My mother was still in Israel, and I gave Caroline a key.

After Caroline left, I settled into a chair next to the hospital bed and took Rowena's hand.

"You need a shave."

"Huh?" I'd fallen asleep. Smiling at me from her bed, as though she'd been watching for some time, was Rowena. "You're back?" I asked.

"I am."

It was no dream. Yet, it seemed unreal. Within a couple of hours of Isobel Marter being vindicated, my wife had come back.

———

The next morning they moved Rowena out of the ICU. We were alone in a semi-private room—the other bed was empty—and sat in the turquoise plastic upholstered chairs with our knees touching. As if the hospital itself were afraid of losing its hold on Rowena, she was still bound by the wires running from her arms and head to wall sockets and in-room monitors.

I'd finished going over what had happened since Solenski had tried to kill us.

"He would have won his cursed prize no matter what, since Aunt Isobel was going to die?" she asked.

"Yes."

"It makes me feel a little bit better to know that she was cheated out of only a few months of life. Maybe the time that was left would have been filled with pain and suffering anyway."

"Yes."

She thought for a moment and then changed her line of questioning.

"You burglarized someone's apartment?"

"No!"

"No? Didn't you get in by falsely representing yourself?" She was my wife and she loved me, but now I was a witness with information she needed to elicit. I was being cross-examined.

"Yes, but I had no intention of stealing anything," I said, remembering the loophole Fletcher had given me.

The deputy D.A. grinned. "That would make it hard to prosecute for burglary, wouldn't it? Hmm. Out-lawyered by a slippery defense attorney. What's going on with Accelenet?"

It took thirty minutes to go through the to-ing and fro-ing with Frankson and the board.

"You accused Ricky Frankson of trying to have me killed?"

"Kind of." I shrugged and made a face.

She laughed. "My knight in shining armor." She patted my knee. "And now you have an offer from this Swiss investor. Like a miracle."

"Like *deus ex machina*," I said.

"Maybe the gods had to even accounts."

"Do you think you should get back in bed and rest?" I asked.

"Good idea," said Dr. Griffith from the doorway.

"I've been lying in bed for a week," Rowena said.

She lost the argument and the doctor busied himself checking monitors as she climbed back into the hospital bed.

"Rowena, could you tell me Ian's birthday?" Griffith asked.

She gave him a funny look. "August 19."

"And your favorite place to get coffee?"

"Peet's at Town and Country."

"Good." Then he had her sit up on the edge of the bed. "Cross one leg over the other, please."

Griffith began a quick exam by hitting a rubber hammer against her knee and then peering into her eyes with a penlight.

"So?" both Rowena and I said together as he stood scribbling notes.

"Everything appears to be okay. We'll set you up with daily rehab."

"When can I go back to work?"

"We'll see."

"Tomorrow?" Rowena asked. She wanted an answer.

"You should be able to go home the day after tomorrow. We'll see about work. Oh, what were those two questions I asked you?"

"About Ian's birthday and my favorite coffee place?"

"Right. What were the answers?"

"August 19 and Peet's."

"Ah, good, good. Still, don't be surprised if you're a little for-getful for a while."

"Okay."

"One last thing. We did a full blood work-up and we did find something unexpected," the doctor said.

Oh, God. "Yes?" I asked and squeezed Rowena's hand.

He smiled and looked from Rowena to me and back at her again. "You're pregnant. How 'bout *that*? What do you say—mazel tov?"

He said the first word as though it rhymed with "dazzle." The doctor's attempt at Hebrew only broadened Rowena's grin, and I squeezed her hand even harder. I didn't know if this was good news or not.

Rowena read my thoughts. "Oh, my God," Rowena said. "The coma, the medication, will any of that affect the baby's health?"

"No, conception goes back only about a week. So you're barely pregnant. Stay healthy the rest of the term, and the baby will be fine."

I let loose all the air in my lungs and leaned over the bed rail and hugged Rowena. She'd gotten pregnant last Thursday? Six hours before she went into the coma?

"Oh, I can't wait to tell our mothers," she said.

Dr. Griffith shifted his weight back and forth, from one leg to the other. Neurosurgeons probably didn't have much practice conveying such good news to their patients.

"Thank you, Doctor," Rowena said. "My mother says good can be found anywhere."

FIFTY-EIGHT

Four days later, on Monday morning, I was sitting on one end of a couch in my mother's living room, with the reclining Rowena's bare legs across my lap. The bruises on her face had faded from shiny purple to mushy olive. Hair from the top of her head draped over the bandage on the back of it.

We'd taken refuge at my mother's, but I still hadn't told her a thing about our accident. At the rate she was healing, Rowena would look almost normal in five days, when Mom was scheduled to return from Israel. Rowena's own mother was back home, but with her daughter pregnant she couldn't stay away. She was planning to be back next week. We would be seeing a lot of her.

"Wouldn't it be great to go on a run?" Rowena asked.

"Griffith said you could be ready in a week or two. That's fast healing in my book. For me, it's at least a three-month wait. That's a long time." I sighed.

Rowena rubbed a heel against my ankle to signal a change in the subject. "Everything going okay with the due diligence at work?" she asked.

"So far. Can I get you something to eat?"

"No, thanks."

"You're eating for two …"

She ignored my attempt to change the flow of conversation. "Are you sure you want to be locked into Accelenet for two more years?"

"Not much of a choice, is there?"

"Do you want to see things through?"

"I'm willing to. Not sure whether I *want* to. The dream was always Paul's, not mine. Still, the Fates have conspired to keep me there."

"The Fates?"

"You know, *deus ex machina*. The offer from Locarno. It really was a miracle from above," I said, my hand stroking Rowena's left shin. The right one still displayed the last remnants of the scab from her shaving mishap.

"Fates? Miracles from the gods? Have you bought into Greek mythology all of a sudden?"

"It provides as good an explanation as any for what happened."

"Maybe, maybe not. What do you always tell me about miracles?"

"What Margot Fulbright keeps saying—if it's too good to be true, then it's too good to be true."

"Maybe she's right?"

"What are you saying? You think someone is trying to put something over on me?"

"Do you think?"

I took my hand off Rowena's leg and rubbed my now smooth chin. Then it came to me. I started to leap up from the couch, but Rowena's legs held me down.

The blue of my wife's irises glinted through narrowed lids. "What?" she asked.

"It's not fate. It's Paul."

"Do you think so?"

"I don't know why I didn't see it. The Swiss bank, the secrecy, the hands-off. Oh, God."

"So what are you going to do?"

I rubbed my now clean-shaven chin. Then I looked at my wife. "I can't take the money from him, can I? I can't take the money if it's really from him. It's blood money. It's for ..." I tried to breathe more slowly. "... but if I go with Torii's deal ..."

"Your stockholders will lose out, and you'll get sued."

"Yeah. Still, I can't take money from him. Not after what happened to your sister. Paul's still manipulating me, still pulling strings to keep *his* dream alive—his, not mine."

"Maybe he's trying to help you."

"Help me?"

"He left you holding the bag at Accelenet and now he's trying to help. He was the best friend you ever had."

"Your sister was killed."

"Yes."

"Is this a test, a test to see if I do the right thing?"

"No. If I knew what's right, I'd tell you. I trust you to make the right call. Robber barons like Rockefeller, Carnegie, and Stanford gave money to charity." I used the tail of my shirt to wipe her eyes. Then she went on, "Nothing is going to bring back Gwendolyn."

We sat on the couch, me breathing almost as hard as I did when trying to keep up with Rowena on a run. After five minutes, I pulled the iPhone out of my pocket. "I'm going to call Peter Reynard at FBS." I listened to the ringing. "Hello, Peter? Ian. Can you talk?"

"Just for a minute," he said. "The due diligence is going fine?" In the background I heard the hubbub of conversation and the clacking of metal on crockery. It was lunchtime in New York.

"Yes, great. I have a question I need answered."

"Shoot."

"Who are the investors in the Locarno Fund?"

"I can't say anything about that."

"Well, I know. The Locarno Fund is Paul Berk."

There was a short pause.

"C'mon, Ian. He's a fugitive. I don't know who the investors in Locarno are. How would you?"

"I can feel he's out there."

"Pretty flimsy."

"Some things don't require documentary evidence. Unless you can promise that his money isn't in the fund, I might have to resign as CEO."

At the prospect of failing to deliver what the Locarno Fund wanted and the attendant healthy fees evaporating, Reynard shed his identity as a mild-mannered Swiss banker who spoke only in modulated tones. "Ian, be reasonable," he shouted over the background clatter. "Locarno won't proceed with its investment unless you're CEO."

"Listen, Peter, I appreciate everything you've done. I really do and I know you might get screwed. I am sorry, but, listen, I have to go think now. We can talk later."

I extricated myself from the pinions of Rowena's long legs and stooped to kiss her.

"You have a plan?" she asked.

"Not exactly a plan."

"Then a what?"

"A Hail Mary," I told her.

FIFTY-NINE

"You know we have an offer for the company," I said to Frankson an hour after I'd left Rowena on the couch.

He didn't answer right away. He wanted me to squirm a little. Turning my head to his office window, I saw that the thirsty hills across the Bay had quaffed the recent rains and turned a seasonal green.

"I'm not sure that Swiss fund is going to come through," he said in a conversational tone.

Ignoring the implicit threat, I took a sip of tea and said, "I guess that means you know the details of what they offered."

"I'm not going to top them. I don't do bidding wars."

"Right. You just make sure that there are no other bidders. Like Intel."

He shrugged. "That's preferable."

"Well, if you're not going to up your offer then I guess we're through."

It was my turn to try rudeness as a bargaining tactic. Without a word I got up and walked out. I resisted the temptation to look back.

In the anteroom, I nodded at the admin without stopping. On my way down the long hall, I didn't slow down, but kept listening for a "Stop." The only sound I heard was the squeaking of my soles on the marble floor.

Out past the guard, I took a left and pushed the elevator's down button. I'd bluffed and lost. Looking up, I watched an amber light skip from the second floor indicator to the seventh and, there, stop for at least two minutes. How many people could be getting on? I beat my right palm against my thigh in a steady tattoo. But when the elevator finally arrived, it was empty, and I pushed the button for the lobby.

My hopes for Accelenet plummeted as fast as the elevator cab. I would have to take blood money or violate my duty to shareholders. Could I allow myself to be Paul's marionette so that shareholders got more?

The elevator doors swooshed open to reveal Frankson's admin in all her Technicolor splendor.

"He wasn't through with you," she told me.

"Could've fooled me."

She smiled through glacier white teeth. "I'm not sure he's used to having people leave before they are dismissed."

"I just learned from him. The way he says goodbye is by hanging up the phone."

She stepped toward me, I retreated and tripped my way back into the elevator. A moment later, we were shooting upward.

I swallowed and my ears popped. "You took a private elevator?"

"Yes."

"Still, I would have beaten you if not for my elevator taking so long to get to the sixteenth floor."

"Which it would have, if I hadn't called an admin on the seventh floor to push a button and hold it five minutes."

Closed in the cab, I felt there were three of us on board—me, her, and her scent of hairspray and perfume. I prefer the smell of clean that I found at the back of Rowena's neck.

I followed the admin's spoor down the hallway until she deposited me back in Frankson's office.

He didn't get up from his chair. I didn't sit down.

"Shall we try again?" he asked.

"I thought we were done. You don't do bidding wars."

"You are a pain in the ass."

"That has nothing to do with the facts. I can't do a deal with you for less than the Swiss will pay. I have a duty to shareholders. We'd both be sued."

"How much of the company do you own?"

Where was he going? "I'll bet you know the answer to that one."

"Okay. I want you to agree to sell me your seven percent right now for the share price I originally offered."

"Why would I do that?"

"Because I'll buy the other ninety-three percent of the shares for the price that Locarno was offering."

"And what makes you think I'd sell my shares for half as much as everyone else gets?"

"Because otherwise you'll be working for Paul Berk again."

My fingers uncurled from the handle of the teacup I was holding. This time Frankson wasn't fast enough. I listened to the shatter of the Imari porcelain, but did not take my eyes off him.

How had he known that Paul was behind Locarno? He'd had our living room bugged?

"You going to say something?" he asked.

"Too bad you weren't working for the CIA a few years ago. If the country had an intelligence network like yours, we would have known there were no weapons of mass destruction in Iraq before the invasion."

"I enjoy what I do at Torii," he said. "I'll be here forever."

"Maybe your investments in biotech companies will make that possible?" I asked.

"Let's discuss portfolio management another time."

"But you wouldn't want me here," I said. "I'm a pain in the ass."

"Want you, no. Need you, to keep everyone in line, yes. Even if you are a pain in the ass."

"I might be a pain in the ass. But you're an out and out asshole."

Still, despite my efforts, he gave not the slightest sign of offense as he nodded. After all, he'd been called worse many times—in print.

Lowering the price paid for my ownership share mattered almost none to Torii with its billions in the bank. And in truth it wouldn't matter much to me either. Even three-and-a-half percent of the purchase price would be plenty for Rowena and me. But it was important because it allowed Frankson to think he'd won.

The corners of Frankson's mouth twitched. Then for the first time, I saw his lips form a smile, or maybe a sadistic grin. He stuck out his hand. Asshole or not, he had me and he knew it.

We shook.

He walked over to his desk, picked up a sheaf of papers, and handed them to me.

I was looking at a term sheet and stock purchase agreement. "You were pretty sure of yourself," I said.

He nodded, his victory smile still manifest. "As Sun Tzu said, 'When you surround an army, leave an outlet free. Do not press a desperate foe too hard.'"

"I was desperate?"

He smiled for a second time. "Why don't you take a look at the term sheet?"

After ten minutes perusal, I called Bryce Smithwick. He joined us in thirty minutes. The lawyer Smithwick and executive Frankson, two Silicon Valley jungle cats, had to spend thirty minutes circling and growling before serious work could begin.

Three hours later, I took the elevator down again, this time with Smithwick.

The other shareholders would get about twice Torii's original offer. Bryce's eloquence could do nothing to raise the price I'd receive for *my* stock, but he managed to strike the provision in the term sheet that required me to go to work at Torii. In fact, Frankson let me go so easily that I figured he hadn't ever really wanted me mucking around inside Torii. So what? I wouldn't be responsible for Paul's dream. Nor would I be chained to Frankson. I was free. And Rowena was back.

EPILOGUE: JUNE 17

I STARTED SCREAMING AS I saw Rowena come into view, long legs pumping, short ponytail swaying. Right next to her was a taller woman with sharp, lean features who loped along as if still herding her family's cattle in the Kenyan highlands. After twenty-six miles, neither had lost her form. They were the only two runners in sight. One or the other would be the first woman to finish the race. A quick glance to my left showed two baseball-capped judges pulling a white tape across the finish line.

"Go, Rowena!" But I knew she didn't hear me over the drumming of her heart, the roaring in her head, the pounding of her feet.

Fifteen yards to go. The race would be decided by luck. If Rowena hit the finish line at the very end of a stride and leaned forward, she could win. There were only about a thousand people cheering, but for the noise they were making, we might as well have been in Rio's Maracanã Stadium after a Ronaldinho goal.

The Kenyan woman kept looking to her left as if her will to win could be sucked from her competitor. Rowena's eyes were fixed on the white tape, paying no attention to her racing doppelganger. Neither relented. The Kenyan leaned forward to cross the line, Rowena caught it in mid-stride.

The people who lined the road roared even louder. It wasn't the Olympics, just the Kona Marathon, but they had seen a race they wouldn't forget. An inch difference after twenty-six miles.

I started pushing my way through the spectators. In the midst of the forest of race fans was a clearing where the two runners had their arms around each other's necks. As the Kenyan started to collapse, Rowena hugged her under the arms to hold her up. A judge and paramedic moved in to assume Rowena's role.

I entered the clearing. Rowena had supported the Kenyan and now I was supporting Rowena. My arms were around her sopping body. When we ran together, she never seemed to breathe hard. Things were different today. Nostrils flaring, lips parting, she sucked air in and blew it out like a filly just past the finish line at Churchill Downs.

She raised her head up and called into my ear, "What was my time?"

"Two hours forty-seven minutes eleven seconds."

"Did I win?"

In February she'd been in a coma. She'd done rehab for two weeks before Dr. Griffith would let her return to light training. He'd been skeptical about the race until he'd spoken to Tammy Russell, now an ob/gyn, who'd qualified for the Olympics in the marathon when just as pregnant as Rowena was.

"The other runner crossed the finish line first, but in my book you won."

The deal with Torii had closed three days before. I'd worked long hours on the due diligence to ensure the transaction got done. I fought enough with Frankson along the way to ensure he was more than pleased with his decision to unlock the shackles that bound me to Accelenet. And the millions I'd given up were worth it.

In any case, I was unemployed. It felt great. The only task in front of me was writing Isobel Marter's biography. I'd already done a four-hour interview with Tompkins that would tweak the history of twentieth-century physics.

One of the race volunteers came over and slipped leis around our necks. Rowena squeezed me closer. For the first time I felt a hint of roundness to her belly. Then after a few seconds, she reached behind her own back, unlaced my fingers, and moved away a few inches. Because the race had started not long after sunrise, it was still early enough for a cool breeze to hit the now-wet front of my aloha shirt. I smiled, looking into the azure blue of her eyes.

"So what now?" she asked me.

"A new baby. A new life."

She returned my smile, and we moved back together and kissed.

THE END

ACKNOWLEDGMENTS

People say novel writing is a solitary profession. Baloney. This book would not exist without the support, encouragement, advice, and wisdom of an entire tribe of relatives, friends, and colleagues. Thank you, everybody. I'm grateful to you all.

One night on a stroll after a restaurant dinner with our wives, I made a comment to the polymathic Brian Rosenthal. His reply sent the synapses in my brain flashing like fireworks on the Fourth of July and provided the inspiration for the plot of *Smasher*. The enthusiasm of my sister Dena, brother Wes, and old friends Loren Saxe, Larry Vincent, and Ellen Bob encouraged me to stick with the book and improved it with cogent comments and suggestions. My brother Corey, a neurosurgeon, prescribed just the right maladies to move the plot along while ensuring the book was true to medical science.

Len Shustek's photos, documents, and memories of the Stanford Linear Accelerator Center helped make the story richer. Len in turn introduced me to Professor Martin Breidenbach. Without Marty's tours of SLAC, encyclopedic knowledge of particle physics, and devil-ish ingenuity, this book would be a far inferior product. I must confess, however, to using a novelist's prerogative to change the history of SLAC to suit the plot. The researchers in the book were not based on the sci-entists who did really win the Nobel Prize for Physics for their work at SLAC. Elements of the back story of Isobel Marter, however, were in-spired by the life of Rosalind Franklin, who did her research not on the make-up of matter in 1960s Palo Alto, but on the structure of DNA in postwar London. If you want to get your blood boiling over the injus-tices and sexism that once existed in the world of science, I recommend reading either Anne Sayre's *Rosalind Franklin and DNA* or Brenda Maddox's *Rosalind Franklin: The Dark Lady of DNA*.

The manuscript benefited in myriad ways from the discerning eye of editor and novelist Donna Levin. My college classmate John Zuss-man spotted errors that other readers glided over. Jeff Rosen and Stacey

Capps provided insight into the county's criminal justice system and life as a deputy district attorney. Any trouble I had focusing on the job at hand disappeared when long-time buddy Bob Finocchio loaned me his noise-canceling headphones, technology that helped me focus my attention on the job at hand. Lexa Logue and Ian Shrank offered me friendship, encouragement, and hospitality while I undertook literary adventures in New York City. The gracious, efficient, and accommodating staff of Quattro provided the sanctuary and caffeine I needed to write this book.

Why is it that mystery and thriller writers, whose fiction features murder and mayhem, are such warm, supportive mensches in the real world? Despite their own deadlines, Steve Berry, M. J. Rose, Cara Black, and Marcus Sakey took time to read the manuscript and provide their comments. They are not only good friends, they are terrific writers at the summit of the crime fiction mountain. Read their books. You'll thank me for the recommendation.

Like any superhero, my agent, Josh Getzler, has a secret identity, his as editor par excellence. I'm so appreciative for what he does for me in both his personas. It took the advice, backing, editing, and enthusiasm of the Midnight Ink team, of Bill Krause, Steven Pomije, Courtney Kish, and Connie Hill, to turn my manuscript into a published novel. I'm grateful for their faith in this book.

I can be a hard-headed person and odds are better than even that I ignored some of the sound advice, corrections, and criticism I was offered. That goes a long way toward explaining the errors in fact and judgment in the book.

And finally, without the support and love of the other five members of my family, this book could not have been written; moreover, my life would have been immeasurably less meaningful.

Keith Raffel

ABOUT THE AUTHOR

As counsel to the Senate Intelligence Committee, Keith Raffel held top-secret clearance to watch over CIA activities. As a Silicon Valley entrepreneur, he founded UpShot Corporation, the award-winning Internet software company, and sold it to Siebel Systems. He has also been a carpenter, college writing instructor, candidate for elective office, and professional gambler. These days he stays busy writing his mysteries and thrillers in his hometown of Palo Alto, California, where he lives with his wife and four children. Check the latest news at www.keithraffel.com.

WWW.MIDNIGHTINKBOOKS.COM

From the gritty streets of New York City to sacred tombs in the Middle East, it's always midnight somewhere. Join us online at any hour for fresh new voices in mystery fiction.

At midnightinkbooks.com you'll also find our author blog, new and upcoming books, events, book club questions, excerpts, mystery resources, and more.

MIDNIGHT INK ORDERING INFORMATION

Order Online:
- Visit our website www.midnightinkbooks.com, select your books, and order them on our secure server.

Order by Phone:
- Call toll-free within the U.S. and Canada at 1-888-NITE-INK (1-888-648-3465)
- We accept VISA, MasterCard, and American Express

Order by Mail:
Send the full price of your order (MN residents add 6.875% sales tax) in U.S. funds, plus postage & handling to:

> Midnight Ink
> 2143 Wooddale Drive, Dept. 978-0-7387-1874-3
> Woodbury, MN 55125-2989

Postage & Handling:

Standard (U.S., Mexico & Canada). If your order is:
> $24.99 and under, add $4.00
> $25.00 and over, FREE STANDARD SHIPPING

AK, HI, PR: $16.00 for one book plus $2.00 for each additional book.

International Orders (airmail only):
> $16.00 for one book plus $3.00 for each additional book

Orders are processed within 2 business days. Please allow for normal shipping time.
Postage and handling rates subject to change.